BEST
TO PERF

BY
JENNIFER TAYLOR

RESISTING
HER REBEL DOC

BY
JOANNA NEIL

MILLS
BOON

Jennifer Taylor has been writing Mills & Boon® novels for some time, but discovered Medical Romance™ books relatively recently. She was so captivated by these heart-warming stories that she immediately set out to write them herself! Having worked in scientific research, Jennifer enjoys writing each book, as well as the chance to create a cast of wonderful new characters. Jennifer's hobbies include reading and travelling. She lives in northwest England. Visit Jennifer's blog at jennifertaylorauthor.wordpress.com

When **Joanna Neil** discovered Mills & Boon®, her lifelong addiction to reading crystallised into an exciting new career writing Mills & Boon® Medical Romance™. Her characters are probably the outcome of her varied lifestyle, which includes working as a clerk, typist, nurse and infant teacher. She enjoys dressmaking and cooking at her Leicestershire home. Her family includes a husband, son and daughter, an exuberant yellow Labrador and two slightly crazed cockatiels. She currently works with a team of tutors at her local education centre, to provide creative writing workshops for people interested in exploring their own writing ambitions.

BEST FRIEND
TO PERFECT BRIDE

BY
JENNIFER TAYLOR

Published in Great Britain 2015
by Mills & Boon, an imprint of Harlequin (UK) Limited,
Eton House, 18-24 Paradise Road, Richmond, Surrey, TW9 1SR

© 2015 Jennifer Taylor

ISBN: 978-0-263-24724-4

Harlequin (UK) Limited's policy is to use papers that are natural,
renewable and recyclable products and made from wood grown in
sustainable forests. The logging and manufacturing processes conform
to the legal environmental regulations of the country of origin.

Printed and bound in Spain
by CPI, Barcelona

Dear Reader,

Should best friends fall in love? That is the question that both Bella and Mac ask themselves after they meet again following Bella's divorce. Their relationship was so clear in the past: they were friends and nothing more than that. However, all of a sudden they find their feelings for one another changing.

It comes as a huge shock to Mac. After all, he's convinced that Bella is to blame for the demise of her marriage. But the more time they spend together, the harder he finds it to believe that. As for Bella— well, she has never been good at relationships. She has always had great difficulty showing her feelings, so to suddenly discover just how hard it is to remain emotionally detached when Mac is around scares her. After all, she doesn't have a good track record when it comes to relationships, does she? Even if it *was* her ex-husband's fault that their marriage failed. Is it realistic to hope that she and Mac can switch from being friends to lovers?

Helping Bella and Mac work through their problems was a real pleasure. I grew extremely fond of them during the course of writing this book. They deserve to find happiness after everything they've been through, and I hope you will agree that they truly earn their happy ending.

Best wishes to you all

Jennifer

Dedication

For Charlotte, who told me about the boat *Gallina*,
and for James, who owns her.

Many thanks for providing me
with the perfect home for my hero.

Books by Jennifer Taylor

Mills & Boon® Medical Romance™

The Doctor's Baby Bombshell
The Midwife's Christmas Miracle
Small Town Marriage Miracle
Gina's Little Secret
The Family Who Made Him Whole
The Son that Changed His Life
The Rebel Who Loved Her
The Motherhood Mix-Up
Mr Right All Along
Saving His Little Miracle
One More Night with Her Desert Prince...

**Visit the author profile page at
millsandboon.co.uk for more titles**

CHAPTER ONE

She hadn't changed. Tall and slender, her red-gold hair coiled into an elegant knot at the nape of her neck, Bella English looked as beautiful today as she had done the last time he had seen her. On her wedding day.

'Mac! I heard you were back. Good to see you, mate. How are you?'

'Great, thanks, Lou.'

James MacIntyre—Mac to all who knew him—turned and grinned at the elderly porter. Out of the corner of his eye he saw Bella move away from the desk but he kept his attention firmly focused on the other man. After what his old friend Tim had told him, he wasn't all that eager to speak to her.

'You're looking well, I must say, Lou. Obviously, moving to the new paediatric A&E unit has done you the power of good. You look a good ten years younger than the last time I saw you!'

'I wish!' Lou's grizzled face broke into a wry smile. 'It'd take major surgery to turn me into Dalverston's very own version of George Clooney.' He glanced over

Mac's shoulder and grimaced. 'Anyway, I'd better get going. Catch you later.'

'Yep.'

Mac didn't need to check to see what had caused Lou to beat a hasty retreat. He could smell her perfume, that subtle fragrance of freesias that Bella always wore. She had told him once that it was made especially for her and that had fitted perfectly with everything he knew about her. Bella was the sort of woman who would have her very own perfume. Nothing about her was ordinary or commonplace.

Mac turned slowly around, taking stock of all the details he had missed before. Although Bella had always been slender, she was verging on thin now, he realised. And even though her complexion was as creamy as ever, there were dark circles under her green eyes that hinted at far too many sleepless nights. Was it guilt that had kept her awake? he wondered a shade bitterly. A noisy conscience clamouring to be heard, even if it was too late in the day? After all, even Bella must feel some degree of remorse about ending her marriage to Tim.

'Hello, Mac. I heard you were back. How are you?'

The greeting was almost identical to Lou's, but Mac had to admit that it made him want to respond very differently. He experienced an uncharacteristic urge to take her by the shoulders and shake her, demand to know why she had done such a cruel thing. She had ruined Tim's life—didn't she care? Didn't she care either that she had broken all those promises she had made three years ago to love, honour and cherish the man she had married? He had sat through the ceremony, listened to her cool clear voice swearing a lifetime's devotion, and had believed every word. If he was honest, he felt almost as let down as poor Tim must do.

The thought shocked him so that it was a moment before he answered. He and Bella had never been anything more than friends—he had made sure of that. So why should he feel so disillusioned? He blanked out the thought, knowing it was foolish to dwell on it. If he and Bella were to work together for the next few months, he couldn't allow recent events to stand in the way.

'Fine, thanks. Looking forward to working in the new unit.' He glanced around and nodded. 'It looks great, I must say. Obviously, no expense has been spared.'

'No. Everything is state of the art. We've been open for almost a month now and I still have to pinch myself when I come into work. I can't believe that we have such marvellous facilities to hand.'

She gave a husky laugh and Mac tensed when he felt the tiny hairs all over his body spring to attention. He had forgotten about her laugh, forgotten how soft it was, how *sexy*. It had been her laugh that he had noticed first, in fact. He had been standing in the lunch queue in the university's refectory when he had heard a woman laugh and he had turned to see who it was…

He ditched that thought as well, not needing any

more distractions. He knew where his loyalties lay, knew that if he had to take sides then he would be firmly allied to Tim. Tim had poured out the whole sorry tale, told him what had happened from start to finish, and whilst Mac was realistic enough to know that it was rarely all one person's fault when a marriage ended, it was obvious that Bella was more at fault than Tim. No, Tim's biggest mistake had been to love Bella too much and be too soft with her. The thought firmed his resolve and he smiled thinly at her.

'Is that what brought you to Dalverston, the chance to work in a wonderful new facility like this? I must confess that I was surprised to learn you had moved out of London.'

'It was one of the reasons, yes.'

Bella's expression sobered and Mac's heart twisted when he saw the pain in her eyes. Maybe Tim *was* hurting but Bella was hurting too, it seemed. The idea affected him far more than it should have done, far more than he wanted it to do. It was an effort not to let her see how he felt when she continued.

'I needed to get away and moving up here seemed like the right thing to do. It's a fresh start for me and, hopefully, it will be a fresh start for Tim as well.'

Bella could feel the animosity coming off Mac in huge waves and it hurt to know that he had judged her and obviously found her wanting. She knew that Tim would have told Mac his version of the story but she had hoped that Mac would wait until he had spoken to her before he started apportioning blame. However, it appeared that he had accepted what Tim had said without question. *She* was the one at fault, the bad guy who had called time on her marriage, while Tim was the innocent victim.

She swung round, refusing to stand there and try to justify herself. She had made up her mind that she wouldn't retaliate after she had found out that Tim had been spreading all those lies about her. She had seen that happen with other couples, had watched as the situation had deteriorated into an unseemly sparring match, and she had sworn that she wouldn't go down that route. People would believe what they wanted to believe anyway. If she tried to contest Tim's claims that she had been unreasonable, that she had ruined his career, that she had ended their relationship rather than have a baby with him, few would believe her.

She had always been the reticent one in the relationship, the one who took longer to make friends, whereas Tim had always been very outgoing. Tim drew people to him and made instant friends of them, and if he tended to drop them just as quickly later, then nobody seemed to mind. No, if there were sides to be taken then most folk would take Tim's. Including Mac, it seemed.

Pain stabbed her heart as she led the way to Reception. Even though she knew it was silly, she hated to think that she had sunk so low in Mac's estimation.

Dredging up a smile, she turned to Janet Davies, their receptionist, determined that she wasn't going to let him know how she felt.

'This is Dr MacIntyre, Janet. He'll be covering the senior registrar's post until Dr Timpson is fit to return to work following her accident.'

'Oh, I know Mac. Who doesn't?' Janet got up and hurried around the desk to give Mac a hug. She grinned up at him. 'So where was it this time? Africa? India? Outer Mongolia?'

'The Philippines.'

Mac hugged Janet back, his face breaking into a smile that immediately warmed Bella's heart. He had always had the most wonderful smile, she thought, then pulled herself up short. Maybe Mac had smiled at Janet with genuine warmth but he certainly hadn't smiled at her that way.

'Oh, grim.' Janet grimaced. 'Was it as bad as it looked on TV?'

'Worse.'

Mac shook his head, his dark brown hair flopping untidily across his forehead. It needed trimming, Bella decided, even though it suited him, emphasising his craggy good looks and that air of toughness he projected. Mac looked exactly like the kind of man he was: tough, unflappable, someone you could depend on, someone who would never let you down. Her heart ached even harder at the thought. She could have done with Mac's support this past difficult year.

'The typhoon destroyed whole cities and left people with nothing except the clothes they stood up in. We had a devil of a job getting hold of even the most basic supplies in the beginning,' he continued.

'How awful!' Janet shuddered as she went back to her seat. 'Makes you grateful that you live here, doesn't it.'

'It does indeed.' Mac grinned. 'Even if it does rain a lot in this part of the world!'

Janet laughed as she reached for the telephone when it started ringing. Bella moved to the whiteboard and checked the list of names written on it, determined to start as she meant to go on. Maybe there were certain issues that she and Mac needed to address, but they were colleagues, first and foremost, and she intended to keep that at the forefront of her mind. There were just three children in cubicles and each of them had been seen and were currently awaiting the results of various tests. She pointed to the last name on the list when Mac joined her.

'I'd like you to take a look at this one, if you wouldn't mind. Chloe Adams, aged eight, admitted at four a.m. this morning complaining of a severe headache. She'd also been vomiting.' She sighed. 'Apparently, she's been suffering from violent headaches for several weeks. Mum took her to their GP, who thought it was probably a sinus infection, but I'm not convinced.'

'So what are you thinking?' Mac queried. 'That it's something more sinister?'

'Yes. I noticed a definite lack of coordination when I was examining her. It made me wonder if it's a tumour. I asked Mum if she'd noticed anything—clumsy gait, frequent falls, that kind of thing—but she said she hadn't.' Bella shrugged. 'Chloe is one of five children and I get the impression that her mother is finding it hard to cope since their father upped and left them at the beginning of the year.'

'I see. It must be difficult for her when she's been abandoned like that,' Mac said blandly, so blandly in fact that Bella knew he was thinking about her situation.

Colour touched her cheeks as she led the way to the cubicles. She hadn't abandoned Tim! She had left because Tim had made it impossible for her to stay. She had tried to help him, tried everything she could think of, but nothing had worked. He had been too dependent on the painkillers by then to give them up. Oh, he had promised that he would, swore that he had umpteen times, but he had lied. The drugs had changed him from the man she had married, turned him into someone who lied and deceived at the drop of a hat. It had reached the point where she simply couldn't take any more and she had left and, amazingly, it had been the best thing she could have done for him.

Tim had sought help after that. He had admitted himself to rehab and finally kicked his habit. Maybe she should have gone back to him then—she had thought about it. But then she had found out about his affair and there hadn't seemed any point. She would only have gone back out of a sense of duty and that hadn't seemed right or fair to either of them.

It made her wonder all of a sudden if she had ever really loved him—loved him with the depth and intensity that people were supposed to feel when they married—if she hadn't been prepared to fight for him. The problem was that she had never been truly in touch with her feelings. As the only child of career-minded parents, she had learned at an early age to keep her emotions in check. Even after she had grown up, she had always held back, had always been wary about letting herself feel. Tim had seemed like a safe bet—the type of man she was used to, someone from her own social circle, someone she felt comfortable with. Unlike Mac. Mac had been very different. Even though they'd only been friends, his self-assurance and experience of life had unsettled her. Everything about him had seemed alien. Dangerous. A threat to her peace of mind. He still was.

Bella's breath caught. If Mac had seemed dangerous all those years ago, he was even more of a threat now that she was so vulnerable.

'Mrs Adams? I'm Dr MacIntyre. Dr English has asked me to take a look at your daughter.'

Mac smiled at the harassed-looking woman sitting beside the bed. He knew that Bella was standing right behind him and forced himself to focus on the other woman. He had sworn that he would behave with the utmost propriety and wouldn't take Bella to task about what she had done. Maybe he *did* believe that she had behaved deplorably by ending her marriage, but it wasn't his place to say so.

'She's feeling a lot better now, aren't you, Chloe?' Donna Adams turned to the little girl, urging her to agree, and Mac sighed. No matter how long this took or how inconvenient it was for the mother, they needed to get to the bottom of Chloe's problem.

'That's good to hear but I still think it would be best if we carried out a couple more tests.' He smiled at the little girl. 'We don't want you having any more of those horrible headaches if we can avoid it, do we, Chloe?'

'No.' She smiled shyly back at him, clutching tight hold of a battered old teddy bear.

Mac grinned at her as he sat down on the edge of the bed. 'What's your teddy's name? I have a bear just like him and he's called Bruno.'

'William.' Chloe gave the bear a hug. 'He's my best friend and I take him everywhere.'

'I expect he enjoys it.' Mac took hold of the bear's paw and solemnly shook it. 'It's nice to meet you, William. My name's Dr Mac.'

Chloe giggled at this piece of nonsense, but Mac knew that it was important to gain her trust. He smiled at her again. 'So, now the introductions are over, I need to ask you some questions, Chloe. There are no right or wrong answers, mind you. And if you want William to help you then that's also fine. OK?'

'OK,' Chloe agreed happily.

'So, Chloe, have you noticed that sometimes you don't seem quite as steady on your feet as normal and fall over?'

'Sometimes,' Chloe murmured. She glanced at her mother then hurried on. 'It happened in school the other day. I got up to fetch a piece of paper to do some painting and fell over. Teacher thought I was messing about and told me off.'

'I see.' Mac glanced at Bella and saw her nod. Poor balance could point towards a disturbance to the function of the cerebellum and was often an indication of a tumour. Although he hoped with all his heart it wasn't that, it was looking increasingly likely.

'And have you found it difficult to walk sometimes, as though your feet don't want to do what you tell them to?' he continued gently.

'Yes. Sometimes they keep going the wrong way,' Chloe told him guilelessly.

'I'm sorry, Doctor, but what has this got to do with Chloe's headaches?' Donna Adams demanded.

'It all helps to build up a picture of what might be wrong with Chloe,' Mac explained, not wanting to go into detail just yet. If their suspicions were correct then there would be time enough for the poor woman to face the fact that her child was seriously ill. He stood up and smiled at Chloe. 'I'm going to send you for a special scan, Chloe, so we can see what's happening inside your head. I just need to make a phone call first and then the porter will take you and your mum downstairs to have it done.'

'Will it take long?' Donna Adams asked anxiously. 'Only I've got to get the others ready for school. They're with my neighbour at the moment but I can't expect her to see to them. She's in her eighties and it's far too much for her.'

'The scan itself won't take very long,' Bella said gently. 'However, Chloe will need to stay here until we get the results back. Is there anyone else you can contact who could see to the children?'

'No.' Donna's tone was bitter. 'There's nobody since their dad upped and left.' She glanced at her daughter and sighed. 'They'll just have to miss school today, I suppose.'

Mac didn't say anything as he followed Bella from the cubicle, but it didn't mean that he wasn't thinking it. Breaking promises was a definite no-no in his view. He only had to recall his own father's despair after his mother had walked out on them to know that it was something he would never do. If he ever made a commitment then he would stick to it, no matter what.

He glanced at Bella and could tell from her expression that she knew what he was thinking, but it was hard luck. Letting Tim down the way she had was beyond the pale, in his opinion. She had promised to love and cherish Tim for the rest of her days but she hadn't meant it. She couldn't have done if at the first sign of trouble she had turned her back on him. He felt guilty enough about not being there when Tim had needed his support, even though he'd had no idea what his friend had been going through. However, Bella *had* been there and, as Tim's wife, she should have been the one person he could rely on. It was little wonder that his friend was so devastated.

Mac's mouth thinned as he followed her into the office. Maybe it was unfair of him to be so judgemental but he had always considered Bella to be the ideal woman. Not only was she beautiful, but she was highly intelligent too. Although he had been deeply attracted to her when they had met at Cambridge, he had been ever so slightly in awe of her as well. The fact that she had kept herself aloof from the rest of their class had only added to her allure, in fact.

He had never been the reticent type. His upbringing, on a council estate on the outskirts of Manchester, hadn't allowed for such luxury. He had learned early on that he needed to be tough to survive, focused and determined if he hoped to achieve his goal of becoming a doctor. Bella had been very different from the girls he had known at home, different too from the rest of the women in their year at university. Although many of them had come from privileged backgrounds too, Bella had stood out: her perfection had made her special. To discover that she wasn't perfect after all had hit him hard. For all these years he had put her on a pedestal but the truth was that Bella was just a woman like any other, a woman who could make and break promises. She wasn't special. And she wasn't out of his league, as he had always believed.

Mac frowned. It was the first time that thought had crossed his mind and he didn't like it. Not one little bit. Or the one that followed it. There was nothing to stop him making a play for Bella now.

Sadly, the results of Chloe's scan only confirmed their suspicions. Bella sighed as she studied the monitor. 'There's no doubt about it, is there? That's definitely a tumour.'

'It is.'

Mac leant forward to get a better look and she tensed when his shoulder brushed against hers. She moved aside, not enjoying the fact that her heart seemed to be beating far faster than it normally did. She cleared her throat. The last thing she needed was Mac thinking that he had any kind of effect on her.

'It's probably a medulloblastoma, wouldn't you say? That's one of the most common types of brain tumour that occur in children.'

'Oh, yes. The fact that it's arisen in the cerebellum makes it almost a certainty,' he concurred.

'Chloe's going to need immediate treatment,' Bella said, focusing on their patient in the hope that it would stop her thoughts wandering again. Maybe she did seem to be unusually aware of Mac, but that was only to be expected. Ever since she'd heard he was back in England, she had been on edge. After all, Mac was Tim's best friend and it must be hard for him to accept what had happened. It was bound to lead to a certain degree of…well, *tension* between them. The thought was reassuring and she hurried on.

'From what I've read, medulloblastomas can grow very rapidly and spread to other parts of the brain as well as to the spinal cord.'

'That's right. Chloe needs to be seen by an oncologist ASAP so we shall have to set that up. She'll probably need radiotherapy as well as chemotherapy if she's to have any chance of surviving this.' He shook his head and Bella saw the sorrow in his eyes. 'I feel sorry for her mother. It's going to be a huge shock for her.'

'It will be a lot for her to deal with, especially with having the other children to look after,' Bella agreed quietly. 'Just travelling back and forth to hospital while Chloe receives treatment will be a major task with her not having any backup.'

'It will.'

Mac's tone was flat. Although there was no hint of censure in his voice, Bella knew that he was thinking about the way she had seemingly deserted Tim in his hour of need. The urge to tell him the truth—the *real* truth, not the version that Tim was determined to tell everyone—was very strong but she refused to go down that path. It wouldn't improve Mac's opinion of her if she tried to apportion blame; it could have the opposite effect, in fact.

It was hard to accept that there was very little she could do, but Bella knew there was no point agonising about it. Switching off the monitor, she turned to leave the office. 'I'll go and have a word with Mrs Adams,' she said over her shoulder. 'The sooner she knows what's going on, the better.'

'Fine. Do you want me to phone Oncology and start the ball rolling?' Mac offered, following her out to the corridor.

'If you wouldn't mind… Oh, they've got a new phone number. They're starting the refurbishments today so they've moved temporarily into the old building. I'll get it for you.' Bella went to go back into the office and staggered when she cannoned into Mac.

'Sorry.' He grinned as he set her safely back on her feet. 'I didn't expect you to turn round so suddenly, or that's my excuse, anyway. It's got nothing whatsoever to do with me being born clumsy!'

'No harm done,' she assured him, although she could feel heat flowing from the point where his hands were gripping her shoulders. She stepped back, setting some much-needed space between them, or much-needed by her, at least. Mac appeared unmoved by the contact. 'Janet should have Oncology's new number, now that I think about it,' she said, hastily squashing that thought. 'Let me know what they say, won't you?'

'Will do.'

He sketched her a wave as he headed to Reception. Bella watched until he disappeared from sight then made her way to the cubicles. She wasn't looking forward to the next few minutes. Breaking bad news to a parent was always difficult and one of the few things she disliked about her job...

Her breath caught as she felt the heat finally consume her entire body. It felt as though she was on fire, burning up, inside and out, and all because Mac had touched her. She couldn't recall ever feeling this way before, couldn't remember when the touch of a man's hands had set her alight, not even when Tim had made love to her. What did it mean? Or didn't it mean anything really? Was it simply the lack of intimacy that had made her so susceptible all of a sudden?

Once Tim had become hooked on the painkillers, they had stopped making love. He hadn't been interested in anything apart from where his next fix was coming from and she hadn't been able to stand the thought of them being intimate when it wouldn't have meant anything. It was almost two years since they had slept together and there had been nobody else since, or at least not for her. Was that why she felt so aware of her body all of a sudden, so emotionally charged? It wasn't Mac's touch per se that had aroused her but the fact that she had been denied an outlet for her feelings for such a long time?

Bella told herself that it was the real explanation; however, as she entered the cubicle, she knew in her heart that it was only partly true. Maybe the lack of intimacy was a contributing factor but she doubted if she would have reacted this way if another man had touched her the way Mac had done. The truth was that she had always been aware of him even though they had never been anything more than friends. There was something about him that she responded to, even though she had refused to acknowledge it. It made her see just how careful she needed to be. The last thing she wanted was to start craving Mac's touch when it was obvious how he felt about her.

CHAPTER TWO

IT WAS A busy day but Mac enjoyed every second. Although he had worked in emergency medicine for some time, paediatric emergency care on this scale was a whole new ball game. The newly opened paediatric A&E unit accepted patients from a wide area and not just from Dalverston itself. Built on a separate site to the main hospital, it boasted the most up-to-date facilities available. Everything was geared up for children, from the bright and airy waiting room, which sported comfortable couches rather than the usual hard plastic chairs, to the on-site Radiography unit. X-rays, CT and MRI scans were all carried out in rooms that had been made as child-friendly as possible. Colourful murals adorned the walls and the staff wore brightly coloured polo shirts instead of their usual uniforms. Even the gowns the children were given to wear were printed with cartoon characters and had easy-to-fasten Velcro tabs instead of fiddly ties.

Whilst Mac knew that all these things were incidentals, they helped to put the children at their ease and that, in turn, helped him and the rest of the team do their job. By the time his shift ended, he knew that he was going to enjoy working there. Not only would it allow him to develop his skills in paediatric medicine, but it promised to be a fun place to work too. Several of the nurses were leaving at the same time as him so he held the door open for them, bowing low as they all trooped past.

'After you, ladies,' he said, grinning up at them.

'Thank you, my man,' one of them replied, sticking her nose into the air as she sallied forth.

They all laughed, Mac included, and it was a pleasant change to enjoy a bit of light-hearted banter. He hadn't been overstating how bad things had been on his most recent aid mission. It had been extremely grim at times and it was a relief to feel that he could legitimately enjoy himself, even though he didn't regret going and would do the same thing again if it were necessary. He often thought that he had the best of both worlds: he got to help people who were in dire need of his skills and he also had a job he loved to come back to. There was nothing else he could wish for…except, maybe, someone to share his life.

'Thank you.'

The cool tones brought him up short. Mac straightened abruptly when he recognised Bella's voice, feeling decidedly awkward at being caught on the hop. Although he and Bella had spoken several times during the day, their conversations had been confined to work. He had made sure of it, in fact. Although he had promised himself that he wouldn't say anything to her about Tim, he had realised how hard it was going to be to bite his tongue. Bella had let Tim down. Badly. And it was painful to know that she was capable of such behaviour when he had expected so much more from her.

'You're welcome.' He forced himself to smile even though his insides were churning with all the conflicting emotions. On the one hand he knew it was none of his business, yet on the other it still hurt to know that she had fallen so far short of the picture he had held of her. 'It's been a busy day, hasn't it?' he said, struggling to get his feelings in check. It wouldn't serve any purpose whatsoever to tell her how disappointed he felt, how let down. After all, why should she care how *he* felt when she obviously didn't care about Tim?

'It has. We're seeing more and more children now that word has spread that we're open. Obviously, the other hospitals know we're up and running, but it's the parents bringing in their children that has made the difference.'

She gave a little shrug, immediately drawing his eyes to the slender lines of her body, elegantly encased in an emerald-green coat that he knew without needing to be told was from some exclusive designer's collection. Bella had money—a great deal of money that she had been left by her grandparents—and it showed in the way she dressed, even though she had never flaunted her wealth. It was a tiny point in her favour and Mac found himself clinging to it. Maybe it was silly but he wanted to find something good about her, something to redress the balance a little. His smile was less forced this time.

'It must take the pressure off the other A&E departments if more kids are being treated here. That can only be a good thing.'

'Yes, although so many A&E units have closed that the ones which are left are still under a great deal of pressure.'

Bella headed towards the car park, making it clear that she didn't expect Mac to accompany her. He hesitated, wondering why he felt so ambivalent all of a sudden. He had been planning an evening doing nothing more taxing than watching television. It was what he needed, some downtime after the hectic couple of months he'd had and yet, surprisingly, he was loath to spend the evening slumped in front of the box. He came to a swift decision even though his brain was telling him that he was making a mistake.

'Do you fancy grabbing a bite to eat?' he said as he caught up with her. He saw the surprise on her face when she glanced round but he ignored it. For some reason he didn't intend to examine too closely, he wanted to spend the evening with her. 'Nothing fancy, just a curry or something.'

'I don't know if it's a good idea.' She stopped and looked him straight in the eyes and he could see the challenge in her gaze. 'It's obvious how you feel, Mac. You blame me for what's happened, don't you?'

'So why don't you set the record straight and tell me your side of the story?'

He shrugged, wishing he felt as indifferent as he was trying to make out. Maybe he was wrong to blame her, but he couldn't help it when he felt so let down. For all these years he had considered her to be the model of perfection and he didn't want to have to change his view of her, especially when he sensed that it could have repercussions. Now that Bella had fallen from her pedestal, she was just a woman like any other. A woman he had always been deeply attracted to.

The thought made his insides churn and he hurried on. 'It seems only fair to me.'

'Sorry, but it isn't going to happen. I have no intention of trying to justify myself to you or to anyone else.'

She carried on walking, ignoring him as she got into her car. Mac stared after her, wondering why she was being so stubborn. Leaving aside his reasons for wanting to get at the truth, surely it would make sense for her to explain why she had called time on her marriage? Nobody liked being blamed for something they hadn't done and Bella must be no different...

Unless the truth was that she was too embarrassed to admit that she *had* been at fault.

Mac's mouth thinned as he watched her drive away. Bella knew that she had been wrong to abandon Tim when he had needed her so desperately and that was why she couldn't face the thought of talking about it. Although his opinion of her had already dropped way down the scale, it slid even further. Bella was a long way from being perfect, it seemed.

Bella spent a miserable evening. Not even the latest bestseller could take her mind off what had happened. Should she have done as Mac had suggested and told him her version—the *real* version—about what had gone on?

She kept mulling it over, wishing that she had and then just as quickly dismissing the idea. Once she set off down that route there would be no turning back; she would have to wait and see if Mac believed her. The thought that he might think she was lying was more than she could bear. It would be better not to say anything rather than have to endure his contempt.

She was due in to work at lunchtime the following day. By the time she arrived, there was quite a long queue of patients waiting to be seen. Janet waved as she crossed Reception and Bella waved back although she didn't stop. There was a child screaming and it seemed propitious to go and check what was happening before the other children started to get upset. The noise was coming from the treatment room so she went straight there, frowning when she opened the door and was assailed by the shrill screams of an angry toddler.

'What's going on?' she asked, dropping her coat onto a chair.

'Alfie fell off his scooter and cut his knee,' Laura Watson, one of their most experienced nurses, told her. She rolled her eyes. 'Unfortunately, he won't let me look at it 'cos it's sore.'

'I see.' Bella crouched down in front of the little boy. He was clinging to an older woman who she guessed was his grandmother. 'That's an awful lot of noise, Alfie. You're going to scare Robbie if you scream like that.'

The little boy stopped screaming and peeped at her through his fingers, distracted by the mention of the unknown Robbie. Bella smiled at him. 'That's better. Have you met Robbie yet? He's rather shy and only comes out of his cupboard when he thinks nobody is looking. I'll go and see if I can find him.'

Standing up, she crossed the room and opened one of the cupboards that held their supplies. Robbie, the toy rabbit, was sitting on a shelf so she lifted him down and carried him back to the little boy.

'Here he is. He must like you, Alfie, because he came straight out of his cupboard and didn't try to hide.' She handed the toy to the child then glanced at the older woman. 'If you could pop him on the bed then I can take a look at his knee,' she said sotto voce.

The woman quickly complied, sighing with relief when Alfie carried on playing with the toy. 'Thank heavens for that! I thought he would never stop scream-ing.' She smiled at Bella. 'You must have children, my dear. It's obvious that you know just how to distract them.'

'Sadly, no, I don't.'

Bella smiled, trying to ignore the pang of regret that pierced her heart. Having a family had always been her dearest wish, something she had assumed would happen once she had got married, but Tim had never been keen on the idea. Whenever she had broached the subject, he had brushed it aside, claiming that he had no intention of being tied down by a baby at that stage in his life. It was only after she had told him that she wanted a divorce that he had tried to persuade her to stay with promises of them starting a family, but she had refused. The last thing she'd wanted was to have a child to hold their marriage together, a sticking-plaster baby.

'Then you should.' Alfie's grandmother laughed ruefully as she ruffled her grandson's hair. 'Oh, they're hard work, but having children is one of life's blessings. And there's no doubt that you'd make a wonderful mother!'

Mac paused outside the treatment room. The door was ajar and he had heard every word. He frowned as he recalled the regret in Bella's voice when she had explained that she didn't have any children. Quite frankly, he couldn't understand it. According to Tim, Bella had refused his pleas to start a family, claiming that her career came first and that having children was way down her list of priorities, but it hadn't sounded like that, had it? It made him wonder all of a sudden if Tim had been telling him the truth.

It was the first time that Mac had considered the idea that his friend might not have been totally honest and it troubled him. He had accepted what Tim had said without question but had he been right to do so? What if Tim had tried to cast himself in a more favourable light by laying the blame on Bella? What if it hadn't been all her fault that the marriage had failed? What if Tim had been more than partly to blame?

After all, it couldn't have been easy for her to cope with Tim's dependence on those painkillers. Mac had worked in a rehab unit and he knew from experience how unreasonable people could be when they were in the throes of an addiction. Bella must have been through the mill—struggling to help Tim conquer his addiction, struggling to support him even when his behaviour probably hadn't been as good as it should have been. As he made his way to the cubicles, Mac realised that he needed to get to the bottom of what had gone on. Although Tim was his oldest friend, he owed it to Bella to ascertain the true facts. The thought that he might have misjudged her didn't sit easily with him, quite frankly.

Mac didn't get a chance to speak to Bella until it was almost time for him to go off duty. He was on his way to the office when he saw her coming along the corridor. She gave him a cool smile as she went to walk past, but there was no way that he was prepared to leave matters the way they were. It was too important that they got this sorted out, even though he wasn't sure why it seemed so urgent.

'Have you got a second?' he asked, putting out his hand. His fingers brushed against her arm and he felt a flash of something akin to an electric current shoot through him. It was all he could do to maintain an outward show of composure when it felt as though his pulse was fizzing from the charge. 'There's something I need to ask you.'

'I'm just on my way to phone the lab about some results I need,' she said quietly. However, he heard the tremor in her voice and realised that she had felt it too, felt that surge of electricity that had passed between them.

'Oh, right. Well, I won't hold you up. Maybe we can meet later? You're due a break soon, aren't you? How about coffee in the canteen?' he suggested, struggling to get a grip. What on earth was going on? This was Bella, Tim's wife—OK, technically, she was Tim's *ex-wife*—but it still didn't seem right that he should be acting this way, yet he couldn't seem to stop it.

'Why? I don't mean to be rude, Mac, but why do you want us to have coffee?'

She stared back at him, her green eyes searching his face in a way that made him feel more than a little uncomfortable. If he came straight out and admitted that he wanted to check if she was solely to blame for the demise of her marriage then it would hardly endear him to her, would it? He came to a swift decision.

'Because we need to clear the air.' He shrugged, opting for a half-truth rather than the full monty. 'I get the impression that working with me is a strain for you, Bella, and it's not what I want. It's not what you want either, I expect.'

'You're imagining it. I don't have a problem about working with you.' She gave him a chilly smile. 'Now, if you'll excuse me…'

She walked away, leaving him wishing that he hadn't said anything. After all, he hadn't achieved anything, probably made things even more awkward, in fact.

Mac sighed as he made his way to the office. That would teach him to poke his nose into matters that didn't concern him. What had gone on between Tim and Bella was their business and he would be well advised to leave alone.

Bella worked straight through without even stopping for a break. Although they were busy, she could have taken a few minutes off if she'd wanted to, but she didn't. Mac's request to talk to her had unsettled her and she preferred to keep her mind on her patients rather than worry about it. She dealt with her final patient, a ten-year-old boy who had fallen off his bike and broken his arm. Once the X-rays had confirmed her diagnosis, she sent him to the plaster room and cleared up. Helen Robertson, one of the new F1s on the unit, grinned when Bella made her way to the nurses' station to sign out.

'Off home to put your feet up, are you? Or are you planning a wild night out?'

'No chance. It's straight home, supper and bed for me,' Bella replied with a laugh. 'My days of tripping the light fantastic are well and truly over!'

'Oh, listen to her. You'd think she was in her dotage, wouldn't you?' Helen looked past Bella and raised her brows. 'Maybe you can convince her that she can forgo the carpet slippers for a while longer!'

Bella glanced round to see who Helen was talking to and felt her heart lurch when she saw Mac standing behind her. She knew that he was supposed to have gone off duty several hours before and couldn't understand what he was doing there... Unless he had stayed behind to talk to her? The thought filled her with dread. She didn't want to talk to him about anything, neither her marriage nor what Tim had and hadn't done. If she told Mac then she would have to face the possibility that he might not believe her and she couldn't bear that, couldn't stand to know that he thought she was lying.

She hurriedly signed her name in the register, adding the time of her departure. Mac was still talking to Helen, laughing at something the young doctor had said, so Bella headed for the door. It hummed open and she was outside, walking as fast as she could towards the car park. She could hear footsteps behind her and knew that Mac was following her but she didn't slow down. He had no business harassing her this way! She had made it perfectly clear that she didn't intend to discuss her marriage with him and he should accept that. All of a sudden anger got the better of her and she swung round.

'Please stop! I don't want to talk to you, so leave me alone.'

'Why? What are you so scared about?' He shrugged. 'If I were in your shoes, I'd want to tell my side of the story, unless I had something to hide. Do you, Bella?'

'No.' She gave a bitter little laugh, unable to hide how hurt she felt at the suggestion. 'I have nothing to hide but Tim's told you what happened, and you obviously believe him, so what more is there to say? Why should I try to justify myself to you?'

'Because I thought we were friends.' He held out his hands, palms up, in a gesture of supplication that she found incredibly moving for some reason. 'I can tell that you're hurting and if there's anything I can do to make it easier for you then that's all I want.'

He paused. Bella had a feeling that he wasn't sure if he should say what was on his mind and she bit her lip because she wasn't sure if she wanted to hear it either. She steeled herself when he continued.

'I guess what I'm trying to say is that I care about you, Bella. It's as simple as that.'

CHAPTER THREE

Mac held his breath, hoping against hope that Bella would believe him. It was the truth, after all—he *did* care. He cared that she was hurting, cared that she had behaved so out of character. The Bella he knew would *never* have broken her marriage vows unless there had been a very good reason to do so.

'Maybe you mean what you say, Mac, but it makes no difference.' Bella's icy tones sliced through the thoughts whizzing around his head and he flinched.

'I do mean it,' he said shortly, annoyed with himself. What possible reason could there be to excuse the way she had treated Tim? Tim had needed her, desperately, and she had failed him. There was no excuse whatsoever for that kind of behaviour, surely? And yet the niggling little doubt refused to go away.

'Fine.'

She inclined her head but Mac could tell that she didn't believe him and it stung to know that she doubted his word. Couldn't she see that he was telling her the truth? Didn't she know that he wouldn't lie about something so important? It was on the tip of his tongue to remonstrate with her when it struck him that he was doing the very same thing. He was doubting *her*, blaming *her* for the demise of her marriage. What right did he have to take her to task when he was equally guilty?

The thought kept him silent and she obviously took it as a sign that he had given up. She went to her car, zapping the locks and getting in. Mac stayed where he was until the sound of the engine roused him. He had no idea what he was going to do but he had to do something. Maybe Bella was at fault, but he couldn't just ignore the pain he had seen in her eyes. Flinging open the passenger door, he climbed into her car, holding up his hand when she rounded on him.

'I know what you're going to say, Bella. You don't want to talk about your marriage. I also know that I'm probably poking my nose in where it's not wanted…'

'You are,' she snapped, glaring at him.

'OK. Fair enough. And I'm sorry. But, leaving all that aside, I meant what I said. I really do care that you're upset.' He reached over and squeezed her hand, hurriedly releasing it when he felt the now familiar surge of electricity scorch along his nerves. He didn't want to scare her, certainly didn't want her to think that he was trying to take advantage of her vulnerability by making a play for her!

Heat rose under his skin, a hot tide of embarrassment that was so unfamiliar that it would have brought him to his knees if he hadn't been sitting down. Making a play for Bella had never been on the cards. From the moment they had met, Mac had known that she was beyond his reach and he had been perfectly happy with that state of affairs too. Although he had earned himself a bit of a reputation at university by dating a lot of women, he'd had no intention of settling down. He had been determined not to get involved with anyone, although he had been genuinely pleased when Bella and Tim had started seeing one another. They had been so well suited, their backgrounds so perfectly in tune that he couldn't have found a better match for either of them.

It had been the same when they had announced their engagement some months later; he had been truly thrilled for them both and absolutely delighted when Tim had asked him to be his best man. It was only at the wedding that he had started to feel a little bit odd. Listening to Bella swearing to love, honour and care for Tim for the rest of her days had, surprisingly, made Mac feel as though he was about to lose something unutterably precious…

He drove the thought from his head. It was too late for it now; far too late to wish that he had said something, done something, stopped the wedding. How could he have jumped up in the middle of the ceremony and declared that he didn't want Bella to marry Tim because he wanted her for *himself*? No, he had done the right thing—sat there and played his part to the best of his ability. And if there'd been an ache in his heart, well, he had accepted that he would have to learn to live with it.

That was why he had decided to sign on with Worlds Together, a leading overseas aid agency, after the wedding. He had been on over half a dozen missions to date and although he knew that he had helped a lot of people during that time, he had gained a lot too. He'd had three years to rationalise his feelings, three years to make sure they were safely under wraps. Why, if anyone had asked him a couple of weeks ago how he felt then he would have confidently told them that he was back on track. But not now. Not now that Bella was no longer Tim's wife. Not now that she was available.

Mac swallowed his groan. Maybe he did want to help Bella but it could turn out that he was creating a lot of problems for himself by doing so.

Bella had no idea what was going on but the tension in the car was making her feel sick. She licked her parched lips, trying to think of something to say, but what exactly? If she ordered Mac to get out of the car, would he do so? Or would he ignore her and stay where he was? It was the not knowing that was the scariest thing of all because it denoted a massive shift in his attitude.

Mac's behaviour towards her had always been impeccable in the past. He had treated her with an old-fashioned courtesy that she had found strangely endearing. Few men in the circles she had frequented had been so polite. The old 'Hooray Henry' syndrome had been very much alive, so that Mac's thoughtfulness and maturity had set him apart. That was why she had enjoyed spending time with him, she realised in surprise. He hadn't needed to shout or tell risqué stories to make himself stand out. Whenever Mac was around, people always knew he was there.

The thought stunned her. She had never realised before just how much Mac had impressed her. He had been an unknown quantity in so many ways, his background so different from hers that she had been afraid of saying something stupid that would betray her ignorance. Now, after working in the NHS for the past ten years, she had a much better idea of the world. She had treated many people from backgrounds similar to Mac's and understood the hardships they faced. That Mac must have had to overcome all sorts of obstacles to qualify as a doctor merely highlighted his strength of character, his determination, his commitment. Few men could have taken on such a challenge and won.

Bella's head whirled as thoughts that she had never entertained before rushed through it. Added to the strain she'd been under since the breakdown of her marriage, it made her feel very shaky. Leaning forward, she rested her throbbing forehead on the steering wheel.

'Are you all right? Bella, what's wrong? Answer me!'

The concern in Mac's voice brought a rush of tears

to her eyes. Although her parents had expressed polite sympathy when she had told them about the divorce, they hadn't really cared about the effect it had had on her. They were too wrapped up in their own lives to put her first. As Mac had just done.

'It's just all too much,' she whispered, unable to lie.

'No wonder!' Anger laced his deep voice as he got out of the car. He strode round to her side and flung open the door. 'When I think what you must have been through recently—' He broke off as he lifted her out of the car. Bella got the impression that he didn't trust himself to say anything more as he carried her round to the passenger's side. He gently deposited her on the seat and snapped the seat belt into place then looked at her. 'Right, where to? You can go straight home or you can come back to my place. You decide.'

Bella bit her lip as she weighed up her choices, even though by rights she knew that she should tell him to take her home. She didn't want to talk to him, especially not tonight when she felt so raw, so emotional, so very vulnerable.

'Come on, Bella. Just choose where you want to go and I'll take you there.' His tone was so gentle, so persuasive, and Bella wanted to be persuaded so much…

'Yours.'

Mac nodded as he closed the door. Walking round to the driver's side, he got in and backed out of the parking space. He didn't say a word as he drove out of the hospital gates. Bella had no idea where he lived and quite frankly didn't care. Wherever it was, it had to be better than the soulless apartment she was renting. They drove for about fifteen minutes, the roads becoming increasingly narrow as they headed away from the town centre. Bella had done very little exploring since she had moved to Dalverston and had no idea where they were going until she saw the pale glint of water in the distance and realised they were heading towards the river. Mac slowed and turned down a narrow lane, drawing up on the grass verge.

'We have to walk from here,' he told her. 'It's not far, just five minutes or so, but we can't take the car any further.'

Bella nodded as she unfastened her seat belt. She slid to the ground, breathing in the musky scent of damp vegetation. She could hear the river now, the softly sibilant whisper of the water providing a backdrop to the sound of the birds performing their evening chorus. It was so peaceful that she sighed.

'It's wonderful not to hear any traffic.'

'One of the big advantages of living out in the sticks,' Mac replied with a smile that made her breath catch.

He turned and led the way along the path, leaving her to follow, which she did once she had got her breath back. It was the way he had smiled at her that had done the damage—smiled at her the way Mac had used to do. Did it mean that he had forgiven her for her apparent misdemeanours? She doubted it, yet all of a sudden she felt better than she had done in ages. The world didn't seem quite so grim now that Mac had smiled at her. How crazy was that?

Mac paused when they reached the riverbank. It was almost nine p.m. and the light was fading fast. In another month, there would still be enough daylight to light their way along the towpath but he was afraid that Bella would trip up in the dark. Holding out his hand, he smiled at her, determined to keep a rein on his emotions this time. He was offering to hold her hand for safety's sake and not for his own nefarious reasons!

'You'd better hold on to me. The path's a bit slippery after all the rain we've had recently. I don't want you ending up taking a dip.'

There was a moment when he sensed her hesitate before she slipped her hand into his. Mac sucked in his breath when he felt his libido immediately stir to life. OK, so, admittedly, he hadn't made love to a woman in a very long time, but that had been his choice, hadn't it? He had grown tired of dating for dating's sake, had become weary of sex that hadn't really meant anything. It had seemed better to step out of the game rather than continue the way he had been doing. However, it was completely out of order for him to start lusting after Bella. She'd been through enough without him making her life even more complicated.

Mac gave himself a stern talking-to as he led her along the towpath and, thankfully, it seemed to work.

There were several boats tied up along the riverbank and he guided her around their mooring lines. They came to the last boat in the row and he stopped, suddenly feeling on edge as he wondered what she would make of his home. Although he loved the old boat—loved everything about it, from the tranquillity of its mooring to the fact that it was the first home he had owned—Bella had been brought up to expect so much more. He couldn't help feeling a little bit...well, *nervous* about what she would make of it.

'This is it,' he announced, wincing when he heard the false note of bonhomie in his voice. It wasn't like him to put up a front and he hated the fact that he'd felt it necessary. If Bella didn't like his home—so what? It wouldn't make a scrap of difference to him... Would it?

'You live on a boat!'

The surprise in her voice made his teeth snap together as he forced down the urge to start apologising.

'Yep. I bought it when I moved here. I couldn't afford a house so I opted for this instead. It's the perfect base when I'm in the UK. Come on. I'll show you round.'

He helped her on board and unlocked the cabin door, turning on the oil lamp so that she could see where she was going. 'The steps are quite steep,' he warned her. 'So take your time.'

Bella nodded as she cautiously stepped down into the cabin. Mac followed her, turning on more lamps as he went so that the cabin was suddenly bathed in light. Bella stopped and looked around, her face looking even more beautiful in the lamplight. And Mac's libido wriggled that little bit further out of its box.

'It's beautiful. So warm and welcoming… Oh, I do envy you living here, Mac. It must be marvellous!'

There was no doubt that she was telling him the truth and Mac's nerves evaporated in a rush of pleasure. He had no idea why it meant so much to hear her praise his home but it did. He laughed out loud.

'I was worried in case you hated it,' he confessed as his confidence came surging back. 'After all, it is *rather* different from what you're accustomed to.'

'And that's why I love it so much,' she said simply. 'You can keep all your architectural gems as far as I'm concerned. I much prefer somewhere like this— a real home.'

She sat down on the old couch that he had spent so many hours reupholstering and smiled up at him. Mac felt himself melt as relief washed over him. Bella liked his home—she *genuinely* liked it! He wanted to leap up and punch the air in triumph even though he knew how stupid it was.

'Thank you, although you'd better not be too lavish with the compliments or I'll get a swelled head,' he said, trying to joke his way through such a truly amazing moment. 'Not a good idea in a place as small as this!'

'Not small—compact. Or maybe that should be bijou if you prefer estate agent speak.'

Her smile was gentle, making him wonder if she had guessed how nervous he'd felt, but how could she? Bella had no idea that he had always felt at a disadvantage around her in the past, thanks to his background. He had gone to great lengths to hide his feelings and had thought that he had succeeded too. Thankfully, he no longer felt that way. The passage of time had given him the confidence to accept himself for who he was, which was why it was all the more surprising that he had been worried about her reaction.

'Hmm, I'm not sure if most estate agents would class it as that,' he replied lightly, not wanting her to guess how disturbed he felt. He hadn't realised that she understood him so well, hadn't thought that she even *cared* enough to try. And that thought was the last one he needed when he and his libido were having such a hard time sorting themselves out.

'Right. I'll make us some coffee.'

He hurriedly set about filling the kettle. Opening a cupboard, he took out a couple of mugs and placed them on the worktop. There was fresh milk in the tiny fridge and sugar in the jar so he fetched them as well. By the time he had done all that, he was feeling far more in control. Maybe it had come as a surprise to discover that Bella knew him rather better than he had thought she did, but he wasn't going to allow it to throw him off course. Maybe he *did* want to hold her, kiss her, do all sorts of things to her he had never even contemplated before, but he wasn't going to forfeit their friendship for a night of rampant sex. Bella was too important to him; he cared too much about her. And not even what Tim had told him could change that.

It was a moment of revelation, a light-bulb moment that suddenly made everything so much clearer. He may have accepted what Tim had told him. He may even have been hurt and angry about what Bella had done, but he still cared about her. And he always would.

'Thank you.' Bella accepted the cup of coffee. It was too hot to drink and she set it down on the table in front of the couch.

Everything was scaled down to fit, yet, surprisingly, it didn't feel cramped. She found herself comparing it to the vast amount of space in her rented apartment and realised that she much preferred it here. In fact, she had never felt so at ease in any of her previous homes, not even the house she and Tim had started their married life in.

Tim's parents had insisted on buying the elegant Georgian town house for them as a wedding present and her parents, not to be outdone, had insisted on furnishing it. However, the designer-styled rooms with their expensive furniture and luxurious fabrics couldn't hold a candle to this place, she decided. The house had been more an expression of wealth than a real home and it was a relief not to have to live there any longer.

The thought immediately made her feel guilty. It reminded her of how relieved she'd been when she had

finally plucked up the courage to leave. It had taken her
months of soul-searching before she had reached her
decision and it still hurt to know that she had broken
her marriage vows, even though she'd had no choice.
Tim's behaviour had become increasingly erratic by
that point; he had become a danger to his patients as
well as to himself. Leaving him had been the only
thing she could think of to shock him into seeking help
and it had worked too. But did Mac understand that?
Did he understand just how hard it had been for her to
break her vows? All of a sudden Bella knew that she
needed to find out.

'It wasn't an easy decision to leave Tim,' she said
quietly. Out of the corner of her eye, she saw Mac
stiffen and experienced a momentary qualm. She had
sworn that she wouldn't try to justify her actions, but
she needed to make Mac understand how impossible
the situation had been. 'I agonised over it for months
but in the end I realised that I didn't have a choice. It
was the only thing I could think of that might bring
him to his senses.'

'Wouldn't it have been better if you'd stayed and
encouraged him to get help?' Mac suggested and she
flinched when she heard the cynicism in his voice.

'I tried that, but Tim refused to listen to anything
I said. He insisted that he didn't have a problem and
that I was making a fuss about nothing.' She shrugged,
recalling the vicious arguments they'd had. The drugs
had changed Tim from the man she had married into

someone she had barely recognised. 'He couldn't see that he was addicted to the painkillers and needed help.'

'So you upped and left him?'

Mac regarded her from beneath lowered lids. It was hard to tell what he was thinking, although she could guess. Mac believed that she should have stayed with Tim no matter what, but he hadn't been there, had he? He hadn't witnessed the rows, the lies, the empty, meaningless promises to stop taking the drugs.

'Yes. I hoped that it would shock him into admitting that he had a problem and it worked too. He went into rehab a couple of weeks later.'

'I see. So why didn't you go back once he was clean?' Mac's brows rose. 'Tim told me that he begged you to go back to him but you refused. If you loved him then surely that would have been the right thing to do?'

'It wasn't that simple,' Bella said quietly. She stared down at her hands, wondering if she should tell him about Tim's affair. Would she have gone back if she hadn't found out about it or had it been the excuse she had needed? Her feelings for Tim had reached rock-bottom by then; the thought of trying to make their marriage work had filled her with dread. The truth of the matter was that she had no longer loved him, always assuming that she had loved him in the first place, which she now doubted.

'No? It seems pretty straightforward to me.' Mac's tone was harsh. 'What about all those promises you made when you got married? Were they just so many empty words at the end of the day?'

'Of course not!' Bella said angrily, hating the fact he seemed determined to blame her for everything. 'I meant every word I said, but it needs two people to uphold a promise, although Tim obviously didn't see it that way.'

'What do you mean?' Mac shot back. 'It was you who left him.'

'Forget it. It doesn't matter.'

Bella picked up her coffee mug, feeling infinitely weary. No matter what she said, Mac would continue to blame her. Even if she told him about Tim's affair, there was no way of knowing if he would believe her. The thought that he might think she was lying about that to save face was more than she could bear. It would be better to say nothing than take that risk.

They finished their coffee in silence. Bella put her mug on the table and rose to her feet. It was gone ten p.m. and time she went home, even though the prospect of going back to the apartment wasn't appealing. 'I'd better go. Thank you for the coffee and everything.'

'Do you know how to get back?' Mac asked gruffly.

'I'll use the satnav.' She bent and picked up her bag, swaying a little as exhaustion suddenly caught up with her. It had been a long day and add to that the ongoing guilt she felt about the divorce and it was little wonder that she felt so drained.

'Sit down.' Mac eased her back down onto the

couch. Taking the bag off her, he placed it on the table then crouched down in front of her. 'There's no way that you can drive yourself home in this state. You'll have to stay here tonight.'

'Oh, but I couldn't possibly,' Bella began but he ignored her. Standing up, he crossed the cabin and opened a door at the far end to reveal a tiny bedroom complete with double bed.

'You can sleep in here,' he informed her brusquely. Picking up one of the oil lamps, he placed it on the shelf next to the bed, turning down the wick so that the room was bathed in a soft golden glow. 'The sheets are clean and you should be comfortable enough. Bathroom's through there,' he continued, pointing to a door leading off from the bedroom. 'It's only basic but there's everything you'll need.'

'But where are you going to sleep?' Bella protested, more tempted than she cared to admit. Maybe it was foolish but the thought of staying on the boat was the most wonderful thing she could think of. She felt safe here—safe, secure, protected: all the things she hadn't felt in ages.

'The couch pulls out into a bed so don't worry about me,' Mac told her. Opening a cupboard, he took out a T-shirt and tossed it onto the bed. 'You can use this to sleep in. I haven't anything else, I'm afraid.'

'It's fine. Thank you,' Bella said softly.

She sank down onto the bed after Mac left, feeling the last vestige of strength drain from her limbs. Picking up the T-shirt, she held it to her cheek, savouring the softness of the cotton against her skin. Tears filled her eyes again and she blinked them away but more kept on coming, pouring down her face in a scalding-hot tide. She hadn't cried before, not even when Tim had said all those awful things to her after she had told him that she wanted a divorce. Now Mac's kindness had unleashed all the feelings she had held in check and they came spilling out, all the hurt and the pain, the guilt and the relief, every single thing, including how she felt about Mac himself.

Bella took a deep breath. She didn't want to think about Mac and how confused he made her feel. It had always been the same and yet she couldn't understand why he made her feel so mixed up. Normally she had no difficulty making up her mind. Every decision she had ever made had been carefully considered, rationalised, even when she had agreed to marry Tim.

Marrying Tim had seemed like the right thing to do. He had come from a similar background to hers, had held the same values as well as the same expectations. To her mind, their marriage was bound to be a success; however, with the benefit of hindsight, she could see that it hadn't been enough. It had needed more than the fact that they had been compatible on paper—her feelings for Tim had needed to be much stronger, especially after he had become addicted to those drugs. She had failed Tim because she hadn't cared enough, because she wasn't sure if she was *capable* of feeling that deeply about anyone.

Lying down on the bed, Bella clutched the T-shirt to her as sorrow overwhelmed her. She had spent so many years ignoring her emotions that she had lost touch with them. No wonder she couldn't understand how she felt about Mac.

CHAPTER FOUR

THE GENTLE MOTION of the boat woke Mac from a restless sleep. It had been the early hours of the morning before he had finally dozed off, his mind too busy to allow him to rest. Last night had been unsettling for so many reasons, the main one being that Bella had slept right here on the boat. Several times he had heard her crying and he'd had a devil of a job to stop himself going to her. However, the thought of what might happen if he did had helped him control the urge. It would have been far too easy to allow the need to comfort her to turn into something more.

His body responded with predictable enthusiasm to that thought and he groaned. He had to stop this! Maybe it was time he thought about breaking his self-imposed vow of celibacy. So what if sex had become merely a physical release, like an itch that needed scratching? Surely it would be better to deal with the itch than allow it to turn into a major problem.

Rolling out of bed, he filled the kettle and set it to boil then opened the hatch to let some fresh air into the cabin. It had been raining through the night and he grimaced as raindrops splashed onto his head and shoulders. Picking up a tea towel, he dried his face then looked round when he heard the bedroom door open, his heart lurching when he saw Bella standing in the doorway. She was wearing the T-shirt he had lent her and although it came midway down her thighs there was still an awful lot of her shapely legs on view. His gaze ran over her, greedily drinking in every detail. Although his T-shirt was huge on her, somehow the washed thin cotton managed to cling to her body, outlining the curve of her hips, the hand-span narrowness of her waist, the swell of her breasts…

Mac sucked in a great lungful of air when he saw her nipples suddenly pucker beneath the cotton. Rationally, he knew that it was no more than a physical response to the chilly air flowing through the cabin, but after the night he'd had, thinking rationally wasn't easy. His wayward thoughts flew off at a tangent as he found himself imagining how it would feel to watch her nipples harden as he caressed her…

He groaned out loud, hurriedly turning it into a cough when he saw her look at him in alarm. 'Hmm, a bit of a frog in the throat this morning,' he muttered, reaching for the coffee.

'It is a bit chilly in here,' she replied, hugging her arms around herself, and Mac saw the exact second when she realised what was happening. Colour rushed up her face as she hurried back into the bedroom. Picking up her sweater from the end of the bed, she dragged it over her head. 'That's better,' she said brightly as she turned round.

Mac wanted to disagree. He wanted to do it so badly that the words got all clumped up in his throat and almost choked him. He had to content himself with nodding, which was probably the safest response anyway.

'Anything I can do? Make the coffee? Or how about some toast—I could make that, if you like?'

Bella hovered uncertainly in the doorway and Mac's feelings underwent yet another rapid change. Tenderness swamped him as he pointed to the bread bin. Bella's composure was legendary. Even when they'd been students, she had always appeared to be totally in control. He couldn't remember her looking so out of her depth before, so that all he wanted to do was to put her at ease.

'Seeing as you've volunteered, you can be on toast duty. There's no toaster, I'm afraid. You have to do it the old-fashioned way under the grill.' He lit the grill for her. 'Butter's in the fridge and there's marmalade in that cupboard over there.' He pointed everything out then headed to the bedroom. 'I'll have a shower while you're doing that if it's OK with you?'

'Of course.'

Bella nodded as she took a loaf out of the bread bin. Picking up the bread knife, she started to cut it into slices, the tip of her pink tongue poking out between her lips. Mac turned away, not proof against any more temptations so early in the day. He didn't want to think about her tongue and how it would feel stroking his…

There was plenty of hot water for a shower but he turned the dial to cold instead. Stepping under the icy spray, he shivered violently. If there was one thing he loathed more than anything else it was a cold shower but he didn't deserve a hot one, not after the way he'd been behaving.

Lusting after Bella simply wasn't on! Quite apart from the fact that it would ruin whatever friendship they had, he couldn't do it to Tim. Tim may have kicked his drug habit but, like any addict, he was very vulnerable. Mac couldn't bear to imagine the harm it could cause if he and Bella had an affair, not that it was on the cards, of course. However, the fact that he was even *thinking* about Bella in such terms was a warning in itself. Now that she had forfeited her married status, it didn't mean that he was free to make a play for her. No, to all intents and purposes nothing had changed. It was still Bella and Tim.

Bella had their breakfast ready by the time Mac re-appeared. He was wearing a pair of navy chinos with a blue-and-white striped shirt, and it was a relief to see him safely covered up. Maybe he had been decent enough before but the T-shirt and shorts he had worn to sleep in hadn't left very much to the imagination. To her mind, there'd been a rather disturbing amount of leanly muscular body on show.

Heat flowed under her skin as she hurriedly placed the toast on the table. She added the coffee pot along with the milk jug and sugar bowl, determined not to allow her mind to get hijacked by any more such foolish ideas. She had seen men wearing a lot less than Mac had worn that morning in the course of her work so it was stupid to start acting like some sort of... *inexperienced virgin*!

'I could grow used to this.' Mac grinned as he sat down and reached for the coffee pot. He filled both of the mugs, adding milk and several spoons of sugar to his. 'It's a real treat to have my breakfast made for me.'

'It's the least I can do,' Bella murmured, sitting down opposite him. Her knees bumped against his and she hastily drew her legs back out of the way, steadfastly ignoring the odd tingling sensation that seemed to be spreading from the point where their knees had touched.

She was bound to feel *aware* of him, she reasoned, adding a dash of milk to her coffee. After all, it wasn't as though she had made a habit of spending the night with a man, was it? She had never had an affair, had never even indulged in any one-night stands like so many of her contemporaries at university had done. She had only ever slept with Tim, in fact, so spending the night with Mac was a whole new experience for her.

The thought unsettled her even more. It seemed to imply that she'd had an ulterior motive for spending the night on the boat. It wasn't true, of course; it had been necessity that had forced her to stay, the need to rest and recoup her strength. The past year had been extremely hard. Between the stress of the divorce and the move to Dalverston, it was little wonder that it had felt as though she had reached rock-bottom last night. However, she felt much better this morning, less anxious and more like her old self. Spending the night here with Mac had worked wonders and it was just a shame that she couldn't do it again.

Bella bit into her toast, more surprised by that thought than she could say. Bearing in mind how confused Mac made her feel, she should be trying to avoid him, surely? And yet there was no denying that if he had offered to let her stay again tonight *and* the night after that, she would have accepted with alacrity. Being with Mac might be unsettling but in a good way.

They finished their breakfast, making desultory conversation as they ate. Mac sighed as he drained the last dregs of coffee from his mug. 'I'd better get a move on or I'll be late. Are you working today?'

'No.' Bella picked up her mug and plate. She carried them to the tiny sink and pumped water into the bowl. 'I'm working over the weekend so I've got today and tomorrow off.'

'Lucky you.' Mac picked up his dishes and brought them over to the sink. He checked his watch and grimaced. 'I really will have to fly. Fingers crossed that they haven't changed the times of the buses, otherwise I am going to be seriously late.'

'Bus? Why do you need to take the bus?' Bella queried, rinsing their mugs and setting them to drain.

'I left my motorbike at the hospital last night.'

Bella sighed. 'Because you drove me back here? Of course. Sorry.'

'It doesn't matter.' He reached for his jacket, patting the pockets to check that he had everything. 'Look, I'm sorry but I'm going to have to cut and run...'

'Here. Take my car.' Bella picked up her car keys. She shook her head when he started to protest. 'I insist. It's my fault that you left your motorbike at the hospital so it's the least I can do.'

'But what about you?' he demanded, his dark brows drawing together. 'How are you going to get home?'

'Don't worry about me. I'll call a taxi.' Bella pressed the keys into his hand. 'Go on, off you go or you'll be late.'

'Yes, ma'am.' Mac grinned at her. 'Has anyone told you how bossy you are?'

'Not lately,' Bella retorted. She followed him up to the deck, pausing when he stopped. His blue eyes were very dark as they met hers.

'Sure you'll be OK? I feel as though I'm abandoning you.'

'Don't be silly,' she said briskly, although she was deeply touched by the sentiment. It had been a long time since anyone had worried about her this way. 'I'll be perfectly fine. I'll tidy up then phone for a cab... Oh, wait, what's the address? I've no idea where we are.'

'Too-Good Lane.' Mac dug into his pockets and pulled out a crumpled supermarket receipt. He jotted down a number on the back and handed it to her. 'Phone Dennis and ask him to come for you. He's a nice chap and very reliable. You'll be safe with him.'

'Oh, right. Thank you.' Bella went to slip the paper into her pocket before she remembered that she didn't have any pockets. She took a hasty step back when she spotted a jogger running along the towpath, suddenly conscious of her state of undress. She could just imagine what people would think if they saw her standing here wearing one of Mac's T-shirts. They would assume that she and Mac had spent the night together and, although they had, they hadn't *slept* together! Heat flowed under her skin as the thought triggered a whole raft of images: Mac's eyes, so deep and dark as he stared down at her; the feel of his hands as he stroked her body from throat to thigh…

A shudder passed through her and she turned away, terrified that she would give herself away. She heard Mac call a cheery goodbye as he leapt off the boat, even managed to respond, but everything seemed to be happening at one step removed. All she could think about were Mac's hands stroking and caressing her.

Bella hurried back inside the cabin and stood there with her arms hugged tightly around herself. She had never felt this way before, never experienced this overwhelming surge of desire. Although she had enjoyed making love with Tim in the beginning, she had never yearned for his touch. However, with a sudden rush of insight she realised that if Mac made love to her it would be very different. She wouldn't be able to remain detached then—she wouldn't want to. If Mac made love to her, she would be unable to hold anything back, not even a tiny scrap of herself. Mac would unleash her passion, awaken her desire and, once that happened, it would be impossible to go back.

She shuddered. She would be changed for ever, a completely different person, a woman who not only felt but *needed* to feel too. She wasn't sure if she could cope with that.

Mac was thrown in at the deep end as soon as he arrived at work. There'd been an accident on the by-pass involving a lorry and a coach ferrying children to the local high school. Thirty-three casualties were brought through their doors and each one needed to be assessed and treated. Fortunately, Trish Baxter, one of their most experienced staff nurses, was on duty and she performed triage. The less seriously injured children—those with only minor cuts and bruises—were told to wait while the rest were farmed out between cubicles, treatment rooms and Resus. Fortunately, there were just two children badly injured enough to require the facilities of resuscitation and Mac dealt with them. Twelve-year-old twins, Emily and Ethan Harris, had been sitting together at the exact spot where the truck had hit the coach.

'Hi, I'm Mac and I'm a doctor,' Mac explained as the paramedics rolled the youngsters in on their respective trolleys. He listened attentively while the crew outlined the children's status. Emily had injuries to her right arm and was in a great deal of pain, while her brother was having difficulty breathing. Ethan had been thrown into the aisle by the force of the impact and trapped under the seat, which had come away from its housing. It was more than likely that he had fractured ribs which could be compromising his breathing if they had pierced the pleura—the two layers of membrane that covered the lungs and the chest wall. If blood had entered the pleura cavity it would compress the lungs and cause a partial collapse. Mac knew that the boy required urgent treatment and turned to Helen Robertson, the F1 student, who was working with him.

'You take the girl. She'll need X-rays first and then we can tell exactly what we're dealing with. If her shoulder has popped out its socket it will need putting back before the nerves are damaged. You also need to check if the humerus is fractured. OK?'

Helen nodded, looking a little daunted at being put in charge of a patient. Mac watched as she hurried to the phone to request the services of the duty radiographer. She would manage fine, although he would keep a close eye on her. However, if she was to develop her skills then she needed to step up to the plate, as every young doctor had to do. He turned his attention to Ethan, checking his pulse and oxygen levels.

Bailey Thomas, the Australian specialist resus nurse, was assisting him and Mac nodded when he asked if Mac intended to aspirate.

'Yep. I reckon there's blood in the pleural cavity, don't you? Let's see if we can drain it off and help him breathe a bit easier.'

Bailey fetched what they needed and Mac set to work, easing the needle through the tough intercostal muscles between the boy's ribs. He was unsurprised when he immediately drew off bloody fluid. 'Definitely a haemothorax,' he said, glancing at Bailey. Out of the corner of his eye, he saw that the radiographer was putting Emily's X-rays up on the monitor. Even from where he was standing, Mac could see that the girl's humerus was fractured although he didn't say anything. He wanted Helen to find her feet and spotting the fracture herself would help her do that.

'Let's see if we can get any more out of there,' he said, turning back to Ethan. He aspirated some more blood before he was satisfied that he had alleviated the problem. Ethan's sats were back to what they should have been and he was breathing steadily so it was time to assess what other injuries he had sustained. Mac called over the radiographer and asked her to do a whole-body X-ray. While she was doing that he went to check on Helen.

'So, how's it going?' he asked, leaving her to explain her findings.

'It's as you suspected—the humerus is fractured

at the upper end.' Helen pointed out the fracture and Mac nodded.

'So it is. Well spotted. Her shoulder's also dislocated so that needs sorting as well.'

'What should I do?' Helen asked uncertainly. 'Should I try to reduce the dislocation and pop the humerus back into its socket or what? I've not dealt with a case where the humerus is fractured as well.'

'It would be far too painful for Emily if we did it here. Plus there's the problem of the fracture, which complicates matters,' he explained. He always enjoyed helping the younger doctors and, unlike a lot of his peers, never considered it to be a waste of his time. The more everyone knew, the easier it was for the rest of the team, he reasoned.

'Phone Theatre and book her in ASAP. They'll take care of the lot and that way Emily won't know a thing about it. You just need to get her parents' permission for the operation to go ahead, so see if they've arrived yet and if not get the police to contact them. Tell them it's urgent.' He grinned at her. 'We don't want to waste any time so lay it on thick. It's the one time you're allowed to lie to the police!'

'Will do!' Helen was laughing as she hurried out of Resus to set the wheels turning.

Mac smiled as he went back to his patient. From what he had seen so far, Helen had the makings of a really good doctor. She would learn a lot from working here too. It made him suddenly glad that he had agreed to cover the paediatric A&E unit until their own registrar returned to work. Oh, he'd had his doubts when he had found out that Bella was working here. After everything that Tim had told him, it was only natural, although now he could see that he had been a little too hasty. OK, so maybe there had been a few teething problems but he and Bella seemed to be getting on remarkably well, all things considered.

The radiographer interrupted his thoughts just then to tell him the films were ready and he turned towards the monitor. There would be time enough to think about his relationship with Bella later.

Mac's heart skipped a beat. When had it turned into a relationship? It definitely hadn't been that before last night, had it? At the very most, he would have classed it as friendship—he and Bella were friends and that was it. However, deep down he knew it wasn't that any longer. At least not *only* that. Friendship had been hiked up to another level, to the point of becoming a relationship. He wasn't sure if that was a good thing or not, but he was powerless to do anything about it.

He took a deep breath as he stared at the screen. He and Bella had a relationship. Pick the bones out of that!

Bella squared her shoulders as she watched the taxi drive away from the hospital. She would collect her keys from Mac and head straight home. The sooner she was back in her apartment, the sooner she would be able to rid herself of the ridiculous notion of asking him if she could spend another night on the boat. Maybe it had helped to stay there last night, but she had to stand on her own two feet. She couldn't expect Mac to *mollycoddle* her.

She went straight to Reception, only to come to a halt when she saw all the children milling around in the waiting area. It didn't take a genius to work out that something major must have happened so she made her way to the nursing station. Trish Baxter was adding more names to the whiteboard, squeezing them in around the edges. She grimaced when she saw Bella.

'We're fast running out of space. I'll have to resort to taping up a bit of paper soon!'

'What's happened?' Bella demanded, glancing at the list. From what she could see, there were fifteen children waiting to be seen, plus another six receiving treatment: three in cubicles, one in the treatment room, plus two more in Resus.

'A lorry ran into the bus taking the kids to the high school,' Trish explained. She put the cap back on the pen and placed it in the tray. 'To say it's been a tad chaotic in here this morning is an understatement.'

'I can imagine,' Bella agreed, shrugging off her jacket. 'Right, who's next on the list? Freya Watson from the look of it,' she continued, answering her own question.

'I thought you were supposed to be off today,' Trish pointed out as they went back to Reception.

'I am. But I can't just take off and leave you to it

when something like this has happened.' Bella picked up the girl's notes and looked around the waiting room. 'Freya Watson?' She smiled reassuringly when a tall red-haired girl hesitantly stood up. 'Come with me, Freya, and we'll get you sorted out.'

Bella led the girl to a cubicle. According to her notes, Freya was sixteen years old and in her last year at the high school. She looked extremely nervous as she sat down on the bed and Bella smiled encouragingly at her. 'This must have been a big shock for you. You're bound to feel rather shaken up and even a little bit tearful, but that's perfectly normal. I'm just going to check you over and make sure you're all right and then, as soon as your parents get here, you can go home.'

Freya didn't say anything as she stared down at the floor and Bella frowned. Although her notes stated that Freya appeared to have suffered only minor bruising, she couldn't rid herself of the feeling that there was something else wrong with her. She didn't say anything, however, as she set about examining her. If there was something wrong then it would soon become apparent. There was quite heavy bruising to the girl's thighs and it was obviously painful because she winced.

'How did this happen, do you know?' Bella asked, gently examining the area.

'A bag fell off the luggage rack and landed on me,' Freya muttered.

'I see. That must have hurt,' Bella said sympathetically. 'Can I just check your tummy? I need to see if it's caused any bruising there as well.'

She went to unbutton the oversized cardigan that Freya was wearing but the girl pushed her hands away. There was real fear in her eyes when she looked at Bella.

'I'm all right!' she said sharply, attempting to stand up. The words were barely out of her mouth, however, when she doubled up in pain.

Bella caught her as she fell and eased her back down onto the bed. 'Obviously you're not all right, Freya, so I need to examine you. Come on, don't be silly. I only want to check that you're not badly injured.'

Tears started to stream down the girl's face as Bella unfastened her cardigan. As soon as she had done so, she realised what was wrong. Freya was pregnant and, from the look of her, at full term too. She chose her words with care, knowing how important it was that she gained the girl's trust.

'Do you know when your baby is due, Freya?'

'No. Not really. I just kept hoping it wasn't actually happening.' She looked up and Bella's heart ached when she saw the fear in her eyes. 'My mum and dad are going to kill me when they find out! They're always banging on about me not getting myself into any trouble.'

'I'm sure they will be fine once they get over the shock,' Bella said soothingly, mentally crossing her fingers.

She quickly examined the girl, her heart sinking

when she realised that the baby's head was engaged. As she'd suspected, Freya was at full term and, when she let out a groan, Bella realised that there was no time to waste; the baby was about to be born. Hurrying to the phone, she rang Maternity and asked them to send over a midwife as soon as possible. In the meantime, she would have to manage as best she could, although it was a long time since she had delivered a baby. Poking her head out of the cubicle, she beckoned to Trish, who had just finished seeing her patient. She lowered her voice, not wanting anyone to overhear. Although there was little hope of keeping the baby's arrival a secret for very long, at least Freya should be able to tell her parents before her classmates found out.

'We've a bit of a situation in here. It turns out that Freya is pregnant and the baby is on its way. I've asked for a midwife to attend but I don't know how long it will be before she gets here, so we're going to have to manage as best we can. Can we move her into Resus to give her some privacy? Apparently her parents have no idea that she's pregnant.'

'Blooming heck!' Trish exclaimed. 'I know her parents and, believe me, they're going to have a fit when they find out. They're very strait-laced, from what I know of them. Pity help the poor kid is all I can say.'

'Great!' Bella sighed. 'I'll get onto Social Services as soon as I can, but my main concern right now is keeping a lid on this so that the rest of the school doesn't find out. Has Mac finished in Resus, do you know?'

'I'll go and check. Won't be a sec.'

Trish hurried away as Bella went back into the cubicle. Freya was moaning softly and clutching her stomach, obviously in the throes of labour. Bella checked her over once again, grimacing when she discovered that Freya's cervix was fully dilated. From the look of her, it wouldn't be long before the baby arrived.

'It shouldn't be long before your baby is born,' she told her gently. 'I know it hurts, sweetheart, but once the midwife gets here she'll sort out some pain relief for you. Do you understand what happens when a baby is born?'

Freya nodded. 'We did it in biology, how the cervix has to dilate and soften so that the baby can make its way out of the birth canal.'

'Good. At least you have some idea of what's happening and that will help.'

Bella looked round when she heard the curtain open, feeling her heart leap when she saw Mac coming into the cubicle. Although it was barely an hour since they had parted, it was as though she was seeing him through fresh eyes. Her gaze ran over him, taking stock of the dark brown hair falling over his forehead, the midnight blue of his eyes, the strongly masculine set to his features. There was no doubt at all that Mac was an extremely attractive man and she couldn't understand why she had never realised it before…

Her breath caught as she was suddenly forced to confront the truth. Deep down, she had always been aware of his appeal, only she had been too afraid to admit it.

CHAPTER FIVE

FREYA'S BABY ARRIVED just twenty minutes later. It was a little girl and she was absolutely perfect in every way, despite the fact that her mother had received no antenatal care. Mac gently placed the little mite in her mother's arms, wondering what was going to happen now. Bella had explained the situation to him and although he understood what a shock it was going to be for Freya's parents, surely they would support their daughter during this difficult time?

He sighed, realising that it could be wishful thinking. He only had to recall what had happened to his own mother to know that the happily-ever-after scenario wasn't guaranteed. His maternal grandparents had refused to have anything to do with his mother after he had been born. As his father had been brought up in care and hadn't had any contact with his family, it had meant that his parents had had to struggle along on their own. Although his dad had done his best, his lack of qualifications had meant that he'd had to take a series of low-paid jobs, so money had been tight. Coming from a comfortable middle-class background, his mother had found it very difficult to adapt to the change in lifestyle, so it wasn't surprising that she had left.

'The midwife should be here shortly.' Bella came back from phoning the maternity unit. 'Apparently they're short-staffed and that's why it's taken them so long to send anyone over here. However, they've promised to get a midwife to us as soon as they can.'

'Not much they can do now,' Mac replied laconically, trying not to think about how much he had missed his mother after she had left. It was all water under the bridge and had no bearing on his life these days.

'No, I suppose not. I'm only glad that you were here. It's been ages since I delivered a baby and I'm rather rusty, I'm afraid.'

'I've delivered my share over the past few years,' he said wryly, returning his thoughts to the matter at hand. After all, he'd had his father, hadn't he? So he'd been far luckier than a lot of kids. 'You have to turn your hand to most things when you're working overseas.'

'Well, all the practice definitely stood you in good stead today.' She smiled but there was a wariness about the look she gave him that made Mac wonder if something had upset her. However, before he could attempt to find out, Trish popped her head round the door.

'Mr and Mrs Watson are here. How do you want to

play this, Bella? Shall I show them straight in here or do you want a word with them first?'

'I'd better have a word with them first,' Bella replied with a sigh. She turned to Mac after Trish left. 'I'll send Jenny in to sit with Freya. You must have loads to do.'

'I need to check how many kids are still waiting to be seen,' Mac agreed, following her to the door. He looked back and frowned as he watched Freya cradling her baby. 'It's going to be a massive shock for her parents so let's hope they can rise to the occasion. That girl is going to need a lot of support in the coming months.'

'She is,' Bella agreed soberly. 'Having a baby at her age is a lot to cope with.'

'It is. My parents were only a year or so older than Freya when they had me.' He opened the door but he could sense Bella's curiosity as she stepped out into the corridor and suddenly wished that he hadn't said anything. Maybe it was the birth of the baby or thinking about his parents, but he was very aware that his emotions were rather too near the surface for comfort.

'I didn't know that your parents were so young when you were born,' she said quietly as they made their way to Reception.

'There's no reason why you should have known,' he countered. 'It's not something that came up in conversation, I imagine.'

'No. Probably not.' She hesitated. 'It must have been difficult for them, though. Did your grandparents help?'

'Nope, Dad was brought up in care and he'd lost touch with his family. As for my mother, well, her parents took the view that she'd made her decision and it was up to her to live with the consequences. They wanted her to have a termination, apparently, but she wouldn't hear of it,' he added when Bella looked at him questioningly. 'They refused to have anything more to do with her after that.'

'Really? Oh, how awful for her!' She touched his arm and he could see the sympathy in her eyes. 'And awful for you, too.'

'I survived.' Mac dredged up a smile, afraid that he would do something really stupid. Maybe it did hurt to know that his grandparents had turned their backs on him but he was far too old to start crying about it at this stage! He swung round, determined that he wasn't going to make a fool of himself. Maybe Bella *had* touched a chord but there was no way that he intended to let her know that. 'Right, I'll go and check how we're doing. Catch you later.'

'I expect so.'

There was a faintly wistful note in her voice but Mac refused to speculate on the reason for it. He went to the desk and checked how many children were still waiting to be seen. There were just half a dozen left so he took the next one to the cubicles and got him sorted out. While his mind was busily engaged it couldn't start wandering, could it? he reasoned.

He sighed, uncomfortably aware that he had never

experienced this problem before. He wasn't someone who wore his heart on his sleeve and yet the minute Bella had expressed her sympathy, he had turned to mush. What was happening to him? First there had been all those crazy thoughts he'd had last night—the ones that had involved him, Bella, and a bed—and now this. He had to get a grip. Maybe Bella *did* make him feel things he had never felt before but he had to remember that, to all intents and purposes, she still belonged to Tim. No way was he going to be responsible for Tim suffering a relapse! No, Bella was off limits. She always had been and she always would be too.

It was almost lunchtime before Bella felt that she could leave. The last of the children had been seen and sent home and the department was more or less back to normal. Granted, there was a lot of paperwork that still needed doing, but she felt that she could justifiably leave that to Mac. After all, it was supposed to be her day off and there was no reason to feel guilty about going home. It was only when she was halfway across the car park that she remembered that she had forgotten to ask Mac for her keys.

She sighed as she turned round and headed back. She could have done without having to speak to him again, if she was honest. What he had told her earlier in the day about his family had affected her far more than she would have expected. She couldn't help thinking how hard it must have been for him to grow up knowing that he had been rejected by his grandparents.

Bella gave herself a mental shake as she reached the main doors leading into the hospital. She had to stop thinking about Mac all the time. Maybe she did feel incredibly aware of him, but she couldn't afford to let it take over her life the way it was doing. The sooner she got it into her head that he was just a colleague, the simpler it would be.

She was just about to enter the hospital when Mac himself appeared. He smiled ruefully as he held up her car keys.

'You need these, don't you? Sorry! I should have handed them back before.'

'Don't worry about it.'

Bella dredged up a smile as she took the keys off him but it was hard to behave naturally. Why had she never noticed before what a gorgeous shade of blue his eyes were, like the sky on a summer evening? And how come she had never realised just how tall he was, not to mention how lean and fit his body looked? Her thoughts skittered this way and that so that it was a moment before she realised that he had asked her a question.

'Sorry,' she said hurriedly. 'What did you say?'

'I was just wondering how it went with Freya's parents.'

Bella felt a shiver ripple through her at the sound of his deep voice. She had to make a conscious effort not to show the effect it was having on her. If she hadn't noticed his eyes or his physique before then she certainly hadn't noticed how seductive his voice sounded!

'Not too good, I'm afraid. They wouldn't believe me at first, insisted that it couldn't be their daughter and that there must have been a mix-up with the names. Then when I took them in to see Freya, they lost it completely and started shouting at her.' She sighed, deliberately reining in her wayward thoughts. 'It was so bad, in fact, that I had to ask them to leave in the end.'

'Sounds grim. How did Freya take it?'

'Pretty much as you'd expect. It took me ages to calm her down but it's a lot to deal with at her age.'

'It is. What's going to happen when she leaves hospital? Are her parents going to take her home and support her?'

'I doubt it, from what I heard.' Bella shrugged. 'I've spoken to Social Services and they've promised to visit her. They said that they will arrange accommodation for her and the baby when she's discharged. In the unlikely event that Mr and Mrs Watson change their minds, they will cancel the arrangements.'

'I'm not sure which is worse,' Mac said grimly. 'Being dumped in some grotty flat or going home and being faced with constant recriminations. That won't do her or the child any good, will it?'

'It won't. But there's not much we can do except pray for a miracle,' Bella said sadly.

'Pray that Freya's parents will have a change of

heart, you mean?' He shook his head. 'In my experience, it rarely happens so I wouldn't hold out too many hopes on that score.'

'Your grandparents never changed their minds?' Bella said quietly, hearing the echo of pain in his voice.

'No. Oh, Mum tried to persuade them to see sense, but they were adamant that they wanted nothing to do with her or me. I never met them, in fact.'

'How sad. Not just for you and your mother, but for them too. They could have had the pleasure of watching you grow up if they hadn't taken such a rigid stance.'

'Obviously, they didn't see it that way. The shame of their unmarried daughter having a baby outweighed everything else.'

'I can't understand why people feel like that,' Bella admitted. 'Oh, I know my parents were more interested in their careers than in me, but I'd like to think they would have supported me if I'd found myself in that position.'

'There wasn't much chance of that happening, though, was there?' Mac observed drily.

Bella's brows rose. 'What do you mean?'

'Nothing. Forget it. Right, I'd better get back. Thanks again for the loan of your car.'

He started to go back inside but Bella knew that she couldn't let him leave without explaining that cryptic comment. She caught hold of his arm, feeling a flutter of awareness run through her as she felt the warmth of his skin seep through her fingertips. It was all she could do not to release him immediately, but she needed to know what he had meant.

'I want to know what you meant,' she said firmly, determined that she was going to put a lid on all these crazy feelings. All she was doing was touching his arm, for heaven's sake, not making mad, passionate love with him! The thought wasn't the best she could have come up with, but she stood her ground. For some reason it seemed vitally important that she found out what he was talking about. 'Well?'

'Tim told me that you'd refused to have a baby.' His eyes met hers and she felt chilled to the core when she saw the condemnation they held. 'It was obvious how upset he was and I don't blame him. Having a child could have been exactly what he needed to keep him on track.'

'Is that what Tim told you? Or is that your expert opinion?' Bella laughed harshly, more hurt than she could say. Once again Mac was blaming her for what had happened and it was even more hurtful after last night. She'd thought that he was starting to accept that she wasn't solely at fault for the demise of her marriage but she'd been wrong. All of a sudden the need to set him straight overcame everything else.

'Don't bother answering that—it really doesn't matter. The only thing that matters is why I refused to have a baby. I don't suppose Tim explained that, did he?' She didn't give him a chance to answer. 'I refused because there was no way that I was bringing a child into the world who wasn't really wanted. Oh, maybe Tim claimed that he wanted a baby but he only wanted one *after* I told him I was leaving him. He'd always refused to start a family before that, told me that he had no intention of having children when they would only tie him down. However, once I asked him for a divorce, he changed his mind.'

She stared back at him, wondering if he would believe her. Maybe he would and maybe he wouldn't, but she intended to tell him the truth. What he made of it was up to him. 'I refused point-blank and I don't give a damn if you think I was wrong to do so. There was no way that I was prepared to have a baby just to try and save our marriage. That was well and truly over, believe me!'

She swung round, ignoring Mac's demands for her to stop. Walking over to her car, she got in and drove out of the car park without a backward glance. She wasn't sure how she felt, if she was honest, whether she was more angry than hurt by his continued refusal to believe that she wasn't solely to blame. However, what she did know was that she wouldn't make the mistake of thinking that he was on her side ever again. Maybe it had appeared that way last night but it wasn't true. Mac's loyalties didn't lie with her but with Tim. It just proved how little he really cared about her, despite his claims to the contrary.

Mac felt absolutely dreadful for the rest of the day. He couldn't rid himself of the memory of how hurt Bella had looked as she had driven away. By the time his shift ended, he knew that he couldn't leave things the way they were. He had to see her and clear the air. If he could.

He collected his motorbike and headed into the town centre. He had got Bella's address from the staff files and knew that she lived in one of the new apartments that had been built on the site of the old brewery. He'd heard that the cost of renting an apartment there was extremely steep, not that it would worry Bella, of course. She was in the fortunate position of having a private income and it was yet another reminder of why he needed to quash any fanciful thoughts he might be harbouring. Although he earned a decent salary, he wasn't in Bella's league!

Mac parked the motorbike and walked to the entrance. There was an intercom system so he pressed the bell, steeling himself when he heard her voice coming through the speaker. He wouldn't blame her if she refused to see him, but he really and truly needed to sort this out.

'Bella, it's me—Mac. I need a word with you.'

'I'm afraid now isn't a good time,' she began, but he didn't let her finish. He had a nasty feeling that if he didn't resolve this issue tonight, he might never be able to do so. If Tim had lied to him then he needed to know.

'I understand that you're angry but we need to sort this out, Bella, once and for all.'

'Why?' She gave a harsh little laugh and his insides

twisted when he heard the pain in her voice. 'What difference will it make to you if Tim was spinning you a line? You're still going to take his side, aren't you, still going to blame me for ending our marriage? As far as you're concerned, Mac, I should have stuck with him come hell or high water, so what's the point of talking about it?'

'The point is that I need to know the truth.' Mac took a deep breath, aware that he was stepping into dangerous territory, yet how could he avoid it? Bella deserved to be given a fair hearing and that was what he intended to do. If she would agree. 'I know it's asking a lot but, please, Bella, let me in so we can talk this all through.'

He held his breath, hoping against hope that he had managed to persuade her. When he heard the door lock being released, he almost shouted out loud in relief. He hurried inside and made straight for the lift, half afraid that she would change her mind. Her apartment was on the fifth floor and he tapped his foot in impatience as the lift carried him upwards. He wasn't sure how he was going to set about this; maybe it would be simpler just to wait and see how it panned out? If he started asking questions, there was always a chance that he would say something to alienate her. He sighed as the lift came to a halt. Normally, he wouldn't have given it a second thought; he would have simply asked Bella what had gone on and that would have been it. But this wasn't a normal situation, was it? Someone was lying and he needed to find out who it was.

Bella must have heard the lift stop because she opened the door. She didn't say a word, however, as she led the way inside the apartment. Mac placed his motorbike helmet on the console table in the foyer then followed her into the living room, stopping abruptly when he was greeted by the most spectacular sight. One whole wall was made of glass and the view of the mountains that surrounded the town was stupendous.

'What a fabulous view!' He went over to the window and stood there for a moment, drinking it in. It was only when he became aware of the silence that he remembered why he had come. He turned slowly around, his heart aching when he saw how distant Bella looked. She had always had a tendency to withdraw into herself if something had upset her and it was obvious that was happening now.

'Thank you for letting me in,' Mac said quietly, trying to rein in the guilt he felt. It didn't make him feel good to know that he had upset her, even though it hadn't been intentional. He sighed, aware that he could make the situation worse if he continued probing, but what choice did he have? He needed to get at the truth.

'What you told me before about Tim not wanting a child until you asked him for a divorce—was it true?' he said before his courage deserted him.

'Yes. Not that I expect you to believe me.'

Mac heard the challenge in her voice but it didn't

disguise the pain it held as well and his heart ached all the more. That she was loath to discuss what had gone on was obvious and in other circumstances he wouldn't have pushed her. However, making sure that he could trust her was even more important than finding out if Tim had lied to him.

The thought stunned him because it aroused feelings that he'd believed he had conquered many years before. After his mother had left, he had found it impossible to trust anyone. He had been only seven when Laura MacIntyre had walked out of their home but he could still remember how terrified he had been in case his father had left him as well.

Was that why he had avoided commitment? he wondered suddenly. Was it the reason why he always called time on a relationship before it became too serious? He was afraid of letting himself fall in love in case he was let down. His breath caught as one thought led to another: was it also the reason why it was so important that he made sure he could trust Bella?

Mac felt panic assail him when he realised just how complicated the situation actually was. His feelings for Bella weren't nearly as clear-cut as he had believed. They seemed to be changing on a daily basis, in fact. He had started out feeling disillusioned, angry even about the way she had behaved, yet he couldn't put his hand on his heart and swear that was how he felt now.

A trickle of sweat ran down his back as he looked at her and remembered how he had felt the night before, how he had ached to touch her, kiss her, feel her body, warm and responsive under his. It certainly hadn't been anger or disillusionment he had felt then!

Bella wasn't sure what Mac was thinking but there was something about the way he was looking at her that made her heart start to race. She bit her lip, determined that she was going to keep a lid on her emotions. If they were to sort this out then she had to remain detached. She had told Mac her version of what had happened, the *true* version, and now it was up to him to decide if he believed her. The one thing she mustn't do was get emotionally involved. Something warned her that would be a mistake of gigantic proportions.

Turning, she went over to the drinks trolley and poured a little brandy into a couple of crystal glasses. Although she rarely drank spirits, she felt in need of some Dutch courage to see her through the next few minutes. Walking over to one of the huge black leather sofas, she sat down, placing the drinks on the glass-and-steel coffee table. She had rented the apartment fully furnished and hadn't made any changes to it. It was merely a place to eat and sleep when she got back from work, yet all of a sudden she found herself wondering what Mac would make of it. Having experienced the welcoming warmth of his boat, she couldn't imagine that it would appeal to him on any level.

For some reason she found the idea upsetting but she refused to dwell on it. It wasn't her taste in furnishings that Mac was interested in but her honesty! Anger rippled through her as she picked up a glass and took a sip of the brandy. She had done nothing wrong and the sooner he accepted that the better.

'So, seeing as you've seen fit to come here to talk to me, I suggest you get on with it.' Bella stared at him over the rim of the glass, wanting to make it clear that she didn't intend to allow this to drag on. She had been genuinely upset when she had got home but she'd had time to calm down now and she had no intention of getting upset again, no matter what he thought. *She* knew she was telling the truth and that was what mattered, wasn't it?

She clamped down on the tiny flicker of doubt, knowing how quickly it could turn into something much bigger. Mac came and sat down opposite her, although he didn't make any attempt to pick up his glass. He stared down at the floor for a moment and her heart surged when she saw how grim he looked when he finally raised his head.

'Why would Tim lie to me, though? That's what I don't understand.' He pinned her with a look of such intensity that she was hard-pressed not to look away, but somehow she managed to hold his gaze.

'You'll have to ask him that.'

'But doesn't it make you angry that he's blaming you for everything that happened?' he retorted.

'Yes, it does.' Bella managed to suppress a shiver when she heard the anger in his voice. Was he angry because Tim had lied to him or because he didn't believe her? She had no idea but she couldn't afford to let it worry her, certainly couldn't allow it to unleash all the emotions that were churning around inside her.

'Then how can you sit there so calmly? Surely, you want to do something to address the situation, Bella.'

'What do you suggest? That I contact everyone I know and tell them that Tim is lying?' She gave a bitter little laugh. 'Maybe some people will believe me, but not very many, I'm afraid. Most will take Tim's side simply because he's always been far more outgoing than me. I have a tendency to keep myself to myself, and that doesn't help if you're trying to get people on your side. I mean, even you aren't sure who to believe, are you, Mac? And you know me better than anyone else does.'

CHAPTER SIX

MAC FELT HIS blood pressure rocket skywards. Bella thought that he knew her better than anyone else? Coming on top of everything that had happened recently, it was almost too much to take in and yet he couldn't pretend that he didn't experience a rush of pleasure at the idea. Knowing Bella, inside and out, was his dearest wish.

'Which is why I want to get to the bottom of this.' He cleared his throat when he realised how uptight he sounded. Until he was sure who was telling the truth, he needed to remain impartial. The thought of how easily he could be swayed by all the emotions rampaging around inside him was sobering. Mac deliberately cleared his head of everything else while he focused on the reason why he had come to see her.

'So you're just going to leave things the way they are and not try to defend yourself?'

'Basically, yes.' She sighed. 'I can't see any point in making a fuss, if I'm honest. Tim obviously has his reasons for blaming me and, quite frankly, I don't intend to end up having a public slanging match with him to clear my name. *I* know what really happened and that's what matters most of all.'

'So what you're saying is that you don't care what anyone else thinks,' Mac said slowly. He shook his head. 'That doesn't seem fair to me. I mean, why should everyone believe you're to blame when it wasn't your fault?'

'It's just the way things are.' Bella shrugged, trying not to get too hung up on the thought that Mac must care if he was so keen to straighten things out. She'd been down that route last night and she wasn't about to make the same mistake again. Maybe Mac did care but out of a sense of justice: it wasn't personal.

'Maybe Tim finds it easier to deal with what's happened by blaming me,' she said flatly, not wanting to dwell on the thought when it evoked so many mixed feelings. She and Mac had never been more than friends and it would be stupid to think that their relationship had changed. 'After all, he's been through a very difficult time. Dealing with his addiction can't have been easy for him. You know as well as I do how hard it is for an addict to get clean and stay off the drugs.'

'Yes, I do.' His tone was flat. 'I grew up in an area where drugs were part of everyday life, so I understand the damage they cause. That Tim managed to overcome his addiction is to his credit but it still doesn't excuse what he's doing, going around telling everyone a pack of lies. He needs to accept responsibility for his actions. Then maybe there's a chance that you two can get back together.'

'That isn't going to happen,' Bella said quietly. 'Our marriage is over and there's no chance of us trying again.'

'But you must still have feelings for him. Oh, I know it's been tough, Bella. Probably tougher for you than it was for Tim, in fact, because he was more concerned about where his next fix was coming from.' He leant forward and she could see the urgency in his eyes. 'But you loved him once, otherwise you wouldn't have married him, would you? So why not give it another shot?'

'As I said, it isn't going to happen.'

She stood up, wanting to make it clear that she didn't intend to discuss the matter any further. She and Tim were never getting back together for one simple reason: she didn't love him and she never had loved him either.

The thought was incredibly painful as it seemed to highlight how out of touch she was with her own emotions. As she led the way to the door, Bella felt a wave of despair wash over her. How could she ever trust her own judgement again? How could she be sure if she did fall in love that it was the real thing this time? The thought of living out her life in a state of lonely uncertainty was more than she could bear, especially with Mac there—Mac, who always seemed so sure of himself, so confident about what he wanted. She couldn't imagine Mac experiencing all these crippling doubts!

Bella opened the door, her heart aching as she fixed a smile to her lips. 'Thank you for coming. I'll see you in work, I expect.'

'So that's it, is it? I've said my piece and you've said yours and that's the end of the matter?' His dark brows drew together as he glowered down at her.

'I can't think of anything else that we need to say.' She gave a little shrug, aiming for a nonchalance she wished she felt. Maybe it was silly, but she had always dreamt of finding the right man and falling in love. However, it seemed unlikely that it would happen now. 'I've told you my side of the story and now it's up to you to decide who you believe.'

'In other words, you don't give a damn if I think you're lying.' He laughed harshly, so harshly that she flinched. 'I have to hand it to you, Bella. Your self-confidence is amazing!'

'You're wrong. I don't feel confident at all,' she shot back. 'I have no idea if you believe me, Mac, but what can I do about it? Should I try to convince you by telling you about all the horrible things Tim said to me or all the lies he told? Should I tell you about his affair to try and gain your sympathy?' She shook her head. 'Sorry, but it isn't going to happen. Either you believe me or you don't—it's as simple as that.'

'Affair? What do you mean? What affair?'

The shock in his voice cut through her anger. Bella

bit her lip, wishing she hadn't told him that. It hadn't been intentional, but the words had somehow slipped out.

'It doesn't matter...' she began.

'Of course it matters!' He gripped hold of her by the shoulders as he bent to look into her eyes, and maybe it was the fact that she was feeling so wrung out, but all of a sudden she couldn't contain her feelings any longer. Tears began to pour down her face and she heard him groan.

'Oh, Bella, I'm sorry! I didn't mean to upset you.' He drew her to him, cradling her against the solid strength of his body, and she cried all the harder. It had been such a long time since anyone had held her like this, since anyone had cared.

'Shh. It's OK, sweetheart. Don't cry. Everything's going to be fine, I promise you.'

He drew her closer, running his hand down her back in a gesture that was meant simply to comfort, and she sighed. She could feel his fingers gliding down her spine, warm and wonderfully soothing as they traced the delicate column of bones. His hand reached the curve of her buttocks and stopped. Bella could feel the heat of his fingers burning through her clothing and shuddered. All of a sudden the air seemed thick with tension, filled with a sense of anticipation that immediately dried her tears. She realised that she was holding her breath as she waited to see what would happen...

His hand slid back up, following the route it had

already travelled. When it reached the nape of her neck it stopped again, resting lightly beneath the heavy knot of her hair. Bella bit her lip, suddenly unsure about what she should do. Should she break the contact, step away from him and make it clear that she didn't welcome this kind of intimacy? But surely that would be a lie? Having Mac hold her, caress her, make her feel all these things *was* what she wanted.

Desperately.

Helplessly, her eyes rose to his and she felt her heart lurch when she saw the awareness on his face. She knew in that moment that Mac understood how confused she felt because he felt the same. Maybe it was that thought, that single mind-blowing thought, that unlocked all her reservations, but she didn't pause to consider what she was doing as she reached up and drew his head down. Their mouths met, clung, and it was like nothing she had experienced before. There was desire, yes, but there was so much more to the kiss than passion. The feel of Mac's mouth on hers made her feel safe, secure, protected. It was as though she had found her way back home after a long and exhausting journey.

Bella wasn't sure how long the kiss lasted. It could have been seconds or a lifetime for all she knew. She was trembling when they finally broke apart, but so was Mac. He ran the pad of his thumb over her swollen lips and his eyes were alight with a tenderness that filled her with warmth. It was obvious that she wasn't the only one to have been so deeply moved by what had happened.

'I didn't plan this, Bella, but I'm not sorry it happened and I hope you aren't either?'

His voice was low, deep, and she shivered when she heard the desire it held. She had done this to him, she thought in amazement. She had aroused his passion and it was a revelation to realise that she was capable of making him want her this much.

'I'm not. I'm not sorry at all,' she said in a husky little voice that made his eyes darken. When he reached out and pulled her back into his arms, she knew what was going to happen. Maybe they hadn't planned it, but there was no point pretending. They had both thought about it—thought about how it would feel to lie in each other's arms and make love. And tonight it was going to happen.

When he swung her up into his arms and carried her into the bedroom, she didn't protest. Why would she when it was what she wanted so much? He laid her down on the huge bed and sat down beside her, his hand trembling just a little as he cupped her cheek.

'Are you sure, Bella? Absolutely certain this is what you want?'

'Yes.' She captured his hand, gently biting the pad of flesh at the base of his thumb, and didn't even feel shocked by her own temerity. This was Mac and whatever happened between them tonight felt right. 'I'm sure, Mac. Completely and utterly sure.'

He made a sound deep in his throat as he stood up and started to strip off his clothes. His body was lean and fit, the muscles in his chest flexing as he dragged his T-shirt over his head and tossed it onto the floor. Bella's eyes ran over him, greedily drinking in the sight of his body, so beautiful in its masculinity. She bit her lip as her gaze came to rest on his erection because there was little doubt about how much he wanted her. Her eyes rose to his and she realised that she must be blushing when he laughed softly and tenderly.

'It's hard for a man to hide how he feels. When he wants a woman as much as I want you, Bella, then it's pretty obvious, I'm afraid.'

'Don't apologise,' she said with a bravado that would have shocked her once upon a time but felt completely natural now. She laughed up at him. 'It's good to know that it isn't all one-sided.'

'Oh, it most definitely isn't!' He lay down on the bed and gathered her into his arms while he kissed her with a passion that made her tingle both inside and out. Propping himself up on his elbow, he smiled into her eyes. 'You're a great kisser, Bella English. I have no complaints on that score.'

'Thank you,' she retorted. 'I hope you don't have any complaints on any other score, either.'

'Maybe just one.' He kissed the tip of her nose and grinned at her. 'You're decidedly overdressed for what I have in mind. Still, it shouldn't take long to resolve the problem.'

His hands went to the buttons on her shirt and Bella sighed. Her lack of experience hadn't prepared her for his relaxed approach to lovemaking. Passion was tempered by humour and, amazingly, that only seemed to heighten her desire for him. By the time he reached the final button, she was trembling with need but it was obvious that he didn't intend to rush things.

He parted the edges of her shirt with exquisite slowness and stared down at her breasts, barely concealed by the lacy white bra she was wearing. His eyes were filled with so many emotions when he looked up that her heart overflowed. Was this how it should be? she wondered giddily. Was this what she had missed, having a man look at her as though she was the most wonderful sight he had ever seen? She had no idea what the answer was but she knew that she would remember this moment for the rest of her life—the moment when she discovered how it really felt to be a woman.

'You're so beautiful, Bella. So very, very beautiful...'

The rest of the words were swallowed up as he bent and drew her nipple into his mouth. Bella cried out at the explosion of sensations that erupted inside her. The moist heat of his tongue, the erotic stimulation of the damp lace against her flesh, the sensual whisper of his breath as he raised his head and blew gently on the hard nub made her tremble with longing. When he turned his attention to her other breast, lavishing it with the same attention, she wasn't sure if she could bear it. She could feel her passion mounting, feel her desire growing more and more urgent with every delicate stroke of his tongue. Lacing her fingers through his hair, she raised his head, uncaring if he could tell how much she needed him.

'Mac, I don't know if I can take much more of this,' she whispered hoarsely.

'Sweetheart!' He kissed her hard and hungrily, then stripped off the rest of her clothes until she was naked to his gaze. His eyes grazed over her and she shivered when she saw the desire they held as he raised his head. 'Tonight is going to be special, Bella. I promise you that. Just give me a second.'

He slid off the bed and, picking up his trousers, took out his wallet and removed a condom from it. Bella closed her eyes as he lay down beside her again and took her in his arms, shuddering as he entered her. There wasn't a doubt in her mind that he was right. Tonight *was* going to be special. For both of them.

Mac lay on his back, one arm resting across his eyes. It was almost midnight and the daylight had disappeared a long time ago, but they hadn't switched on the lamps. Maybe they had both felt a need to preserve the status quo. Casting light onto the scene might spoil things; it might make them question the wisdom of what they had done. He didn't want to do that and he sensed that Bella didn't want to do it either.

He sighed softly. He was still finding it difficult

to accept how quickly his feelings had changed. The anger he had felt about the way Bella had treated Tim seemed to have melted away. Finding out that his friend had had an affair had been a shock but it wasn't only that which had made him see that he had been unfair to her. Holding her in his arms, being close to her had done more than merely satisfy his desire for her. It had made him remember exactly who she was, and that certainly wasn't the sort of woman who would turn her back on someone in need. No, Bella had been forced into ending her marriage by Tim's appalling behaviour and it made him feel incredibly guilty to know how badly he had misjudged her. Now he could only pray that he hadn't made her life even more difficult by what they had done.

'Penny for them, Dr MacIntyre.'

Her voice was low but Mac heard the uncertainty it held and lowered his arm. Rolling onto his side, he pulled her to him and kissed her softly on the lips. Maybe he did have doubts, but he intended to keep them to himself. He didn't want her worrying unnecessarily.

'I'm not sure they're worth as much as a penny,' he countered, clamping down on the rush of desire that flooded through him. They had made love not once but twice and he really shouldn't be feeling this need again, he told himself sternly, but to very little effect. 'I was just letting my mind drift rather than thinking actual thoughts.'

'So you weren't regretting what we've done?' She looked steadily into his eyes and he sighed, unable to lie to her.

'No. I don't regret it, but I do wonder if it was right. I…well, I don't want it to affect our friendship, Bella, and make life even more complicated for you.'

'Neither do I.'

She smiled but there was something about her expression that made him wonder if he had phrased that badly. Getting into a discussion about the problems it could cause if they had an affair didn't seem right, but maybe he should have made his feelings clearer? However, before he could try to make amends, she tossed back the quilt and stood up. Mac gulped as he was treated to a tantalising glimpse of her beautiful body before she pulled on a robe.

'I'll have a shower then make us some coffee. There's a second bathroom along the corridor if you want to use that,' she told him briskly.

'Thanks.'

Mac stayed where he was until she had disappeared into the en-suite bathroom. Getting out of bed, he gathered up his clothes and made his way to the bathroom. There was a heavy feeling in his heart, a suspicion that he had upset her, and he hated to think that his clumsiness had caused her any pain, but what should he do? Sit her down and explain how awkward he felt about encroaching on Tim's territory?

Although Bella had claimed that there was no

chance of her and Tim getting back together, she could change her mind. He had seen it happen to other couples, watched as time had softened the bad memories and brought the good ones into focus. He wouldn't want to stand in the way of that happening. Neither would he want to be left with a broken heart if it did. If Bella did rediscover her love for Tim then how would it affect him?

Once again the fear of finding himself rejected reared its ugly head. As Mac got dressed, he tried his best to rationalise it away. He was a grown man, after all, not a scared seven-year-old child, and if anything happened he would deal with it. However, no matter how he tried to reason the fear away, it wouldn't budge. In all those dark places he didn't visit very often, he knew that losing Bella would be far worse than anything that had happened to him before. Once he had allowed himself to fall in love with her, his heart would no longer be his. It would belong exclusively to her.

Bella had the coffee ready by the time Mac appeared. She loaded everything on to a tray and carried it through to the sitting room. He was standing by the window, ostensibly enjoying the view, but she sensed that his thoughts were far removed from the charms of the moonlit scene. Was he afraid that he had allowed his judgement to be swayed by passion? Was he worried in case she had used sex as a means to convince him of her innocence? That thought stung more than any other could have done. The only reason she had slept with him was because she had wanted to!

She plonked the tray on the table with a thud that made him swing round and she felt her heart scrunch up in her chest when she saw the strain on his face. Whatever thoughts he was harbouring obviously weren't pleasant ones. Picking up the pot, she poured coffee into the mugs, wishing that some passing genie would spirit her away. She wasn't up to this! She couldn't face the thought of explaining why she had slept with him when it was obvious that her reasons were a world removed from his. Oh, so maybe he had wanted her; she'd seen definite proof of that! However, it meant nothing if he now regretted what they had done.

Bella's hand shook as she put the pot back on the tray. She couldn't believe how painful it was to know that Mac wished tonight had never happened. It felt like another rejection, just like the way Tim had rejected her when he'd had that affair. What was wrong with her? Was it her inability to show her emotions that drove men away?

That was what Tim had said during one of those terrible rows they'd had. He had accused her of being so cold that she had driven him into the arms of another woman. He had even blamed her coldness for his drug addiction and, although Bella knew that he had been trying to excuse his behaviour by blaming her, the words had stuck in her mind. Now they rose to the surface again to taunt her.

She was incapable of showing her true emotions because there was something missing from her make-up, some vital element she was lacking. No wonder Mac was having second thoughts about what had happened tonight. After all, what man would want to get involved with someone like her? Someone who wasn't a *real* woman.

Mac drank his coffee as quickly as he could. It was scalding hot but, he gulped it down anyway, uncaring if it burnt his tongue. He needed to get away and the sooner the better, preferably. He had never gone in for the *wham, bam, thank you, ma'am* routine; he'd had far too much respect for the women he had slept with to treat them that way. However, he would have given his right arm to simply cut and run without offering up any explanations. If he started to explain to Bella why he wanted to leave so desperately, who knew what he'd end up admitting? The thought of laying his soul bare gave him hot and cold chills and he stood up abruptly. He had to leave. Right now, this very second. No matter what Bella thought of him!

'I have to go.'

He headed for the door, hating himself for leaving her like this, yet unable to do anything about it. He knew that he was within a hair's breadth of falling in love with her and the thought scared him witless. It was all very well telling himself that he could cope with anything that happened, but could he if it involved losing Bella? Could he honestly see himself carrying on if he loved and subsequently lost her? Just the thought made his head spin, round and round, faster and faster, until it felt as though his thoughts were swirling on a merry-go-round. Losing Bella would be the one thing he couldn't handle, the thing that would bring him down, and he couldn't take that risk.

He stopped when he reached the front door, forcing himself to smile as he turned to her. His heart stuttered to a halt when he saw the pain in her eyes but he had to be strong, had to do what was right for her as well as right for him. It wasn't just himself he had to think about, after all. How Bella was going to feel was even more important. He couldn't bear to think that she would be consumed by guilt about what they had done if she did decide to go back to Tim.

'I know we crossed a lot of boundaries tonight, Bella,' he said gruffly, trying to batten down the thought of how he would feel if that happened. 'But there's no need to feel...well, *awkward* about what's happened. We've always been friends and I hope that we can still be friends from now on too.'

'If that's what you want.'

Her voice echoed with scepticism and Mac grimaced, understanding completely why she had difficulty believing him. Friends didn't usually make mad passionate love, did they? They definitely didn't cross that boundary! The thought of how hard it was going to be to think of her as a friend after tonight was too much to handle and he shrugged, opting for the easier route, a half-truth.

'It is. I value our friendship, Bella. I always have.' Bending, he dropped what he hoped was a friendly kiss on her cheek, drawing back when he felt his body immediately respond. So much for friendship, he thought wryly as he opened the door. All it took was one chaste little kiss and he was up and running again!

He made his way to the lift, pausing briefly to wave before he stepped inside. He heard the apartment door close as the lift set off and sighed. If only that was the end of the matter, but there was no point kidding himself: tonight was going to have far-reaching consequences for both of them. He and Bella had slept together and even if they ignored what had happened, it wouldn't go away. It would be like the proverbial elephant in the room whenever they were together, always there but never acknowledged.

He groaned. What in heaven's name had he done?

CHAPTER SEVEN

THE DAYS FLEW PAST. With the schools breaking up for the long summer holiday, there were a lot of visitors in the area and that meant they were busier than ever in the paediatric A&E unit. Bella started early and finished late but she didn't complain. It was easier when she was working. It was when she was on her own that it became a problem. With nothing to distract her, her mind kept returning to what had happened that night in her apartment. She and Mac had made love and whilst she knew that a lot of women would have taken it in their stride, she couldn't do that. That night had been a turning point for her. She had not only discovered how it felt to be a real woman but she had also realised how inadequately suited she was to the role. It was much easier not to have to think about it.

It was a Saturday evening, three weeks after that fateful night, when Bella found herself working with Mac. Up till then their paths had crossed only fleetingly; if she'd been working days, he had been working nights. However, that night they were both rostered to work and she knew that she would have to deal with it. He was already there when she arrived, standing by the desk, laughing at something Laura Watson was saying to him. Bella felt her heart jolt as the memories came flooding back. Mac had looked like that when they had made love. His expression had been softened then by pleasure. If she lived to be a hundred, she would never forget that night, no matter how hard she tried.

He suddenly glanced round and she took a steadying breath as his gaze landed on her. Although neither of them had said anything, they were both aware of the rules. If they were to continue behaving as friends then there must be no harking back to what had happened. They must focus on the here and now, not on what they had done that night.

'It sounds as though you two are having fun,' she said lightly, going over to the desk to sign in.

'Laura was just telling me about one of the children she saw this morning,' Mac explained. He stepped back, ostensibly to give Bella some room, although she suspected that in reality he was trying to avoid touching her. A spurt of anger suddenly shot through her. He had been more than eager to touch her that night, hadn't he?

'Oh, yes?' She smiled up at him, her green eyes holding a hint of challenge. Maybe they had agreed to behave as though nothing had happened, but it wasn't true. They had made love and not once either, but twice. Whether he liked the idea or not, he couldn't just ignore what they had done. 'So what happened?'

'Oh, nothing much. The kid just got a bit confused, that's all.' He glanced round when the phone rang. 'I'll get that.'

He headed to the phone, leaving Bella seething even though she wasn't sure why exactly. After all, it made far more sense to pretend that nothing had happened, especially when there was no chance of there being a repeat. She snorted in disgust as the thought slid into her head. There definitely wasn't going to be a repeat. One night in Mac's arms had caused enough upheaval in her life!

Bella worked her way through the list. There was nothing really serious, just a lot of cuts and bruises, as could be expected when so many children were on holiday. She patched up several cut knees and sent a couple of youngsters for X-rays, and that was it. By the time she was due to take her break, there was just one child waiting to be seen. Mac had finished with his patient and arrived at the desk at the same time as her. He shrugged as he reached over and picked up the last file.

'I'll take this if you want to go for your break, Bella. We may as well make the most of it while it's quiet.'

'Fine.'

Bella headed for the lift. Although she wasn't hungry, a cup of tea would be very welcome. Mac had taken his patient to the cubicles and the waiting room was empty. She was about to step into the lift when

the main doors opened and a couple of police officers
came in. The female officer was carrying a baby in her
arms and Bella paused, wondering what was going on.
When Janet, their receptionist, beckoned to her, she
hurried over to them.

'What's happened?'

'We received a report to say that a baby had been left
at home on its own,' the male officer explained. 'When
we got to the flat, we found the front door open. The
child was inside, screaming its head off. It doesn't appear to be injured, from what we can tell, but we need
you to check it over, just to make sure.'

'Of course.' Bella led the way to the treatment room.
'If you can put the baby on the bed, I'll examine it.'

She undid the poppers down the front of the child's
sleepsuit and slipped it off then removed its vest and
nappy. It was a little girl and she appeared to be both
clean and well-nourished. Bella carefully checked her
over and shook her head.

'No, there's nothing wrong with her. She's a little
bit dehydrated but that can soon be sorted out once we
give her a drink. Do you know where the mother is?'

'No idea. The neighbour who phoned in the report
wasn't able to tell us very much.' The officer sighed.
'Apparently, she's little more than a kid herself, from
what we can gather. We've been on to Social Services
and we're hoping they might be able to help us.'

'Do you know her name?' Bella asked slowly,

although she had a feeling that she already knew the name of the baby's mother.

'Yes. The neighbour was able to tell us that much at least.' The officer consulted his notebook. 'Freya Watson. We're trying to find out if she's local. If we can trace her family then they might know where she's gone.'

'I can give you their address.' Bella brought up Freya's file on the computer. She gave the policeman the Watsons' address then quickly explained the situation. 'I'd like to think that Freya's parents know where she is, but they were furious when they found out about the baby and refused to have anything more to do with her,' she concluded. 'If Freya has been living in the flat on her own with the baby then it doesn't look as though they've had a change of heart, does it?'

'No. It doesn't.' The policeman sighed as he wrote everything down in his notebook. 'Right, then. It might turn out to be a waste of time but I'll get on to the station and ask them to send someone round to speak to the girl's parents. The sooner we find out what's happened to her, the better.'

Both officers went outside to make the call, leaving Bella alone with the baby. She sighed as she picked her up and cradled her in her arms. It was no wonder that Freya had found it difficult to cope. Caring for a child on your own was a lot for any woman to deal with. Why, even she would find it hard and she was a lot older than Freya and had far more resources at her disposal. Quite frankly, she couldn't imagine how she would cope if she found herself in the position of being a single parent, not that it was likely to happen. Mac had taken great care to ensure she didn't get pregnant that night they had made love.

A tiny ache awoke in her heart, even though she knew how stupid it was. However, his determination to make sure that there were no consequences from their night of passion simply proved how he really felt about her. Maybe he'd been keen enough to sleep with her but he certainly wasn't looking for anything more.

Mac was surprised to see the police there when he got back from attending to his patient. He went over to the reception desk and asked Janet what was going on.

'They brought in a baby that had been left home alone.' She lowered her voice. 'From what I overheard just now, they seem to think it's Freya Watson's baby.'

'Really?' Mac exclaimed.

He glanced round when he heard footsteps, feeling a whole raft of emotions hit him when he saw Bella walking towards him, carrying the baby in her arms. He had never really thought about having children. Although he liked kids, the fact that he had always avoided commitment meant that it had never been an issue before. Now, however, as he looked at Bella holding the baby, he realised all of a sudden what he was missing.

He could picture it now, imagine how wonderful it would be to have a child of his own, a son or a daughter to love and cherish. His vision blurred as the image inside his head grew stronger. He could see a chubby little baby laughing up at him from its mother's arms now. It was only when the mother's face started to become clearer that Mac realised what was happening and groaned. Picturing Bella as the mother of his children was something he mustn't do! It was a mistake of gigantic proportions to allow himself that much licence. Maybe Bella would have children one day, but one thing was certain: their father would be someone very different from him, a man who came from a background similar to her own.

Bella was relieved when her shift finally ended. It had been a stressful night for so many reasons. The police were still searching for Freya Watson and it was obvious that they were becoming increasingly concerned as time passed and they failed to find any trace of her. The baby had been placed with a foster carer so at least she had the comfort of knowing that the infant was being looked after. However, as she left the hospital, she couldn't shake off the feeling of gloom that weighed her down.

Tim had only wanted to have a child with her to stop her divorcing him—he'd certainly not wanted one before then. And Mac had been at pains to ensure that nothing untoward happened in that department either. Even though she couldn't blame him for behaving responsibly, she couldn't rid herself of the thought that her inability to get in touch with her emotions had a huge bearing on the way both men had acted. The future had never seemed bleaker than it did right then and she realised that there was no point going home as she would never be able to sleep with all these thoughts whizzing around her head.

She left the hospital and headed to a supermarket on the outskirts of town that should open shortly. She hadn't done any food shopping for several weeks and the cupboards were bare. She filled a trolley then paid for her shopping and loaded everything in to her car. At least it had helped to distract her but, as she set off home, she found the same thought churning round and round inside her head: unless she got in touch with her emotions she would never be truly happy.

Maybe it was the stress, but somehow she must have taken a wrong turning because she found herself on a road she had never driven along before. She drove on for a few more miles, searching for any clues as to where she was. The car's satellite navigation system wasn't any help; it just showed an unmarked road and nothing else. When the road suddenly petered out into a track, Bella decided to turn round rather than risk going any further and getting completely lost. She carefully manoeuvred the car, shunting it backwards and forwards across the narrow track. She had almost completed the turn when there was an almighty bang from the rear of the vehicle.

She got out, her heart sinking when she discovered

that one of the back wheels had hit a boulder and had buckled under the impact. There was no way that she could change the wheel herself, but maybe there was a farm up ahead and people who would help her?

Lifting her bag out of the car, she started walking. Although it was almost the middle of the morning, heavy black clouds hung overhead, obscuring the tops of the surrounding mountains, and she shivered. Although she was wearing a jacket, it wouldn't be much use if it started to rain.

She must have walked a couple of miles before she decided to give up. There had been no sign of a farmhouse and it seemed pointless carrying on. She turned back, grimacing when she felt the first drops of rain start to fall. Within seconds, it was pouring down, sheets of water falling from the sky and soaking through her clothing. Bella walked as fast as she could but the increasingly slippery ground hampered her progress and it took her twice as long to get back to the car.

She climbed in, shivering violently as she started the engine and switched on the heater. Digging in to her bag, she found her mobile phone, intending to call the local garage and ask them to come out and fetch her. It was only when she saw the phone's blank screen that she realised the battery was flat. Tipping back her head, she groaned. What a perfect end to a miserable night!

Mac couldn't shake off the feeling that there was something wrong with Bella. Oh, he understood that it must have been a strain for her to work with him—heaven knew he hadn't found it easy, either. Nevertheless, he couldn't rid himself of the nagging thought that there was something else troubling her. As he left the hospital, he knew that he wouldn't rest until he found out what was the matter, even though he doubted Bella would appreciate his concern. If last night was anything to go by, she would much prefer it if he steered well clear of her!

He drove into town, drawing up in front of the apartment block where she lived. There was no sign of her car in the courtyard and he frowned. He had assumed that she would go straight home after working all night but maybe she had stopped off along the way. He decided to wait but when she still hadn't appeared an hour later, he realised that he might as well give up. There was no point in him hanging around if she had gone off somewhere. He would just have to try again later.

Mac headed home and went straight to bed but, even though he was tired after the busy night, he couldn't sleep. His mind kept churning over all the reasons why Bella might be upset. The fact that Freya had gone missing was bound to have upset her, but was it really that which was troubling her or something of a more personal nature? Try as he might, he couldn't come up with an answer and it was frustrating, to say the least, not to be able to find an explanation.

In the end he gave up any attempt to sleep and got up. He made himself a cup of coffee and stood on the deck while he drank it. It had started to rain but he barely noticed. Was it something he had said? Or was he deluding himself by thinking that anything *he* did could affect her?

He sighed. The truth was that he had no idea how Bella really felt about him. Maybe he should be glad that she seemed to have put what had happened that night behind her, but in his heart he knew it wasn't relief he felt. It was something far more disturbing, an emotion he shouldn't allow himself to feel. To wish that Bella would never forget that night, as he would never forget it, was selfish in the extreme.

Bella trudged on. Although the rain had eased off, it hadn't stopped and cold little flurries of raindrops stung her face as she made her way back along the track. She had decided to walk back to the main road and try to flag down a car in the hope that she could beg a lift into town. However, she hadn't realised just how far she must have driven. At this rate it would be midnight before she reached the road!

Spurred on by the thought, she quickened her pace then had to slow down again when she came to a section where the hillside had caved in. Mud and boulders had been washed down by the rain and covered the track. Bella carefully made her way around the obstruction, pausing when she heard a cry coming from somewhere to her left. She looked around, trying to determine where it had come from, and gasped when she spotted a woman huddled against some bushes. She hurried towards her, her feet slipping this way and that on the muddy ground. It was only as she got closer that she realised it was Freya Watson.

'Freya! What are you doing out here?' she demanded, crouching down beside her.

'I've hurt my ankle,' the girl told her. She ran a grimy hand over her face and Bella's heart went out to her when she realised that she was crying.

'It's OK,' she said, putting her arm around the girl's shoulders. 'We'll get it sorted out so don't worry. Here, let me take a look.'

She eased up the leg of Freya's jeans, hiding her grimace when she saw her ankle. It was very badly bruised and swollen, the flesh black and purple in places. 'Can you wiggle your toes?' she asked, trying to assess if it was broken or badly sprained, not that it made much difference. It must be extremely painful whichever it was.

'No. I can't move them. Is it broken, do you think?' Freya asked miserably.

'It looks like it.' Bella unwound her scarf from around her neck. 'I'm going to use this as a temporary support. I'll be as gentle as I can but it might hurt a bit.'

Leaving the girl's shoe and sock on, she carefully wound the scarf in a figure of eight fashion around Freya's foot and ankle. 'That should help,' she said after she had finished. 'How did it happen, though? And what were you doing out here in the first place?'

'I was hiding from a man who gave me a lift,' Freya told her. She bit her lip, looking for all the world like a child who knew she had done something wrong.

Bella sighed. 'I think you'd better start from the beginning. But, before you do, have you a mobile phone I can use to call the mountain rescue services? My battery's flat.'

'No. My dad used to pay for my phone but he stopped it after I had Ava and I can't afford to pay for it myself.'

'Don't worry. We'll work something out,' Bella told her, wondering what sort of parents could treat their child the way the Watsons were doing. She would never do that to *her* child, she thought angrily, then sighed when it struck her that it was highly unlikely that she would ever be in the position of having a child of her own.

'So what happened, sweetheart?' she asked, trying not to think about how bleak the future seemed. 'I know you walked out of your flat because the police brought Ava into the hospital to be checked over. She's fine,' she said hastily when she saw the fear in Freya's eyes. 'She's with a foster carer at the moment so she's being well looked after. But what made you leave her in the first place?'

'She wouldn't stop crying,' Freya explained. Tears began to stream down her face once more. 'I tried everything I could think of, too. I fed her and changed her, rocked her and sang to her, but she wouldn't stop.

I know I shouldn't have left her on her own but I just couldn't stand it any longer.'

'It must be hard when you don't have anyone to help you,' Bella said gently. 'I take it from what you just told me that your parents haven't had a change of heart?'

'No. They won't even speak to me when I try phoning them.' Freya dried her eyes with the back of her hand. 'I know I was stupid, but it's not as though I've *murdered* someone or anything like that!'

Bella wholeheartedly agreed although she didn't say so. To her mind, the Watsons had behaved deplorably. 'So what happened after you left your flat?'

'I got on a bus. I've no idea where it was going 'cos it really didn't matter. I just needed to get away, you see. The trouble was that when I tried to catch a bus back home, it was after midnight and they'd stopped running.' Freya sighed. 'I started walking when this car drew up and the driver offered me a lift.'

'And you accepted?' Bella asked, her heart sinking at the thought of Freya getting into a stranger's car.

'Yes. He said he'd drive me home but he brought me here instead.' Freya's eyes welled with tears again. 'I was so scared! I managed to jump out of the car when he stopped and hid until he had left. It was pitch-dark and I had no idea where I was so I just stayed here until the morning. I was making my way back to the road when I slipped and hurt my ankle. If you hadn't come along then, I don't know what I'd have done,' she added tearfully.

'Well, I did come so let's not think about that,' Bella said rousingly. She stood up. 'Now, we need to get you back to the main road. Do you think you can hop if I support you? It's either that or leave you here while I go for help.'

'Oh, don't leave me!' Freya exclaimed, obviously terrified by the thought of being left on her own once again.

Bella looped the girl's arm across her shoulders as she helped her to stand up. It wasn't going to be easy to get Freya back to the road, but what choice did she have? Nobody knew they were here and nobody would come looking for them either. Just for a second the thought that Mac might notice her absence crossed her mind before she dismissed it. Mac wouldn't miss her, as he had made it abundantly clear.

CHAPTER EIGHT

MAC WAS GROWING increasingly concerned. He had tried phoning Bella several times but she hadn't responded. He would have put it down to the fact that she didn't want to speak to him, only it appeared that her mobile phone had been switched off. It seemed odd to him, bearing in mind how conscientious she was. How would work contact her in case of an emergency if her phone was switched off?

In the end he went back to her apartment. Although there was still no sign of her car, he rang the bell anyway. There was always a chance that her car had broken down and she had made her way home by some other means. However, after half a dozen rings on the bell, he gave up. She obviously wasn't here, so where was she?

He stood there, trying to think where she might have gone. He knew for a fact that she had made very few friends since she had moved to Dalverston. Although she was well regarded by their colleagues, the fact that she kept herself to herself didn't encourage close friendships—he definitely couldn't picture her dropping in to someone's house for coffee and a chat! No, what friends she did have were all in London, so was it possible that she had driven down there?

It seemed unlikely but it was the only lead he had. He phoned half a dozen mutual friends but drew a blank. Nobody had seen or heard from Bella in months, it seemed. That left him with just one other option, the least appealing one too. He dialled Tim's number, filled with such a mixture of emotions that it was difficult to speak when Tim answered. He had come to Dalverston, sure in his own mind that Bella had been responsible for the demise of her marriage. However, he no longer believed that and it was hard to behave with equanimity as he asked Tim if he had heard from her. He had been wrong to blame her—so very, very wrong. If he lived to be a hundred he would always regret it.

Once again Mac drew a blank. Tim hadn't heard from Bella either, apparently. Mac cut him off, knowing that he would lose it completely if he had to listen to Tim blackening her name again. Although she hadn't gone into any detail about Tim's affair—she'd not had time!—he believed her. And the thought filled him with all sorts of uncharitable feelings towards his former friend. Tim had deliberately lied to him and he wasn't sure if he would ever be able to forgive him for that.

He went back to his motorbike, his face set as he revved up the engine. He was going to find Bella even if it took him all day!

* * *

Progress was excruciatingly slow. They had to stop every few minutes while Freya rested. Bella glanced at her watch, sighing as she realised how much time had passed. They'd barely travelled half a mile and it was already gone midday. She helped Freya sit down in the lee of a large rock and sat down beside her while she tried to decide what to do. It had started to rain again, which would only exacerbate the problem. With the ground becoming increasingly slippery there was a very real danger that Freya might fall again. Bella came to a swift decision, prompted by necessity.

'Look, Freya, this isn't working. I know you don't like the idea of being left on your own but I need to fetch help.' She patted Freya's hand when she started to cry, feeling terrible about abandoning her. However, she would be much faster on her own. 'I'm going to leave you here while I go back to the main road. There's bound to be a car coming along it and I'll flag it down and get them to phone the mountain rescue people. Once they receive the call, it won't be long before we're out of here.'

'You will come back for me?' Freya asked anxiously. She looked round and shuddered. 'What if you can't remember where I am? I mean, it all looks the same to me!'

'I'll use my blouse as a marker.' Bella hurriedly undid her jacket and stripped off her blouse. Rooting around on the ground, she found a sturdy branch and knotted the blouse's sleeves around it. 'Look, I'll push the end of the branch into this crevice in the rock—it will act as a marker so that we'll be able to find you.'

'I suppose so,' Freya agreed reluctantly, obviously unsure about what she was proposing.

'It will be fine, Freya. I promise you.'

Bella gave her a hug then hurried away before *she* started doubting the feasibility of her plan. She had to leave Freya here, otherwise they could be stuck out in the open all day long. The thought spurred her on and she made rapid progress, although it still took her over an hour to reach the main road. She stood at the side of the carriageway, praying that a car would come along soon. She was cold and wet and unutterably weary and all she wanted was to go home and have a long hot bath then climb into bed. Just for a second the image of Mac lying beside her popped into her head before she drove it away. Mac wouldn't be sharing her bed today or in the foreseeable future!

Mac drove all around the town but he still couldn't find any sign of Bella. He tried to imagine where she might have gone but his mind was blank. He sighed as he pulled up outside a coffee shop. Maybe a shot of caffeine would help restore some life to his flagging brain cells. He went in and ordered a triple espresso to go. He added a couple of sachets of sugar to the brew to give it an extra kick then left, stopping when he came face to face with Helen Robertson, their F1 student. She grimaced as she studied the concoction he was nursing.

'You're obviously in need of some serious stimulation if you're thinking of drinking that. It looks lethal to me.'

'Hmm, it probably is. But needs must, and my brain definitely needs a major pick-me-up,' Mac replied with a grimace as he gulped down the coffee.

'It must have been a rough night,' Helen observed, laughing. 'I saw Bella at the supermarket earlier and she looked really washed out.'

'You saw her!' Mac exclaimed. He grabbed hold of Helen's arm. 'When was this?'

'First thing this morning,' Helen told him, looking startled. She glanced over at a young man who was obviously waiting for her and shrugged. 'David and I had been out at a club all night and we popped into the supermarket for some breakfast on our way home. We saw Bella at the checkout, although I don't think she saw us.'

'Thank you so much!' Mac impulsively hugged her. He let her go and grinned. 'I've been worried sick because she wasn't at her apartment or answering her phone. At least I have some idea where she went now.'

'Probably needed to stock up, from the amount of shopping she had,' Helen said lightly.

'Probably,' he agreed.

He said his goodbyes and hurried over to his motorbike. Climbing astride it, he headed out of town to the supermarket, mentally crossing his fingers that he would find Bella there. He sighed. And if he didn't find her, then what? He could hardly report her missing and call out a search party on such flimsy evidence, could he? After all, there was no proof that anything had happened to her—nothing, apart from this gut feeling he had.

He snorted in disgust. Try explaining that to the authorities. They would think he was deranged!

It must have been half an hour before a car finally appeared. Bella stepped into the middle of the road and flagged it down. There was an elderly couple inside and she could see how nervous they looked as she approached the driver's window. Bending down, she smiled reassuringly at them.

'Thank you for stopping. Do you have a mobile phone I can use to call the mountain rescue service? There's been an accident, you see—a young girl has been injured and she needs help.'

The man quickly gave her his phone. Bella made the call, checking with the driver as to their location. Fortunately, he was a local man and he was able to explain exactly where they were. Bella thanked him as she handed back the phone. When the couple asked her if she would like to sit in the car while they waited for the mountain rescue team to arrive, she gratefully accepted. It would be wonderful to get out of the rain even for a short time.

The first of the rescue vehicles arrived just fifteen minutes later and was quickly followed by several others. In a very short time, Bella was leading the team back to where she had left Freya. Thankfully, her makeshift marker had survived the wind and the rain and proved a big help in locating her. Once Freya was loaded onto the stretcher, they headed back. Bella was exhausted by then and finding it difficult to keep up. Relief overwhelmed her when she saw the road up ahead. Just a few more minutes and that would be it, she thought. It was only when she spotted the motorbike parked behind the other vehicles and the man standing beside it that her heart began to pound.

What on earth was Mac doing here?

It had been pure chance that Mac had happened upon the scene. After failing to find Bella at the supermarket, he had driven around, trying to decide what to do next. Although reporting her missing might have seemed premature, that gut feeling he had that something was wrong was growing stronger by the minute. When he came across the mountain rescue vehicles parked beside the road, he could hardly contain his fear. He just *knew* that Bella was involved!

He climbed off the bike, his legs trembling as he went over to speak to one of the team. He was just about to ask the man if he knew the name of the casualty when a shout went up and he turned to see the rest of the group walking towards them. His heart started to pound when he saw the figure lying on the stretcher. Was it Bella? Was she badly injured? All of a sudden the strength came flooding back to his limbs and he raced towards them. It was only as he drew closer that he realised it wasn't Bella on the stretcher but Freya Watson and he didn't know whether to feel relieved or terrified. Where on earth was she?

'Mac? What are you doing here?'

The sound of her voice had him spinning round. Mac just had a second to take in the fact that she was right there in front of him before instinct took over. Dragging her into his arms, he held her to him, held her as though he would never let her go again. Maybe he wouldn't, he thought giddily. Maybe he would follow his heart and not allow his fear of being rejected, of being left, to ruin things. If he could find the courage to believe in her, to believe in *them*, he could have everything he wanted: Bella in his arms and in his life for ever more.

The next hour passed in a blur. Although Bella did everything that was expected of her, her mind was far removed from what was happening. She kept thinking about the expression on Mac's face, about the way he had held her so tightly, so desperately, and it didn't make any sense. He had behaved as though he truly cared about her but that couldn't be true…

Could it?

The question nagged away at her as she and Freya

were ferried to hospital in one of the rescue vehicles. They were taken straight to A&E, where they were met by the senior registrar. Bella quickly explained what had happened, nodding when he immediately decided to send Freya down to X-ray. Once they knew for certain if Freya's ankle was fractured, he could decide on the appropriate course of treatment.

After Freya left, Bella reluctantly agreed to be checked over as well. Although she was sure she was fine, there were procedures to follow and it would be wrong to create a fuss. As expected, she was given a clean bill of health and told that she could leave whenever she wanted. And that was when the tricky bit started. As she exited the cubicle and saw Mac sitting in the waiting room, she had no idea what to do. Had she correctly interpreted his reaction as rather more than relief for the safe deliverance of a friend?

Bella's heart began to race as that thought unlocked the door to several others. Did she want him to feel more than friendship for her, maybe even love? But if he did then how could *she* be sure that she wouldn't ruin things and that her inability to show her true feelings wouldn't destroy whatever he felt? Pain shot through her. Quite frankly, she didn't think she could bear knowing that yet again she had failed as a woman.

Mac could feel the tension building inside him as he waited for Bella to return. He knew that his behaviour must have aroused her suspicions and he was honest enough to admit that the thought scared him too. However, if he intended to win her then he couldn't back down. He had to fight for her. Tooth and claw!

'They said I could go home whenever I liked.'

He started when he realised she was standing in front of him. He shot to his feet, almost overturning the chair in his haste. 'No damage done, then?' he said and winced at the sheer inanity of the comment.

'No, I'm fine.'

She gave him a quick smile and headed for the door. Mac followed her, pausing when he realised that it was still raining outside. Bearing in mind the soaking she'd had already that day, it seemed decidedly off to drive her home on the back of his motorbike.

'I'll phone for a cab,' he said, hunting his mobile phone out of his jacket pocket.

'What's wrong with your bike?' she asked, one brow arching in a way that made all sorts of complicated things start to happen inside him.

'Oh, ahem, nothing,' he murmured, trying to wrestle his libido back into its box. 'I just thought you'd prefer not to get drenched again.'

'I don't think it matters. I'm soaked as it is, so a drop more rain isn't going to make much difference.'

She gave a little shrug, her breasts rising and falling beneath the clinging folds of her wet jacket, and Mac's libido won the battle, hands down.

'Oh, well, if you're sure, then.'

Mac didn't give her chance to reply as he led the

way to where he had left his motorbike. Quite frankly, he couldn't believe how crassly he was behaving. Usually, it took more than the lift of a brow or the wiggle of a woman's breast to arouse him. He groaned as he took the spare helmet out of the box beneath the seat. Who was he kidding? Bella only had to look at him and he was putty in her hands!

He helped her on with the helmet then swung his leg over the bike, tensing when she settled herself behind him on the seat. He could feel her body pressing against the length of his back and sent up a silent prayer that he would manage to hold out. There must be no stopping along the way, he told himself sternly. And absolutely no thoughts of pulling into a secluded lay-by. He wasn't a teenager but a mature adult who had given up such behaviour years ago. No, he would drive Bella home, make sure she was safely inside her apartment and leave…

'Can we go back to the boat?'

Mac jumped when she leant forward and spoke directly into his ear. He could feel the warmth of her breath on his skin and shuddered. It took every scrap of willpower he could muster not to respond as he yearned to do. 'You don't want to go home to your apartment?' he said hoarsely.

'No. I…well, I would prefer to go to the boat, if you don't mind.'

There was something in her voice that made his skin prickle. Mac nodded, not trusting himself to speak.

He drove out of the car park, trying to get a grip, but it was impossible. How could he behave calmly when every instinct was telling him that the reason Bella wanted to go back to the boat was because she wanted to be with *him*?

As he followed the familiar route, he could feel his tension mounting, could feel all sorts of things happening which he had steadfastly avoided in the past. He had refused to allow himself to fall in love before—completely and totally rejected the idea, in fact. He had witnessed his father's devastation when his mother had walked out on them and he had sworn that love wasn't for him; but not any more. Not now that Bella was in his life.

His breath caught as he was forced to confront the truth. How could he *not* fall in love with her when he wanted her so desperately?

Bella took a deep breath as she stepped down from the motorbike. Had she been mad to ask Mac to bring her here? Oh, she knew what was going to happen—there was no use pretending that she didn't. She and Mac would make love again because it was what they both wanted. But surely that would only complicate matters even more?

'Come on. Let's get you inside before you're completely waterlogged.'

Mac placed his hand at the small of her back to urge her onto the boat and she shivered. Just the feel of his fingers pressing against her flesh made her senses reel. She stepped on board, waiting while he unlocked the cabin door. He turned to her and she could see the uncertainty in his eyes even though he smiled. Did he have doubts about the wisdom of what they were doing too? she wondered. And knew it was true. He was no surer about this than she was.

'Take care on the steps,' he advised her. 'They can be a bit slippery when it rains.'

Bella nodded as she made her way inside the cabin, feeling her nervousness crank itself up another notch or ten. The fact that Mac had doubts only seemed to heighten her own misgivings so that all of a sudden she found herself wishing that she had never suggested coming back here. She should have gone straight home to her apartment, chosen the sensible option rather than placed herself in this position. If they made love again it would be that much harder to do the right thing. No matter how she felt about Mac, she wouldn't *coerce* him into having a relationship with her. It wouldn't be fair. Mac needed a woman who didn't have all these hang-ups. A woman who understood her own feelings and was able to show them too. What he didn't need was someone like her.

The thought was more than she could bear. Bella knew that she had to leave before anything happened. She spun round so fast that she cannoned right into Mac as he stepped down from the last tread. There was a moment when they both froze, when it felt as though time itself had stood still, and then the next second he was hauling her into his arms.

'I was so scared when I couldn't find you!'

His voice grated with fear and a host of other emotions, and she shuddered. It was hard to believe that she had made him feel all those things. Her eyes rose to his and she knew that he could see how she felt—how shocked, how amazed, how overjoyed.

'I didn't think anyone would notice I was missing,' she said truthfully.

'Well, I did!' He rested his forehead against hers and she felt the tremor that passed through him and was shocked all over again.

She had never believed that she was capable of arousing such strong emotions in another person. She had always been so diffident in her approach to life that she had honestly thought it was beyond her, but maybe she had been mistaken. Maybe her experiences with Tim weren't the yardstick by which she should measure any future relationship? The thought made her head reel even more because it opened up so many possibilities that she had thought were denied to her. If she could make Mac feel this way then perhaps there was a future for them after all?

When he bent and kissed her, Bella didn't hesitate. She simply kissed him back, wanting him to know just how much she needed him. When he murmured something deep in his throat, her heart overflowed with joy. That he wanted her too was blatantly obvious. Swinging her up into his arms, he carried her into the tiny bedroom and laid her down on the bed and she shuddered when she saw the desire burning in his eyes.

'I want to make love to you, Bella, but only if it's what you want as well.'

'It is.' She held out her hand. 'It's what I want, Mac. More than anything.'

He didn't say a word as he took hold of her hand and raised it to his lips, but he didn't need to. The expression on his face said everything that she wanted to hear. Bella could feel herself trembling as he lay down beside her and drew her into his arms. No one had ever looked at her like this before. Looked at her as though she held the key to their future. In that second she knew that, no matter what happened, she would make sure that he didn't get hurt. She loved him so much—far too much to risk his happiness. Maybe she always had loved him too, she thought as she closed her eyes and let their passion sweep her away. She had just been too afraid to admit it before.

They made love with a voracious hunger that had them both trembling. Every kiss, each caress only seemed to fuel their desire for one another. Mac's whole being was consumed by the need to be inside her, but somehow he managed to hold back. He wanted this to be as amazing for Bella as it was for him.

'Mac, *please*!'

The desperation in her voice tipped him over the edge and he entered her with one powerful thrust. He couldn't have held back then even if he'd tried but he didn't need to. Bella was with him every step of the way, her body arching under his as he drove them both to the heights of passion and beyond. They were both shaking when they came back down to earth, both stunned by the sheer intensity of what had happened. Mac knew that he had visited a place he had never been before and that he would never visit again without Bella. It was only with Bella that he could experience such rapture, such a feeling of completeness. Only Bella whom he loved.

The need to tell her how he felt was very strong but something stopped him, a tiny vestige of that fear of rejection that had blighted his life for so long. Although he hated himself for being such a coward, he knew that he needed to come to terms with how he felt before he could take the next step.

Rolling onto his side, he smiled into her eyes, loving the way her face lit up when she smiled back at him. If that weren't proof that she felt something for him, he thought, then what was?

'Now that I've had my wicked way with you, Dr English, I suppose I'd better feed you,' he said, battening down that delicious thought. Maybe she *did* care about him but he had to be sure—one hundred per cent *sure*—before he went any further. 'How about bacon and eggs—would that hit the spot?'

'Mmm, lovely.' She batted her eyelashes at him. 'I don't suppose you offer your guests breakfast in bed, do you? I'm feeling far too relaxed and comfortable to get up.'

'I suppose I could stretch a point just this once.' He huffed out a sigh, playing up the role of martyr to the full. 'I must warn you, though, that I don't plan to provide such luxuries on a regular basis.'

'Oh, so there are going to be other occasions like this, are there?'

She grinned up at him, her green eyes filled with laughter, and Mac couldn't resist. Bending, he dropped a kiss on her lips, feeling his body immediately stir. Catching hold of her around the waist, he lifted her on top of him.

'I think so. In fact, I'd go so far as to say that I *know* there will.'

He ran his hand down her back, feeling her tremble as her hips were brought into intimate contact with his. That she could feel how much he wanted her wasn't in any doubt. He kissed her long and hungrily, not even surprised by the depth of his desire. Even if he made love to her a dozen times a day, he would still want her, he thought.

Their lovemaking was just as fulfilling the second time round. Mac had to drag himself out of bed afterwards. He knew that Bella must be hungry and he wanted to feed her and take care of her every need. The thought filled him with tenderness as he dragged on his clothes and went to start preparing their meal. Bella had decided to take a shower and he smiled when he heard the water running. He could get used to sharing his life here on the boat with her. Very easily too.

It was the first time he had ever considered such an arrangement and it shocked him. Although he'd had many girlfriends over the years, he had never lived with any of them. It had seemed like a step too far and yet he knew without even having to think about it that living with Bella was what he wanted more than anything. He wanted the intimacy that came from living together, wanted to get to know all the little things that made her tick, like her favourite food and which programmes she enjoyed watching on television. His head began to spin because if he went down that route then it was just a small step to the next, but was he ready for that, ready for the ultimate commitment—marriage?

He wished he knew, wished with all his heart that he could simply close his eyes and *know* it was what he wanted but he couldn't. Not yet. That last pesky remnant of fear was still niggling away at the back of his mind and, until he had rid himself of it, he couldn't make the final decision. He sighed heavily. Please heaven, he prayed he wouldn't leave it too late and end up losing her.

CHAPTER NINE

'I AM ABSOLUTELY STUFFED!'

Bella groaned as she laid down her knife and fork. She had eaten far too much but it had been hard to resist when Mac had placed the meal in front of her. Now she smiled at him, loving the way his eyes lit up as he smiled back—another indication of how he felt about her, perhaps?

'Are you trying to make me fat, Dr MacIntyre?' she said, trying not to get too hung up on the idea. Maybe they *had* made love and maybe it *had* been marvellous but she mustn't take anything for granted. 'Because you're definitely going to succeed if you keep cooking me meals like that!'

'From what I can recall, there's no danger of you getting fat.'

He smiled into her eyes and Bella felt a wave of heat flow through her when she realised that he was remembering how she had looked when they had made love. She bit her lip as she was suddenly assailed by the memory of his powerful body. The strange thing was that she had never been aroused by a man's physical appearance in the past. Even as a teenager she hadn't done what most teenage girls did and stuck posters on her wall of the latest male heart-throb. Looks hadn't aroused her and yet the memory of Mac's body, so lean and yet so powerful, made her tremble. Picking up her cup, she buried her face in it, praying that he wouldn't guess what she was thinking. Lusting after him definitely wasn't something a woman of her age should be doing!

'Bella?' His voice was so bone-meltingly gentle that she reacted as though he had actually touched her. Her hand was trembling as she placed the cup on the table and she saw him look at her in concern. Leaning forward, he covered her hand with his. 'You're not upset about what we did, are you, sweetheart?'

'No.' She shook her head to emphasise that she meant what she said. She didn't regret making love with him again, although she couldn't help wondering what was going to happen from here on. Would Mac expect them to be friends who occasionally slept together from now on? She hoped not, even though she wasn't sure exactly what she did want them to be.

'Then what's wrong?' He squeezed her fingers. 'Tell me. I want to know if there's something worrying you.'

'There isn't. I'm fine.'

She smiled brightly back at him, not wanting to admit her fears when she felt so ambivalent. Did she want Mac in her life for ever and ever or simply for the foreseeable future? Oh, she loved him—she was sure about that. But *for ever* was a long time and she had no idea if it was expecting too much to aim for that.

All of a sudden the situation seemed way too complicated. Bella pushed back her chair and started gathering up their plates. She needed time to think, time to work out what she really wanted… Her breath caught as she turned to carry the plates to the sink and saw Mac watching her. She wanted Mac. But did she have the right to want him when she wasn't sure if she could fulfil his needs?

'I think I'll have a shower.' Mac stood up. Picking up their cups, he brought them over to the sink. He put them down on the counter then bent and dropped a kiss on the nape of her neck. Bella shuddered when she felt his lips brush against her skin. It was hard to be sensible and act responsibly when she felt this way!

'Bella.'

Her name on his lips was like a caress. When he turned her into his arms, she didn't hesitate. Maybe she didn't know what was going to happen in the future but she did know what she wanted to happen right now. Lifting her face to his, she kissed him back, her mouth clinging to his as she sought reassurance. Surely this desire they felt for one another could be seen as a good omen?

They made love once again and once again it was unlike anything Mac had experienced before. The feel of Bella's satin-smooth skin gliding beneath his fingertips aroused him as nothing had ever done in the past. He could only marvel at how different it was to make love to her. How special. How totally fulfilling. It wasn't just his senses that were engaged when they made love but his spirit too. It felt as though he had found himself in her arms, discovered the real person beneath the public image. He hadn't realised to what extent he put up a front between himself and the world, but he did now. With Bella he could be himself. Completely and wholly himself. The thought was so poignant that it washed away the last remnants of fear. Framing her face between his hands, he looked deep into her eyes.

'I love you, Bella.' He had to break off at that point because words failed him; only to be expected when it was the first time he had ever uttered them. Not once had he told a woman that he loved her because it wouldn't have been true, but it was true now. He loved Bella with all his heart and with every atom of his being too.

'I...' Bella started to speak and then stopped. Mac could see the shock on her face and understood. It was a momentous occasion for both of them. He laughed softly as he dropped a kiss on the tip of her nose.

'I know. I feel as stunned as you do, my love. I think we both need a few minutes to get our heads round the idea, don't you?'

He stood up, feeling tenderness engulf him when

he saw the expression on her face, a mixture of shock mingled with a growing excitement. Obviously, his announcement hadn't come as an unwelcome surprise then, he thought a shade smugly. As he made his way into the bathroom, Mac could feel happiness bubbling up inside him. Telling Bella how he felt had been a huge gamble, but it appeared to have paid off. Clearly, she had feelings for him too, and now all he needed to do was to persuade her to admit that she loved him back and they could look towards the future.

He grinned as he poured shower gel into his palm and started to lather himself. Maybe he was guilty of putting the cart before the horse, but it looked very much as though he and Bella might be riding off into the sunset. Together!

Bella washed the dishes and put them away in the cupboard. Mac kept the boat immaculately tidy and she didn't want to leave everywhere in a mess. After all, she would hate to think that he considered her to be a nuisance…

She sat down abruptly on the couch as all the strength suddenly seeped from her limbs. From what Mac had said before, there seemed little danger of that! He had told her that he loved her, but could it be true?

A tremor ran through her as she recalled the expression on his face as he had made the admission. He was either a brilliant actor or he had been telling her the truth and all of a sudden she knew which she wanted it to be. She wanted Mac to be a permanent part of her future!

Her breath caught as her mind raced away with the idea. Being with Mac, day in and day out, would be like a dream come true. He would always be there for her, always support her, always put her first. His loyalty and steadfastness were qualities she had admired ever since they had first met. Even though she had been a little wary of him initially because of the differences in their backgrounds, she had always known that he would be there for her. That was why it had hurt so much when he had blamed her for the failure of her marriage. She had expected him to understand why she'd had to end it and the fact that he hadn't done so had knocked her for six. Did he now accept that she wasn't at fault? she wondered suddenly. She hoped so. If they were to have that glorious future she longed for then they had to trust one another completely.

It was a tiny doubt, like a black mark on an otherwise bright and shiny canvas. Bella knew that she needed to talk to him about it before they went any further. She made a fresh pot of coffee while she waited for him to finish showering, feeling her nervousness increasing by the second. If Mac didn't believe in her innocence then this could be the beginning and the end for them.

'Mmm, coffee.' Mac came into the cabin. He grinned as he came over and caught her around the waist. 'Not only beautiful and sexy, but you can read my mind as well. It's no wonder that I love you, Bella English.'

He kissed her lingeringly, his lips teasing hers until Bella's head reeled. She kissed him back, feeling the tiny niggling doubt disappear. Mac wouldn't feel this way unless he believed in her. And it was the most marvellous feeling in the world to know that his love for her was everything he professed it to be. When he raised his head, she knew that this was the moment she should tell him how she felt too. She loved him and now that all her doubts had been erased, she wanted to make that clear.

'Mac, I…' She got no further when at that precise moment his phone rang. Mac groaned as he glanced over at where it lay on the table.

'Typical! Why do the wretched things always ring at the most inconvenient times?' Reaching over, he picked it up and she saw his expression change as he glanced at the screen.

'Hello, Tim,' he said flatly. He paused while he listened to what the other man was saying. 'Yes, I found her and she's fine… Of course. She's right here.'

Bella's heart bumped painfully against her ribs as he handed her his phone. She wasn't sure why Mac looked so distant all of a sudden. Surely he didn't think that she was eager to speak to her ex after what had just happened between them?

She was curt almost to the point of rudeness as she

told Tim that she had taken a wrong turning on her way back from the supermarket and that was why she had gone missing. She didn't add anything about Freya and what else had happened because she wanted to end the call as quickly as possible.

She glanced at Mac, who had gone to stand by the sink, and felt her heart start racing when she saw how grim he looked. Mac obviously believed that she was pleased to hear from Tim, but nothing could be further from the truth. That part of her life was over and there was no chance of her and Tim getting back together. She realised that she needed to make that clear to Tim, so when he asked if they could meet up, she agreed. She couldn't move forward until she had drawn a line under the past.

'Tim was just calling to check that I was all right,' she said quietly as she ended the call. Mac didn't say anything and she hurried on, wanting to make the situation clear to him as well. 'He wants to see me and I've agreed.'

'So I heard.' Mac's expression held a contempt that chilled her to the core. 'Maybe I should congratulate you. It appears that you two have resolved your differences at last. I hope you will be very happy together.'

'No! It isn't like that,' she began but he didn't let her finish.

'Don't bother explaining. It's obvious that Tim still loves you if he's so eager to talk things through with you. And you obviously still love him if you've agreed to meet him after everything that's happened.' He gave a dismissive shrug that made her heart curl up inside her. 'I'm only glad that I was able to help in some small way. It appears that sleeping with me has helped you realise exactly what you want from life, and it certainly isn't an affair with me.'

Bella couldn't believe what she was hearing. Oh, she understood the words all right—they were plain enough. However, the fact that Mac believed that she had slept with him to help her decide if she should go back to Tim was beyond her comprehension. If he loved her, as he claimed to do, then he would *know* that she was incapable of such behaviour.

All of a sudden she couldn't take any more, couldn't bear to stand there and listen to him accusing her of such terrible deeds. Snatching up her bag, she pushed past him and ran up the steps to the deck. She heard him shouting her name but she didn't stop. What was the point? He had said everything that needed to be said, made it abundantly clear how he felt. Oh, maybe he had thought that he loved her but it wasn't true. It couldn't be when he didn't know in his heart that she would *never* go back to Tim after what they had done. Once again the thought that it was all down to her rose to the surface to taunt her. If she had only shown Mac how she really felt, convinced him that it was *him* she wanted and no one else, told him she loved him too even just once then maybe things would have turned out very differently.

Tears streamed down her face as she ran along the towpath, tears of grief for what she'd had so fleetingly and lost so quickly. It hurt so much, far more than when her marriage had ended, but that was to be expected. This time she had given her heart and had it ripped to shreds and thrown back at her. It had to be the most painful rejection of all.

Mac sank down onto the couch after Bella left. He knew that he should go after her but he felt incapable of doing anything at that moment. Bella was planning to go back to Tim; could it be true? But if it wasn't true then why had she agreed to meet Tim?

His head reeled as question after question assailed him. He realised that he needed to find out the answers before he drove himself mad, and leapt to his feet. There was no sign of Bella when he reached the deck so he set off at a run, expecting to catch up with her in the lane, but there was no sign of her there either. His heart began to thump as he wondered where she had gone. It was only when he caught a glimpse of the bus disappearing around the bend that he had the answer to that question at least. As for all the others, well, he would need to speak to her. She was the only one who knew the truth.

Mac made his way to where he had parked his motorbike. He started the engine, feeling his stomach churning with dread as all his old fears of rejection surged to the forefront. Maybe he did need answers but he could only pray that he was strong enough to hear them.

* * *

'Four-year-old in cubicle three—Oscar Starling. Mum thinks he's swallowed some detergent. Who wants it? You or Mac?'

'I'll take it.'

Bella grabbed the child's notes, turning away when she saw Trish look at her in surprise. There was no way that she intended to explain why she was so eager to take the case. Mac had been trying to get her on her own all morning long, but she had no intention of talking to him. That was why she hadn't answered the door when he had turned up at her apartment yesterday after she'd got back from the boat. What was there to say, after all? That she had no intention of going back to Tim? Why should he believe her when she had such difficulty expressing her true feelings?

Bella pushed back the curtain, preferring to focus on her patient's needs rather than her own problems. There was a little boy sitting on the examination couch and he smiled when she went in.

'I've got a new tractor,' he told her importantly, holding up a bright green toy tractor for her to admire.

'You lucky boy. It's beautiful.' Bella took the toy off him and ran it across the couch, making appropriate tractor noises. She handed it back then turned to his mother and smiled. 'Hello, I'm Dr English. I believe Oscar may have swallowed some detergent— is that right?'

'Yes.' Louise Starling sighed. 'He was playing in

the kitchen with his tractor. He never normally goes in the cupboard where I keep the detergent but he did today. I'd gone upstairs and when I came down, he had the box on the floor. I use those liquid capsules and one of them was broken open. The liquid in them is bright blue and I could see that Oscar's lips were stained blue as well.'

'I see.' Bella turned to the little boy. 'Did you swallow a lot of mummy's detergent, Oscar?'

He shook his head. 'No, 'cos it tasted funny.' He zoomed the tractor across the couch and grinned at her. 'I spat it out on the floor.'

'Good boy.'

Bella ruffled his hair, thinking how adorable he was. It must be wonderful to have such a bright and happy child. The thought naturally reminded her of her own situation and she swallowed her sigh. There was little chance of her ever having a child when she ended up driving away every man she met. She tried to put the thought out of her mind as she asked Louise Starling if she had brought any of the capsules with her.

'I brought the box.' Louise handed Bella the box of detergent capsules. She grimaced. 'I saw something on TV about taking the container with you if your child swallows something he shouldn't. I remember thinking that it would never happen to Oscar as I'm so careful, but it just goes to show, doesn't it?'

'You mustn't blame yourself,' Bella said sympathetically. 'Even the most careful parents can't always predict what their children are going to do. Right, I'll go and phone the National Poisons Information Service and see what they advise. However, I don't think that you need to worry too much. From what Oscar has told us, he didn't ingest very much of the detergent.'

Bella went to the desk and called the NPIS helpline. They kept a list of household products on file and were able to advise her on the best course of treatment. Fortunately, these particular capsules weren't highly toxic and, because so little of the detergent had been ingested, they agreed that Oscar wasn't in any immediate danger. Bella went back and broke the good news to the little boy's mother then set about treating him, which involved getting him to drink a large tumbler of water. He was as good as gold and drank it all without a murmur, making her smile.

'You are a good boy, Oscar. I want you to drink another glass of water when Mummy takes you home—will you do that for me?'

Oscar nodded, more interested in his tractor than in what was happening. Bella laughed as she lifted him off the couch. 'Come with me and I'll see if I can find you a sticker for being such a good boy.'

He happily held her hand as she led the way from the cubicle. They kept a pile of stickers behind the desk so Bella sorted through them until she found one with a tractor on it. Crouching down, she stuck it onto the child's T-shirt. 'There you go. It says, "I'm a star patient!"—which you are.'

Bella smiled as Oscar excitedly showed the sticker to his mother. She told Louise to bring him back if she was at all worried then sat down to write up the child's notes after they left. It was almost lunchtime and, once she had finished her notes, she would go to the canteen and make herself eat something. She hadn't been able to force down anything except a cup of coffee that morning and she couldn't keep going on that alone. If she was to do her job properly then she needed to look after herself. After all, if she was never going to have that family she had longed for then she would need to focus on her career.

It seemed like a poor substitute even though she loved her job but Bella knew that she had to be realistic. Oh, maybe she did have dreams and maybe it was hard to relinquish them, especially the dreams she'd had about her and Mac and the golden future they would enjoy together, but the longer she clung to her dreams, the more painful it would be. She and Mac had had their chance and it hadn't worked out. The sooner she accepted that, the better.

By the time lunchtime rolled around, Mac was finding it difficult to contain his frustration. Bella had evaded his every attempt to speak to her. Oh, he had tried—tried umpteen times, in fact—but she had managed to avoid him. It was fast reaching the point where the rest of the team were bound to notice that something was going on, but hard luck. It wasn't his doing; it was

Bella's. And if people started gossiping about them then she only had herself to blame!

Mac grimaced, aware that he was being very unfair. He had started this by making those accusations. He had spent a sleepless night, thinking about what had happened, and by the time morning arrived he knew that he had been wrong to jump to such hasty conclusions. Bella would never have tried to use him that way—it simply wasn't in her nature. He had allowed his fear of getting hurt to skew his judgement and he owed her an apology, but the big question was: would she accept it? From the way she had behaved towards him that morning, he very much doubted it.

His spirits were at an all-time low as he saw his patient out and returned to the desk. He paused when he spotted Bella sitting at the computer. There was nobody else around so maybe this was the moment he'd been waiting for. The thought of losing her if she went back to Tim was bad enough, but it would be so much worse if they parted on such bad terms. He needed to make his apologies and at least try to salvage something from the situation even if it was all too little. He took a couple of hurried strides then stopped when the emergency telephone rang. It felt as though he was being torn in two. Part of him desperately wanted to ignore the phone and speak to Bella, while another part urged him to respond to the summons.

In the end duty won. Mac snatched up the receiver, listening intently while the operator relayed the details.

There'd been an accident at a level crossing on the outskirts of town. A train had hit a car that had stalled on
the track and a number of people had been seriously
injured, including several children. Mac confirmed
that they would send a team and hung up then pressed
the call button to summon the rest of the staff. Once
everyone had gathered around the desk, he explained
what had happened and what they would do.

'Bella, Laura and I will attend the accident as we've
all done the major incident training course. That leaves
Helen, Trish and Bailey to cover here.' He turned to
Janet. 'Can you phone Adam and ask him to come in?'
he asked, referring to their consultant, Adam Danvers.
'He was at a finance meeting this morning but it should
be over by now so it shouldn't be a problem.'

Once everything was organised, Mac led the way
to the room where they kept all their equipment. After
they had donned weatherproof suits, they each collected a backpack containing everything they might
need, from basic dressings to surgical instruments.
It was impossible to foretell what they would have to
deal with and they needed to be prepared. A rapid response car was waiting when they exited the building.
Bella didn't look at him as she climbed into the back
and beckoned to Laura to sit beside her.

Mac's mouth compressed as he slid into the passenger seat. He had missed his chance to try and sort
things out with her and, if she had anything to do with
it, he wouldn't get another opportunity either. Maybe

he should think about cutting short his contract and signing on for the next aid mission? He had planned on staying in England for a while, but it would be better than having to work with Bella if she and Tim got back together. To see her day in and day out, knowing that she didn't love him but someone else, would be unbearably painful. Quite frankly, he doubted if he could handle it.

He closed his eyes as they set off with lights flashing and siren blaring, trying to blot out the thought of the dark and lonely future that lay ahead of him. Without Bella in his life, it felt as though he had very little to look forward to.

CHAPTER TEN

IT WASN'T THE FIRST major incident that Bella had attended but it had to be the most serious. The train was a high-speed express and many of its carriages had been derailed. The fire and rescue crews were working their way along the track, searching for any injured passengers, and by the time they arrived there were over a hundred people gathered at the side of the railway line. It was more than a little daunting to be faced with so many people who needed help, but Mac took it in his stride.

'We need to find out where the children are. It may seem hard-hearted to ignore the adults but there are other teams of medics who can deal with them. Our brief is to concentrate on the kids first and foremost.'

Bella nodded, feeling her initial panic subside in the face of his calmness. 'So what do you want us to do?' she asked, her heart lifting when he smiled at her. She battened it down, knowing how easy it would be to allow herself to think that it meant something. Mac had proved beyond any shadow of a doubt that he didn't really love her and she must never forget that.

'I'll have a word with the officer in charge. Incident control said that there were two children who'd been seriously injured, although there may be others. However, we'll start with them.'

'Fine. Laura and I will go and check on that group over there,' Bella replied dully, confining her thoughts to what was happening. There was no point thinking about how much she loved him when it wouldn't make any difference. Mac may have thought that he loved her; however, the way he'd reacted yesterday proved it wasn't true. If he had loved her, as he'd claimed, then he would have known that she would never go back to Tim!

Her heart felt like lead as she and Laura made their way over to a group of teenagers huddled beside the track. There were three boys and two girls in the party and they all looked deeply shocked. One of the boys had a large gash on his forehead so Bella cleaned it up and applied butterfly stitches to hold the edges together. He would need to go to hospital and have a scan to check that he hadn't suffered a head injury. The rest of the group had suffered only minor cuts and bruises so she told them to wait there until they were told they could go home. They all had mobile phones and they'd called their parents so she guessed it wouldn't be long before they were collected.

As for the aftermath of what they had witnessed, that was something no one could predict. Some would put it behind them and get on with their lives, while others might be permanently affected. It all depended on the type of person they were. Take her, for instance. She had spent her life distancing herself from other people so it was doubly ironic that now she had finally got in touch with her emotions, it was to have them thrown back in her face. It was a sobering thought but thankfully she didn't have time to dwell on it as Mac came over just then and drew her aside.

'The injured children are still on the train. The crew who found them decided it was too risky to try and move them.'

'Sounds bad,' Bella said quietly, her heart sinking. 'Do you know which carriage they're in?'

'One of the crew's going to take us to them.' Mac looked at her. 'Are you OK about this, Bella? I know how upsetting this kind of situation can be, so say if it's too much for you.'

'I'm fine,' she snapped, determined that she wasn't going to let her newly discovered emotions get the better of her. Mac didn't love her. If she said it often enough then maybe she would believe it and not keep reading too much into everything he said.

'Fair enough.'

He shrugged but she saw the hurt in his eyes and had to bite her tongue to stop herself saying something. He didn't need her reassurances. He didn't need anything at all from her. The thought stayed with her as they followed one of the fire crew along the track. They came to the first two carriages, the ones directly behind the engine, and Bella grimaced. The carriages were lying on their side, in a mangled mess halfway down the embankment, and it was hard to believe that anyone sitting in either of them had survived.

'You're going to need to be extremely careful,' the fireman warned them. 'There's a lot of broken glass and metal in there. We've tried to stabilise the carriages as best we can to stop them sliding any further down the embankment but if we tell you to get out then no arguing—just do it. One of the kids is in the first carriage and the other is in the second, but you'll need to make your way inside through here. A couple of our guys are waiting with them.'

Bella nodded, saving her breath as she set about levering herself up into the carriage. It was a long way and there were very few footholds so it wasn't easy.

'Here. Put your foot in my hands and I'll give you a boost up.'

Mac made a cup with his hands and after a moment's hesitation Bella placed her foot in it. He boosted her up until she could grab hold of the fireman's hand. He hauled her the rest of the way, waiting until Mac joined them before he led them inside. It was strangely disorientating to walk along what was actually the side wall of the carriage, scrambling over seats and tables that had sheared away from their housings. Bella was glad when they reached the first casualty, a young girl, roughly ten years of age.

'You stay with her and I'll check out the other child,'

Mac told her as they paused. His eyes darkened. 'Just mind what you're doing, Bella. It's only too easy to have an accident yourself in this kind of situation.'

Bella nodded, unable to speak when her throat felt as dry as a bone. She crouched down and began examining the girl, focusing all her attention on what she was doing. It would be a mistake to read anything into the way Mac had looked at her, she reminded herself sternly. Her heart began to thump because there was no way that she could stop herself. Despite what had happened, she wanted Mac to be concerned about her.

She took a deep breath but the truth had to be faced. She wanted him to feel all *sorts* of things when he looked at her, and especially love.

Mac did his best but the boy's injuries were just too severe. He died a short time later and now all that was left to do was to inform his parents. They had been injured as well and had already been ferried to hospital.

His heart was heavy as he made his way back through the train. Breaking bad news to relatives was always hard and even worse when it concerned a child. He couldn't imagine how people coped with such a tragedy; he knew he'd find it impossibly difficult. If he had a child then he would love it with every fibre of his being, and it was such a poignant thought in the circumstances. Bella was the only woman he had ever wanted to have a child with and it was never going to happen.

It was hard to hide how devastated the thought made him feel as he stopped beside her. She looked up and he had to bite back the words that were clamouring to get out. It wasn't fair to put her under any pressure, to make her feel guilty because she loved Tim and not him. People couldn't choose who they fell in love with, although even if he could have done he would have still chosen Bella. Right from the first moment they had met, he had known in his heart that she was the only woman for him.

It was hard to contain his emotions at that thought but somehow he managed to get them under control. 'Have you nearly finished here?'

'Yes. She's stable and ready to be moved. How about the other child?'

Mac shook his head, feeling tears welling behind his eyelids. He was at emotional overload and it would take very little to make him break down. 'He didn't make it.'

'Oh, I'm so sorry!' Reaching up, she touched his hand, just the lightest, briefest of contacts, but he felt the touch like a brand burning into his skin.

He turned away, terrified that he would do something crazy. He mustn't beg her to stay with him, mustn't try to *coerce* her. She had to want him as much as he wanted her, otherwise there was no point. She would only end up by leaving him and he couldn't bear the thought of that happening... Although could it be any worse than what was happening right now? Could he feel any more devastated than he did at this very moment, knowing that he had lost her?

The questions thundered inside his head as he made his way from the train. He had intended to find the officer in charge and update him about what had happened to the boy. However, he'd only gone a couple of yards when he heard shouting behind him and spun round. His heart seemed to seize up as he watched the wrecked carriages start to slide down the embankment. There was a sickening screech of metal being ripped apart, the sound of glass shattering, and then silence.

Mac stood where he was, unable to move as fear turned his limbs to stone. Bella was trapped somewhere inside that tangle of broken glass and metal!

Bella had been about to stand up when she heard someone shouting and the next second she felt the carriage begin to move. Grabbing hold of a table, she clung on as it gathered momentum, jolting and bouncing its way down the embankment. Bits of broken glass and metal were being flung around and she gasped when a shard of metal cut into her neck. She could feel the warm stickiness of blood pouring from the cut but she was too afraid to let go of her handhold to check it out. Fortunately, Katie, the young girl she'd been treating, was wedged between a couple of overturned seats and they provided some protection for her. However, Bella could see the fear in her eyes and reacted instinctively.

'It's OK, sweetheart. The carriage has just slipped a little but it will stop in a moment.'

Reaching out, she squeezed Katie's hand, praying that she wasn't being overly optimistic. The bank was very steep at this point, falling away to the river at the bottom, and she didn't want to imagine what would happen if it slid all the way down. When they suddenly came to a jarring halt, she was overwhelmed by relief. She gingerly straightened up, holding on to the table when she felt the carriage sway. She could see out of the window now and her heart sank when she realised that the carriages had come to rest against some scrubby-looking trees. It seemed unlikely that they could support their weight for very long.

'We need to get you out of here.' The fireman who had accompanied them onto the train appeared. His expression was grim as he glanced out of the window. 'Those trees won't be able to support this weight for much longer, so we're going to have to move you and the girl straight away.'

'I understand,' Bella said quietly, doing her best to hide her concern for Katie's sake. Crouching down, she concentrated on making sure that the supports she had placed around the girl's hips and legs were securely fastened. Katie had a fractured pelvis plus fractures to both femurs and it was essential that the breaks were stabilised before they attempted to move her. Once Bella was sure that she had done all she could, she stood up. 'Right, there's nothing more I can do. Let's get her out of here.'

The fire crew carefully eased the girl out from between the seats. They had a stretcher ready and they slid her onto it, passing it from hand to hand as they lifted her over all the debris. Bella followed them, biting her lip against the pain from the cut in her neck. It had stopped bleeding, thankfully, but it was definitely going to need stitching from what she could tell. They reached the door at last and the lead fireman turned to her.

'We'll get you out first. That way, you'll be on hand if she needs anything.' He lowered his voice. 'It won't be easy to get her out of here, so be prepared, Doc.'

Bella nodded, understanding how difficult it was going to be. Not only would the crew need to lift the stretcher up to reach the opening, they would have to raise it at an angle to get it through the gap. She could only pray that the pain relief she had given the girl would be sufficient. In other circumstances, she would have insisted on them waiting while she topped it up but that wasn't an option right now. At any moment, the carriages could start to move again and the consequences of that happening didn't bear thinking about. She allowed one of the crew to boost her up to reach the opening, gasping when she discovered that Mac was there waiting to help her down. He gripped tight hold of her hands and she could see the relief in his eyes.

'Are you all right?' he asked, his deep voice throbbing with an emotion that made her heart start to race.

'I…I think so.'

'Good.'

He squeezed her fingers then quickly lowered her down to the ground where another member of the crew was waiting to escort her to safety. Within seconds Bella found herself at the top of the embankment. She sat down abruptly on the grass as her head began to whirl. Maybe it was the stress of what had happened the previous day allied to the amount of blood she had lost, but all of a sudden she felt incredibly dizzy. Putting her head between her knees, she made herself breathe slowly and deeply but the feeling of faintness simply got worse. As she slid into unconsciousness, the last thing she heard was Mac's frantic voice calling her name.

CHAPTER ELEVEN

MAC WAS ALMOST beside himself with fear by the time he returned to Dalverston General. He would have happily sold his soul to the devil if it had meant he could have gone with Bella in the ambulance that had ferried her and Katie to the hospital, but there'd been no way that he could have left Laura on her own. He'd had to stay, even though it had been the hardest thing he had ever done. Bella was injured and he needed to be with her even if it wasn't what she wanted.

The thought weighed heavily on him as he made his way to A&E. Nick Rogers, one of the senior registrars, was on duty and he grinned when he saw Mac coming in. 'Bit of excitement today, eh? I drew the short straw and had to stay here. Story of my life—I never get the really interesting jobs!'

Mac knew that Nick was joking and that he was as committed to his job as they all were, but he took exception to the comment. 'You wouldn't say that if you'd seen the state of those poor souls who were on the train,' he snapped.

'Sorry.' Nick held up his hands in apology and Mac sighed, aware that he had overreacted.

'No. It's me. Take no notice. Anyway, you've got Bella in here. Can I see her?'

'Sure. She's in cubicle four... No, wait a sec; she's just gone down to radiography.'

'Radiography?' Mac repeated. His heart gave a little jolt as he looked at Nick in horror. 'She's having an X-ray?'

'Yep. That cut on her neck is deep and I wanted to check there was nothing lodged in it so I've sent her down for an X-ray.'

'I was hoping it would just need stitching,' Mac murmured, his stomach churning sickeningly. If there was something lodged in the cut—a piece of glass or a sliver of metal, perhaps—then Bella might need surgery and he couldn't bear the thought of her having to go through such an ordeal.

'Probably will,' Nick replied cheerfully. 'It's just best to err on the side of caution, as I said.'

'I...er... Yes, of course.'

Mac did his best to pull himself together as he thanked the other man. He knew he was overreacting but he couldn't help it. This was Bella and he simply couldn't take a balanced view where she was concerned. He hurried to the lift, tapping his foot with impatience as it carried him down to the radiography unit. There was nobody in the waiting room so he pressed the bell, his impatience mounting as he waited for someone to answer. When the door to one of the X-ray suites opened, he spun round, his heart leaping when he saw Bella being wheeled out by a porter.

'Mac, what are you doing here?' she exclaimed when she saw him. 'I thought you'd still be at the accident.'

'All the children have been either moved to hospital or sent home,' he explained as he went over to her. 'Nick told me you were here, having an X-ray done on your neck.'

'Yes. Thankfully, there's nothing in it. Once it's stitched up I should be right as rain.'

She dredged up a smile but Mac could see the wariness in her eyes and realised that she wasn't sure what was going to happen. All of a sudden he couldn't stand it any longer, couldn't bear to tiptoe around any more. He loved her! He wanted her! And he wanted her to know that too.

His heart was thumping as he turned to the porter and told him that he would take Dr English back to A&E. Once the man had disappeared, he pushed Bella to a quiet corner where they wouldn't be disturbed. Crouching down in front of the wheelchair, he looked into her eyes, knowing that he was about to take the biggest gamble of his life. Telling her that he loved her had felt like a huge risk at the time, but it wasn't nearly as massive as this. This was so enormous that it scared him witless and yet it was what he *had* to do if he was to have a chance of achieving what he wanted so desperately—Bella and that happy-ever-after he yearned for.

Capturing her hands, he raised them to his mouth, feeling his panic subside as soon as he felt the warmth of her flesh against his lips. He could do this. He really could! 'I love you, Bella. I know I already told you that but then I went and ruined things by overreacting when Tim phoned. There's no excuse for what I said. I was wrong and I bitterly regret it.'

'I would never have slept with you just to work out how I feel about Tim,' she said softly.

'I know that.' Mac had to force the words past the lump in his throat when he heard the pain in her voice. He knew that she was telling him the truth and the fact that he had caused her such anguish filled him with guilt. 'I am so sorry, my love. Can you ever forgive me?'

'Yes. If I'm sure that you believe me.' She looked steadily back at him. 'I couldn't cope if you kept on doubting me all the time. I have to know that you believe in me, Mac. Our relationship won't work if you're continually wondering if I'm telling you the truth.'

'I know that.' He sighed as he leant forward and kissed her gently on the mouth. He drew back when he felt his body immediately stir. It was too soon for that. They needed to sort this out before they went any further. *If* they went any further. The thought spurred him on.

'I hate myself for hurting you, Bella. However, the

truth is that I've always had a problem about trusting people since I was a child and my mother left.' He dredged up a smile, uncomfortable about admitting to what he considered a weakness. 'I know I should have got over it years ago, but sometimes it comes back to haunt me.'

'We're all the product of our upbringing, Mac.' She lifted his hand to her lips and pressed a kiss to his palm and her voice was so gentle, so tender that it brought a lump to his throat.

'Think so?' he murmured huskily.

'Oh, yes.' She smiled into his eyes. 'Look at me. My parents aren't demonstrative people and they didn't encourage me to show my feelings either. That's why I've always had such difficulty relating to other people—I tend to hold everything inside me rather than show how I really feel.'

'Really?' His brows rose and he grinned at her. 'I would never have guessed from the way you responded when we made love.'

'That was different,' she protested, a rush of colour staining her cheeks.

'Was it? Why?' He brushed her lips with the lightest of kisses, drawing back when he felt her immediately respond. His heart filled with joy, although he shouldn't assume that her response meant that it was *him* she wanted…

All of a sudden Mac couldn't wait any longer. Cupping her face between his hands, he looked into her eyes, knowing that this was the most important moment of his life. Whatever happened in the next few seconds was going to determine his whole future.

'Do you love me, Bella? I know I shouldn't put you on the spot like this, but I need to know before I drive myself crazy!'

Bella could feel her heart thumping. It was beating so hard that she could barely think, let alone answer the question. And then slowly through all the confusion in her head one thought rose to the surface. Of course she loved him. There was no doubt about that.

'Of course I love you,' she said indignantly, glaring at him. 'I'd have thought that was obvious.'

'Not to me.'

His voice was filled with a mixture of pure amazement and utter joy. Bella felt her indignation melt away as fast as it had appeared. Placing her hand on his cheek, she smiled at him, stunned by the fact that he was so vulnerable. Mac had always been so together, so in charge of himself—or so she had thought. To suddenly discover this whole different side to him was a revelation. She realised in that moment that she would do everything in her power to make sure that he never regretted letting her see the real man beneath the confident façade he presented to the world at large.

She kissed him softly on the mouth, letting her lips show him in no uncertain terms how she felt. She loved him so much and she wanted nothing more than to spend the rest of her days proving it to him…

If he would let her.

She drew back, feeling the first tiny doubt gnawing away at her happiness. Mac had asked her if she loved him. He had told her that he needed to know. However, he hadn't said why.

'I love you, Mac, but are you sure that you love me? You were so quick to think that I'd used you to clarify my feelings for Tim and you wouldn't have done that if you'd really loved me. You would have known that I would never have slept with you for that reason.'

It was the hardest thing Bella had ever done. She had never done anything like this before, never delved into emotional issues, and it scared her to do it now when it was so important. Whatever Mac told her would affect the rest of her life and she wasn't sure if she could handle the thought.

She stood up abruptly, suddenly too afraid to sit there and listen to what he had to say. If Mac didn't want her then there was nothing she could do about it. She had to accept his decision and not make a scene, certainly not make a fool of herself by begging him to reconsider! Tears stung her eyes as she went to push past him but he was too quick for her. Reaching out, he drew her to a halt, his arms closing around her so that she couldn't move, couldn't escape him or the truth.

'Bella, stop! I know you're scared because I'm scared too, but you can't run away. I won't let you.'

Bending, he pressed a kiss to her lips and she felt the shudder that passed through his body and into hers. Raising his head, he looked steadily at her. 'We both need to be brave if we're going to make this work. I love you and I want to spend my life with you. I think… *hope*…that you feel the same. Do you, my darling? Do you love me enough to live with me from now to eternity because I warn you that's what I want. Nothing less.'

Bella could feel her heart thumping. This was it. Whatever she said now would determine her future. Did she want to be with Mac for ever? Did she want to live with him and spend each and every day making him happy? Of course she did!

Reaching up, she drew his head down and kissed him, letting her lips answer his question. There was a moment when he held back, a tiny beat of time when he seemed to hesitate as though he wasn't sure that what was happening was real, and then he was kissing her back, kissing her with a hunger he didn't attempt to hide. They were both trembling when they broke apart, both shaken by the depth of their feelings for each other. Mac cupped her cheek and she could hear the love resonating in his voice.

'I didn't know it was possible to feel this way, Bella, to want someone *this* much.'

'Me neither.' Turning her head, she pressed a kiss against his palm and felt him shudder. It felt like the most natural thing in the world to tell him how she felt, to lay bare her emotions completely and totally. 'I want you so much that it hurts, Mac. I want to spend my life with you and spend every single second of every minute loving you. Even then it won't be enough. Nothing would be when I feel this way.'

'And you're sure? Sure that you want me and not Tim? After all, you agreed to meet him—'

'Yes, I did.' She laid her fingertips against his lips to silence him. 'And the reason I agreed was because of how I feel about you. I wanted to draw a line under past events and, if possible, make my peace with Tim. I want the future—our future, together—to be perfect and not tainted by anything that's happened in the past.'

'Oh, my love!'

He kissed her again, hunger replaced by a bone-melting tenderness that brought tears to her eyes. He smiled as he wiped them away with his fingertips. 'Don't cry, sweetheart. Although I have to confess that I feel very much like shedding a tear or two myself.'

'Just not right for your macho image,' she teased, smiling up at him through her tears.

'Definitely not. I should really be beating my chest right now, shouldn't I?' He grinned back at her. 'I mean, I've just won the woman I love and I should be celebrating before dragging you back to my cave.'

'Hmm. Let's not get too carried away by the macho theme.' She laughed up at him. 'I'm a modern woman, after all, and I value my independence.'

'And so you should. I don't want you to change,

Bella. I want you to stay exactly the same as you've always been.'

'I don't think that's possible,' she said quietly. 'I've changed a lot in the past few weeks and changed for the better too. I now understand my feelings and I'm not so afraid to show them, thanks to you. And, hopefully, I shall get even better at it as time passes too.'

'I've always thought you were perfect from the moment we met.'

His voice grated and Bella's eyes filled with tears once more because it was obvious that he was telling her the truth. Mac loved her exactly how she was and it was marvellous to know that he didn't want her to change. Reaching up, she kissed him, showing him without the need for words how much she loved him and how much she needed him. He'd said she was perfect but to her mind he was perfect too!

EPILOGUE

One year later...

MAC CAREFULLY LAID the baby in her crib. It was two a.m. and the rest of the town was sleeping. With a bit of luck, three-week-old Isobel Grace MacIntyre would follow suit.

'Has she dropped off at last?'

'Not yet.'

He turned, thinking that Bella had never looked more beautiful as she sat there propped against the pillows in their bed. They had married as soon as they had discovered that she was expecting the baby. He knew that they would have got married anyway but he had discovered that he was surprisingly old-fashioned in many ways and had wanted their child to be born in wedlock. The simple ceremony in the hospital's chapel had been perfect too, the final seal on their happiness, not that they had needed to prove it. He loved Bella with every fibre of his being, just as she loved him, and anyone could see how they felt too!

'I think she's debating whether or not to give her poor mum and dad a break.'

He lay down on the bed and gathered Bella into his arms, inhaling the warm womanly smell of her. She had decided to feed Isobel herself and he loved watching her do so, loved how her face filled with adoration for their baby, loved how fulfilled she looked with the infant nursing at her breast. Love, as he had discovered, was infinite and expanded on a daily basis.

He kissed her gently on the lips, drawing back when he felt his body immediately stir. It was too soon for them to make love because Bella needed time to heal after the birth. Anyway, waiting only made his desire for her even stronger, not that it hadn't been pretty strong to begin with!

'Mmm. I think I can guess what's on your mind,' she said, pulling back so she could look into his eyes, and he chuckled.

'Is it that obvious?'

'Yes.' She snuggled against him and sighed. 'Not just on your mind either.'

'Never mind. Just another couple of weeks and we can resume relations, as they say,' he said comfortingly, pulling her back to him.

'I can't wait,' she murmured against his chest. She suddenly drew back again. 'Did I tell you that I spoke to Freya this morning? Apparently, the results of her mock A-levels were so good that she's been offered a place at Lancaster. She will make a brilliant nurse, don't you think?'

'I do. I'm so glad that her parents saw sense in the end. She needs their support if she's to make a success of uni,' he said, pulling her back into his arms. He kissed the tip of her nose and smiled. 'Another set of grandparents who've been won over.'

'Like my parents, you mean.' She burrowed against him. 'Dad phoned as well this afternoon to let me know they're coming up to visit us at the weekend.'

'Again?' Mac laughed softly. 'That's the third time in as many weeks. Why do I get the feeling that they're going to turn into doting grandparents?'

'Oh, I've no idea, but don't knock it. Dad mentioned something about him and Mum babysitting if we wanted to go out for dinner. Sounds good to me.'

'Me too. So long as Isobel is all right, of course,' he added, glancing over at the crib.

'She'll be fine.' Bella snuggled even closer. 'Now, why don't we take advantage of the fact that she seems to have dropped off at last?'

'Mmm, sounds interesting. What do you suggest?' he asked, leering comically at her.

'I'm not sure. I shall leave that up to you.'

Mac laughed as he pulled her to him and kissed her hungrily. Maybe they couldn't make love just yet but there were other ways to show how they felt about one another. They just needed to be creative...

* * * * *

RESISTING
HER REBEL DOC

BY
JOANNA NEIL

Published in Great Britain 2015
by Mills & Boon, an imprint of Harlequin (UK) Limited,
Eton House, 18-24 Paradise Road, Richmond, Surrey, TW9 1SR

© 2015 Joanna Neil

ISBN: 978-0-263-24724-4

Printed and bound in Spain
by CPI, Barcelona

Dear Reader,

First love, young love…such an intense, wonderful experience. Is it possible that it can survive the ravages of time and be a 'for ever' kind of love?

Well, the answer to that is *maybe*. Sometimes it needs to change and mature, to grow into something else before young lovers can reach the fulfilment they long for.

Life in general—along with a broken romance and a troublesome background of family secrets—manages to get in the way and mess things up for Caitlin and Brodie when they meet up again in the beautiful surroundings of rural Buckinghamshire.

I hope you enjoy reading about their skirmishes and triumphs as they find one another once more.

With love

Joanna

Books by Joanna Neil

Mills & Boon® Medical Romance™

Dr Right All Along
Tamed by Her Brooding Boss
His Bride in Paradise
Return of the Rebel Doctor
Sheltered by Her Top-Notch Boss
A Doctor to Remember
Daring to Date Her Boss
Temptation in Paradise

**Visit the author profile page at
millsandboon.co.uk for more titles**

CHAPTER ONE

'WHAT WILL YOU DO?' Molly stood by the desk at the nursing station, riffling through the papers in a wire tray. 'Will you go to the wedding?' She sent Caitlin a sympathetic glance. 'It must be a really difficult situation for you.'

Caitlin nodded. 'Yes, it is, to be honest. These last few weeks have been a nightmare. It's all come as a complete shock to me and right now I'm not sure how I'm going to deal with it.' She pulled a face, pushing back a couple of chestnut curls that had strayed on to her forehead. Her shoulder-length hair was a mass of wild, natural curls but for her work at the hospital she usually kept it pinned back out of the way. 'I don't want to go but I don't see how I can avoid it—when all's said and done, Jenny's my cousin. My family—my aunt, especially—will want me to be there for the celebrations. I don't want to be the cause of any breakdown in family relationships by not going. It will cause a huge upset if I stay away.'

Yet how could she bear to watch her cousin tie the

knot with the man who just a short time ago had been the love of her life? She and Matt had even started to talk about getting engaged and then—*wham!*—Jenny had come along and suddenly everything had changed.

Her usually mobile mouth flattened into a straight line. When she'd opened the envelope first thing this morning back at the flat and taken out the beautifully embossed invitation card, her spirits had fallen to rock-bottom. She'd had a sick feeling that the day was headed from then on into a downward spiral.

Sure enough, just a few minutes later as she had opened the fridge door and taken out a carton of milk, her prediction was reinforced. She'd shaken the empty carton in disbelief. One of her flatmates must have drained the last drops of milk and then put it back on the shelf. She'd stared at it. No coffee before starting work? It was unthinkable!

'I can see how awkward it is for you.' Molly sighed, bringing Caitlin's thoughts back to the present. 'Families are everything, aren't they? Sometimes we have to do things we don't want to do in order to keep the peace. I just wish you weren't leaving us. I know how you feel about working alongside Jenny and Matt but we'll miss you so much.'

'I'll miss you too,' Caitlin said with feeling. Molly was a children's nurse, brilliant at her job and a good friend, but now, as Caitlin looked around the ward, she felt sadness growing deep inside her. She'd been working at this hospital for several years, specialising as a children's doctor, making friends and getting to know the inquisitive and endearing children who had come into her care.

It would be such a wrench to put it all behind her, but she knew she had to make a fresh start. She couldn't bear to stay while Matt was here. He had betrayed her and hurt her deeply. 'We'll keep in touch, won't we?' she said, putting on a bright face. 'I won't be going too far away—Buckinghamshire's only about an hour's drive from here.'

Molly nodded. She was a pretty girl with hazel eyes and dark, almost black hair cut in a neat, silky bob. 'Are you going to live at home? Didn't you say your mother needed to have someone close by her these days?'

'Yes, that's right. Actually, I thought it would be a good chance for me to keep an eye on her now that she's getting on a bit and beginning to get a few aches and pains. It's been worrying me for quite a while that I'm so far away.' She smiled. 'I think she's really quite pleased that I'll be staying with her for a while, just until I can sort out a place of my own.'

She started to look through the patients' charts that were neatly stacked on the desk. Her whole world was changing. She loved this job; she'd thought long and hard before giving in her notice, but how could she go on working here as long as Matt was going to be married to her cousin? And, worse, Jenny was going to take up a job here too.

She shuddered inwardly. It was still alien to her to

think of him as her ex. They'd been together for eighteen months and it had been a terrible jolt to discover that he'd fallen out of love with her and gone off with another woman.

'I shall have to look for another job, of course, but there are a couple of hospitals in the area. It shouldn't be too difficult to find something. I hope not, anyway.' She straightened up and made an effort to pull herself together. No matter how much she was hurting, she knew instinctively that it was important from now on to make plans and try to look on the positive side. She had to get over this and move on. She glanced at Molly. 'Perhaps we could meet up from time to time— we could go for a coffee together, or a meal, maybe?'

'Yeah, that'll be good.' Molly cheered up and began to glance through the list of young patients who were waiting to be seen. 'The test results are back on the little boy with the painful knee,' she pointed out helpfully. 'From the looks of things it's an infection.'

'Hmm.' Caitlin quickly scanned the laboratory form. 'It's what we thought. I'll arrange for the orthopaedic surgeon to drain the fluid from the joint and we'll start him on the specific antibiotic right away.' She wrote out a prescription and handed it to Molly.

'Thanks. I'll see to it.'

'Good.' Caitlin frowned. 'I'd like to follow up on him to see how he's doing, but I expect Matt will take over my patients when I leave here. I'll miss my little charges.'

Caitlin phoned the surgeon to set things in motion and then went to check up on a four-year-old patient who'd been admitted with breathing problems the previous day. The small child was sleeping, his breathing coming in short gasps, his cheeks chalky-pale against the white of the hospital pillows. He'd been so poorly when he'd been brought in yesterday and she'd been desperately concerned for him. But now, after she had listened to his chest and checked the monitors, she felt reassured.

'He seems to be doing much better,' she told his parents, who were sitting by his bedside, waiting anxiously. 'The intravenous steroids and nebuliser treatments have opened up his airways and made it easier for him to breathe. We'll keep him on those and on the oxygen for another day or so and you should gradually begin to see a great improvement. The chest X-ray didn't show anything untoward, so we can assume it was just flare-up of the asthma. I'll ask the nurse to talk to you to see if we can find ways of avoiding too many of those in the future.'

'Thank you, doctor.' They looked relieved, and after talking with them for a little while longer Caitlin left them, taking one last glance at the child before going back to the central desk to see if any more test results had come in.

'There's a phone call for you, Caitlin.' The clerk at the nurses' station held the receiver aloft as she approached the desk. 'Sounds urgent.'

'Okay, thanks.' Caitlin took the receiver from her and said in an even tone, 'Hello, this is Dr Braemar. How may I help?'

'Hi, Caitlin.' The deep male voice was warm and compelling in a way that was oddly, bone-meltingly familiar. 'I don't know if you remember me—it's been quite a while. I'm Brodie Driscoll. We used to live near one another in Ashley Vale?'

She drew in a quick breath. Brodie Driscoll! How could she possibly forget him? He was the young man who had haunted her teenage dreams and sent hot thrills rocketing through her bloodstream. Just hearing his name had been enough to fire up all her senses. He had been constantly in her thoughts back then— and to be scrupulously honest even now the sound of his voice brought prickles of awareness shooting from the tips of her toes right up to her temples.

Not that she'd ever let on that he had the power to affect her like this—not then and certainly not now! Heaven forbid she should ever fall for the village bad boy, let alone become involved in any way with him. He was a rebel, through and through, trouble with a capital T… But who could resist him? His roguish smile and his easy charm made him utterly irresistible.

'Oh, I remember,' she said softly. She couldn't imagine why he was calling her like this, out of the blue. Not to talk about old times, surely? Her pulse quickened. Maybe that wouldn't be such a bad idea, after all…?

'That's good, I'm glad you haven't forgotten me.'

There was a smile in his voice but his next words brought her out of her wistful reverie and swiftly back to the here and now. 'I'm sorry to ring you at work, Caitlin, but something's happened that I think you need to know about.'

'Oh? That's okay…what is it?' She'd no idea how or why he'd tracked her down, but he sounded serious, and all at once she was anxious to hear what he had to say.

'It's about your mother. I'm not sure if you know, but I moved into the house next door to hers a couple of weeks ago, so I see her quite often when she's out and about on the smallholding.'

She hadn't known that. Her mother was always busy with the animals and the orchard; knowing how friendly she was with everyone it was easy to see how she and Brodie would pass the time of day with one another. Her mouth curved. It was good that she had someone nearby to take an interest in her.

'What's happened?' she asked. 'Are the animals escaping on to your property?' Her mother could never resist taking in strays and wounded creatures and nursing them back to health. 'I know the fence was looking a bit rickety last time I was there. I made a few running repairs, but if there's a problem I'll make sure it's sorted.'

'No, it isn't that.' There was a sombre edge to his tone and Caitlin tensed, suddenly alert. 'I'm afraid it's much more serious,' he said. 'Your mother has had an accident, Caitlin. She had a fall and I'm pretty sure she's broken her hip. I called the ambulance a few minutes ago and the paramedics are transferring her into it right now. I'll go with her to the hospital, but I thought you should know what's happening.'

Caitlin's face paled rapidly. 'I— Yes, of course. I… Thank you, Brodie. I'll get over there… I need to be with her.' She frowned. 'What makes you think she's broken her hip?' She added tentatively, 'Perhaps it's not quite as serious as that.'

'That's what I was hoping, but she can't move her leg and it's at an odd angle—it looks as though it's become shorter than the other one. I'm afraid she's in a lot of pain.'

'Oh, dear.' Those were typical signs of a broken hip. The day was just going rapidly from bad to worse. 'Will they be taking her to Thame Valley Hospital?'

'That's right. She'll go straight to A&E for assessment.' He paused as someone at the other end of the line spoke to him. She guessed the paramedic had approached him to say they were ready to leave.

'I'm sorry, I have to go,' he said.

'All right…and thanks again for ringing me, Brodie.' She hesitated then said quickly, 'Give her my love, will you, and tell her I'll be with her as soon as I can?'

'I will.' He cut the call and Caitlin stood for a moment, staring into space, trying to absorb what he'd told her.

'Are you all right?' Emerging from one of the patients' bays, the senior registrar came over to the desk and looked her over briefly. 'You're as white as a sheet,' he commented. 'What's happened? Is it something to do with one of the patients?'

She shook her head. 'My mother's had an accident— a fall. A neighbour's going with her to the hospital—it sounds as though she's broken her hip.'

'I'm so sorry,' he said with a frown. 'I know how worrying that must be for you, especially with her not living close by. You'll want to go to her.'

'Yes, I do… But are you sure it's all right?' She wanted to jump at the chance to leave but she had patients who needed to be seen.

'It's fine. I'll take over your case load. Don't worry about it. I'm sure Molly will fill me in on some of the details.'

'Thanks,' she said, relieved.

She left the hospital a short time later, walking out into warm sunshine. The balmy weather seemed so at odds with what was happening.

She picked up an overnight bag from her flat. The news was dreadful and she was full of apprehension about what she might find when she caught up with her mother. It was a relief at least to know that Brodie was with her. She must be in shock and in terrible pain but it would be a comfort to her to have someone by her side. Caitlin would be eternally grateful to Brodie for the way he had responded to her mother's predicament.

Guilt and anxiety washed over her. She should have been there; somehow she should have been able to prevent this from happening… She tried as best she could, but it wasn't always possible for her to get away every week, with shift changes and staff shortages and so on. It was frustrating.

Her heart was thumping heavily as she drove along the familiar route towards her home town. She had the car window wound down so that she could feel the breeze on her face, but even the heat and the beautiful landscape of the Buckinghamshire countryside couldn't distract her from her anxiety.

How bad was it? Being a doctor sometimes had its disadvantages—she knew all too well how dangerous a hip fracture could be, the complications involved: perhaps a significant amount of internal bleeding and the possibility of disabling consequences.

She gripped the steering wheel more firmly. Think positively, she reminded herself. Her mother was in good hands and she would be there with her in just a short time.

A few minutes later she slid the car into a parking bay at the Thame Valley Hospital and then hurried into the Accident and Emergency department, anxious to find out how her mother was getting on.

'They've been doing some pre-op procedures, X-rays and blood tests and so on,' the nurse said. 'And as soon as those are complete the surgeon will want to talk to her. Mr Driscoll thought maybe you might like to have a cup of coffee with him while you're waiting. He asked me to tell you he's in the cafeteria.' She smiled and added good-naturedly, 'If you leave me your phone number, I'll give you a ring when it's all right for you to see your mother.'

'Okay, thanks, that'll be great.' Caitlin wrote down her number on a slip of paper and then hurried away to find Brodie.

He caught her glance as soon as she entered the cafeteria. 'Hi there,' he said with a smile, coming to greet her, his blue gaze moving fleetingly over her slender figure. She had discarded the hospital scrubs she'd been wearing and had on slim, styled black jeans topped with a loose, pin-tucked shirt. 'It's good to see you, Caitlin.'

'You too.' Her voice was husky, her breath coming in short bursts after her rush to get here. That was the excuse she gave herself, but maybe the truth was that it was a shock to see Brodie in the flesh after all these years.

The good-looking, hot-headed youth she remembered of old was gone and in his place stood a man who simply turned her insides to molten lava. This man was strong, ruggedly hewn, his handsome features carved out of…adversity, she guessed, and…success? There was something about him that said he had fought to get where he was now and he wouldn't be giving any ground.

He was immaculately dressed in dark trousers that moulded his long legs and he wore a crisp linen shirt, the sleeves rolled back to reveal bronzed forearms.

His hair was black, cut in a style that added a hint of devilishness to his chiselled good looks. Tall and broad-shouldered, his whole body was supple with lithe energy, his blue eyes drinking her in, his ready smile welcoming and enveloping her with warmth.

'Come and sit down,' he said, laying a hand gently on the small of her back and ushering her to a seat by the window. 'Let me get you a coffee—you must be ready for one after your journey.' He sent her a quick glance. 'I expect you've been told that your mother is having tests at the moment? The surgeon's going to see her soon to advise her about what needs to be done.'

She nodded. 'The nurse told me.' She sat down, her body stiff with tension. 'How is my mother?'

'She's okay,' he said cautiously. 'She's been conscious all the while, and the paramedics were with her very quickly after her fall, so that's all in her favour.'

'I suppose that's something, anyway.'

'Yes. The doctor who's looking after her gave her a pain-relief injection so she's comfortable at the moment. She's had an MRI scan to assess the extent of the injury—it's definitely a fracture of the hip, I'm afraid.'

She winced. 'Will the surgeon operate today, do you know?'

He nodded. 'Yes. I was told it will probably be later this afternoon—the sooner the better, in these cases. Luckily she hadn't had any breakfast to slow things up. You'll be able to see her before she goes to Theatre.'

'That's good.' She finally relaxed a little and when

he saw that she was a bit more settled he left her momentarily to go and get her a coffee.

Caitlin glanced around the cafeteria. It was a large room, with light coming in from a wall made up entirely of windows. The decor was restful, in pastels of green and cream, and there were ferns placed at intervals, providing a touch of the outdoors.

Brodie came back to the table with a loaded tray and handed her a cup of coffee. It was freshly made, piping hot, and it smelled delicious. 'I thought you might like to try a flapjack,' he said, putting a plate in front of her. 'Something to raise your blood sugar a little—you're very pale.' He took a small jug and a bowl from the tray and slid them across the table towards her. 'Help yourself to cream and sugar.'

'Thanks.' She studied him thoughtfully. She couldn't imagine what it would be like having Brodie as a neighbour. 'How is it that you came to be living next door to my mother?' she asked.

He sat down opposite her. 'I'd been staying in a room at the pub,' he said, 'while I looked around for something more permanent. Then the place came on the market as a suitable property for renovation. The old gentleman who owned it found the upkeep too much for him when his health failed. He went into a nursing home.'

'Lucky for you that the opportunity came your way,' she murmured.

He nodded. 'It's a substantial property—an invest-

ment project, possibly—and I thought it would be interesting to do up the house and sort out the land that
goes along with it.'

'An investment project?' It didn't sound as though
he was planning on staying around for too long once
the place was renovated. 'Does it mean you might not
be staying around long enough to make it a home?'

He shrugged negligently. 'I haven't really made up
my mind. For the moment, I'm fed up with living in
rented accommodation and wanted something I could
renovate.'

'I see.' She picked up one of the golden-brown oat-
cakes and bit into it, savouring the taste. 'I didn't get
to eat breakfast this morning,' she explained after a
moment or two. 'Someone emptied the cupboards of
cereals and bread.' She spooned brown-sugar crystals
into her cup and sipped tentatively, all her regrets about
missing the first coffee of the morning finally beginning to slip away. He watched her curiously.

'You were right,' she murmured at last. 'I needed
that.' She told him about her flatmate drinking the last
of the milk. 'It had to be Mike who was the culprit. Neither of the girls I share with would do something like
that. He probably finished off the cornflakes as well.'

Brodie grinned. 'I guess he's down for a tongue
lashing at some point.'

Her mouth twitched. 'Definitely, if only so I can
vent…not that he'll take any notice. He never does—
why should he when he leads a charmed life?' She took

another sip of coffee. It was reviving and she savoured it for a moment or two before her thoughts shifted to her mother once more. 'Can you tell me anything about what happened this morning with my mother? I'm guessing you must have been outside with her when she fell.'

He nodded. 'I was about to head off for a meeting. Your mother usually feeds the hens first thing, and then checks up on the rabbits, and we say hello and chat for a minute or two. Today she seemed a bit preoccupied— she was worried a fox might have been sniffing around in the night—so she didn't say very much. She started to pull a few weeds out of the rockery and I went to my car. Then I heard a shout and when I looked around she had fallen on to the crazy paving. I think she must have lost her footing on the rocks and stumbled.'

Caitlin winced. 'I've told her to leave the rockery to me. I see to it whenever I'm over here. This is why I worry about leaving her on her own for too long. She's not so nimble on her feet these days, but she's always been independent, and if something needs doing she'll do it.'

'You can't be here all the time. You shouldn't blame yourself.'

She sighed. 'I do, though. I can't help it. I love her to bits and I often think I should never have taken the job in Hertford. It seemed like such a good opportunity at the time.'

He nodded agreement. 'Jane told me you're a children's doctor; she's always singing your praises. She's very proud of your achievements, you know.'

Caitlin smiled. 'She's always been the same. She sees the best in everyone.'

'Yeah.' Brodie gave a wry smile. 'She was the only one who ever saw any good in me. Of course, she'd been friends with my mother since they were at school together, so that must have helped.'

'Yes, I expect so.' Sadly, Brodie's mother had died in a car accident when he was a teenager. That was probably another reason why Jane Braemar had taken him under her wing. Caitlin had lost her father and there had been an immediate bond between her and Brodie because of their shared circumstances. They had each understood what the other had been going through, and in their own way had tried to comfort one another. It had given them a unique closeness, and it had also been good, a source of consolation, that her mother had looked out for Brodie in his darkest times. She'd stood by him all through his unruly, reckless phase.

She hadn't been able to do anything to stem the tide of hostility that had grown among the locals with Brodie's exploits, though.

After a whirlwind period of rebellion—of cocky, arrogant defiance, trespass, petty vandalism, and a 'love 'em and leave 'em' way with girls—even Brodie must have realised he'd gone too far and that he'd worn out any vestiges of goodwill people might have felt for a motherless boy. He'd finally used up all his chances.

On his eighteenth birthday, his father had kicked him out of the family home and Brodie had had to hunt around for somewhere to live. He'd stayed with various friends, Caitlin recalled, before he'd left the village a year or so later. At the time, she'd been broken-hearted. She'd suddenly realised she didn't want him to leave.

Her phone trilled, breaking into her thoughts and bringing her sharply back to the present day. 'My mother's back on the ward,' she told Brodie after a second or two. 'The nurse said she's a bit drowsy from the pain medication but I can go and see her.'

'That's good. It might help to put your mind at rest if you can spend some time with her.'

She nodded. 'Thanks again for looking after her,' she said softly, her grey eyes filled with gratitude. 'I owe you.'

'You're welcome any time, Caitlin.' He stood up with her as she prepared to leave. He reached for her overnight bag. 'Let me help you with that,' he said.

'Thank you.' She watched him lift the heavy bag effortlessly. In it, she'd packed everything she thought she might need over the next few days, including her hairdryer, laptop, make-up bag and several changes of clothes.

'Have you thought about what will happen when your mother leaves hospital?' he asked as they set off for the orthopaedic ward. 'She'll need a lot of help with mobility. Perhaps she could go to a convalescent home for a few weeks?'

She shook her head. 'That won't be necessary. I'd planned on coming back to live in the village in the next week or so—this has just brought it forward, that's all.'

He frowned. 'You're leaving your job?'

'Yes. I'll have to find something else, of course, but I'd made up my mind that it was something I needed to do.'

'Are you doing this for your mother's sake or for some other reason?'

'A bit of both, really.' He was astute—she should have known that he would suspect an ulterior motive. 'I have some personal reasons for wanting to leave.'

'There wasn't a problem with the job, then?'

'Heavens, no.' She looked at him wide-eyed. 'I love my work. I just hope I can find something as satisfying to do here.'

They approached the lift bay. 'Hmm. Maybe I could help you out there,' he said. 'No promises, but I've just taken over as head of the children's unit here and I'm fairly sure I'll be able to find you a position.'

She stared at him in disbelief. 'You're a doctor?' Not only that, he was in charge of a unit. How could that be?

He nodded, his mouth quirking. 'I know that must seem strange, with my background, but thankfully I managed to get my head together before it was too late. I used a legacy from my grandfather to put myself through medical school. I didn't know anything about it until the lawyers contacted me but as far as I was concerned it came in the nick of time.'

She was stunned. 'I can't get used to the idea—you were an unruly, out-of-control teenager. You were always playing truant, going off with some friend or other to spend time in the woods.' She shook her head. 'Are you making this up?'

He laughed. 'No, it's all true. I took stock of myself one day and realised I was going nowhere fast. For all that I missed out on some of my schooling, I managed to get through the exams without too much bother, so when I made up my mind what I wanted to do it wasn't too difficult for me to get a place at medical school.'

They stepped inside the lift. 'What made you decide you wanted to be a doctor?' She still couldn't get her head around it.

His mouth flattened. 'I think my mother's accident had something to do with it, although I didn't consciously think of it in that way until some years later. I did some work with troubled teenagers and then I spent some time helping out in a children's home, supervising leisure activities and so on. I suppose that's what guided me towards a career working with young children. They aren't at all judgemental and I think that's what I liked most. They accept you for what you are; I find I can get along with them.'

The lift doors pinged and opened out on to the floor where the orthopaedic ward was housed. Brodie walked with her to the doors of the ward and then handed over her bag. 'I'll leave you to go and spend some time with your mother,' he said. 'Perhaps you'll think over what I said about the job? We always need paediatricians and even though I'm fairly new to the hospital I'm sure the bosses will accept my judgement on this.'

'I will give it some thought, of course—though I can't help thinking you're taking a bit of a risk offering me something like that when we've only just met up.'

'I suppose some might think that. Actually, though, I know your boss in Hertford. Jane told me you were part of his team and I knew then you must be good at your job. He's a decent man; he picks out good people.'

Her mouth curved. 'It sounds as though my mother has been giving you my life history.'

'Like I said, she thinks the world of you.' He scanned her face briefly. 'In fact, your boss actually mentioned you to me once. He said he had this dedicated young woman, Caity, working with him—though at the time I didn't realise he was talking about you.' He was thoughtful for a moment or two, then added, 'If you like, if you're stuck for something to do while your mother's in Theatre, you could maybe come over to the children's unit? The surgery will take a few hours and rather than you waiting about I could show you around. I'm on duty, but you could tag along with me, if that doesn't sound too off-putting?'

She nodded cautiously. 'It sounds fine to me. Perhaps I'll do that.'

He smiled then turned and walked away down the corridor. She watched him go. He was tall, straight backed and sure of himself. He'd always been that way, but whereas once there had been a brash recklessness about him it seemed to have been replaced with a confident, shrewd perception.

He'd made up his mind quickly about her and decided she would be capable of doing the job. She had accepted his explanation but perhaps his decision also had something to do with knowing her from years before.

She didn't know what to make of him. He seemed calm, capable, efficient and friendly—all good attributes. But could he really have changed so completely? Were there still vestiges from the past lurking in his character?

He was certainly impulsive. Was he still the same man who had girls clamouring for his attention? He'd enjoyed playing the field back then; he and his younger brother had caused havoc among the village girls.

She remembered one girl in particular, Beth, who'd been upset when Brodie had broken off their relationship.

He'd told her things were getting too heavy between them. He didn't want to settle down, wasn't looking for anything serious. He was still young and the world was his oyster. He wanted to get out there and explore what was on offer.

Caitlin frowned as she pushed open the door to the

ward. What was she to think? Could she work with a
man like that?

His personal life shouldn't matter to her, but she
couldn't help wondering about him. Was he still the
same man at heart—a man who could turn on the
charm, make a girl desperate to be with him and then
when someone more interesting came along simply
cut things dead?

Wasn't that exactly what Matt had done to her when
Jenny had arrived on the scene? It had hurt so badly to
be treated that way. She had never thought it possible
that he could do such a thing.

The truth was, she simply didn't trust men any more.
From now on, she would keep her independence and
wrap herself around in an impermeable, defensive coat
to ward off any attempt to break her down and make
her vulnerable again. That way, no one could hurt her.

Even so…she thought about what Brodie had said.
A job was a job, after all, and that had to be top of her
priorities right now, didn't it? She'd be a fool to turn
down his offer, wouldn't she? Maybe she would talk it
through with him in a while.

A small shiver ran through her. Right now, all these
years later, he seemed like a good man, someone great
to have around in a crisis, but you could never tell,
could you? Agreeing to come and work with him would
be a bit like making a date with the devil…albeit a
devil in disguise, maybe. Would she come to regret it
before too long?

CHAPTER TWO

'How are you feeling, Mum? Are you in any pain?'
Caitlin sat by the bedside and reached for her mother's
hand, squeezing it gently. It upset her to see how pale
and drawn she looked.

'I'm okay, sweetheart. They gave me something for
the pain. You don't need to worry about me. I'm just
so glad to see you, but I'm sorry you were pulled away
from your work.' Her mother tried to stifle a yawn and
closed her eyes fleetingly. 'I don't know what's happening to me… I'm so tired.'

Caitlin smiled reassuringly. 'I expect there was a
sedative in the injection you had. The nurse told me it
won't be too long now before you go for your operation. That's good—they seem to be looking after you
really well. I'm very pleased about that.'

Her mother nodded, causing the soft brown waves of
her hair to flutter gently. 'They've all been so kind, explaining everything to me, telling me to take it easy and
saying how I shouldn't fret. I can't help it, though—
I keep thinking about the animals back home.' She

frowned and Caitlin could see that she was starting to become agitated. 'They need to be fed and the crops have to be watered. It hasn't rained for a couple of days. With this warm, sunny weather everything will dry out.'

'I'll see to all of that,' Caitlin promised. 'You don't need to stress yourself about any of it. All you have to do is concentrate on getting better.'

'Oh, bless you—but there are so many things…' Her mother's brow creased with anxiety. 'You don't know about Ruffles' sores. He's the rabbit—someone brought him to me after they found him wandering in their garden.' She sighed. 'He needs a special lotion putting on his back. I should have collected it from the vet—I forgot to bring it home with me the other day. And the quail needs his claws clipping—he's another one a neighbour brought to me in a bit of a state. I was going to see to the clipping today—' She broke off, her breathing becoming laboured.

'It's all right, Mum,' Caitlin said in a soothing voice. 'Don't worry about it. I'll see to all of it and if anything else comes up I'll deal with that too.' She couldn't help but respect her mother for the way she coped with the smallholding, seeing to repairs, harvesting the crops and looking after various animals. Her mother had had a lot to cope with since she'd been widowed when Caitlin was a teenager, but she'd accepted the way things were, set to and got on with it. She was an incredible woman. 'Trust me,' Caitlin murmured. 'I just need to know that you're all right. Everything else will be fine.'

Her mother smiled wearily but she seemed comforted. 'I'm so glad you're home, Caity. I mean, I'm sorry for the reason for it—for this trouble with Matt, that must be so hard for you—but it'll be wonderful to have you close by.'

Caitlin patted her hand. 'Me too. I'm glad to be with you.' Even so, a faint shudder passed through her at the mention of Matt's name. She didn't want to think about him, and did her best to push him from her mind, but it was difficult.

She watched her mother drift in and out of sleep. It was worrying, not knowing how the surgery would go… It was a big operation… She'd already lost her father to a heart attack and she didn't want to lose her mother too.

She shook off those unreasonable fears. After the surgery her mother would need physiotherapy and would have to use crutches or a walker for some weeks or months.

'Oh, is she asleep?' A young porter came over to the bedside and spoke softly, giving Caitlin a friendly smile.

'She's drowsy, I think.'

'That's okay. It's for the best. It's time to take her to Theatre.'

Caitlin nodded and lightly stroked her mother's hair.

'I'll be here when you wake up,' she murmured, and the young man carefully wheeled his patient away.

'The operation could take up to three hours,' the nurse told her. 'You might want to take a walk outside, or go and get something to eat, if you don't want to go home. I can give you a ring when she's back in the recovery room, if you like?'

'Oh, thanks, that's really kind of you. I do appreciate it,' Caitlin said. She thought for a moment or two. What should she do? There might be time to go home. But perhaps she ought to follow up on Brodie's invitation… It was important that she found work quickly, though how she would manage her mother's day-to-day care when she was back home was another problem.

Decision made, she glanced at the nurse once more. 'Actually, I think I'll go over to the children's unit for a while. Dr Driscoll—the man who came in with her—said he'd show me around.'

'He's a doctor?' The girl's eyes widened. 'He must be new around here. I thought I knew most of the staff in the hospital. Wow! Things are looking up!'

Caitlin smiled. That was probably a fairly typical reaction from women where Brodie was concerned. He'd always turned heads. Perhaps she'd better get used to seeing that kind of response all over again. Of course, she knew how these women felt. Try as she might to resist him, she wasn't immune to his seductive charm.

She made her way to the children's unit, uneasily conscious of the quivering in her stomach now that she was to see him again. It was hard to say why he had this effect on her, but it had always been the same. There was something about him that jolted all her senses, spinning them into high alert the minute she set eyes on him.

The children's wards were on the ground floor of the hospital, a bright and appealing place with colourful walls, decorative ceiling tiles and amusing animal designs on the floor. There were exciting murals created to distract the children from the scariness of a hospital environment, and she noticed that the nurses were wearing patterned plastic aprons over their uniforms.

'Hi there.' The staff nurse came to greet her as she walked up to reception. 'I saw you admiring our wall paintings. They're very recent additions—Dr Driscoll brought in artists to do them the first week he started here.'

'Really?' Caitlin was astonished by that piece of news. 'My word, he doesn't let the grass grow under his feet, does he?'

'Too right. I heard he'd been talking with designers while he was working out his notice at his previous hospital. We all love the changes he's made. It's only been a few weeks and everything's so different here.' She paused by the entrance to the observation ward. 'You must be Caitlin,' she said with a smile. 'Am I right?'

'Well, yes…' Puzzled, Caitlin frowned. 'How did you know?'

The nurse's bright eyes sparkled. 'Dr Driscoll asked me to look out for you—he said I wouldn't be able to miss you. You had glorious hair, he said, beautiful auburn curls, and he told me what you were wearing. He's with a patient in Forest right now but he said to send you along.' Still smiling, she led the way. All the wards, Caitlin discovered, were divided into bays with names derived from the environment, like Forest, Lakeside, Beechwood.

'Ah, there you are,' Brodie murmured, looking across the room, his mouth curving briefly as Caitlin entered the ward. 'I'm glad you could make it.'

She smiled in acknowledgment. He looked good, and the muscles in her midriff tightened involuntarily in response. He was half sitting on the bed. One long leg extended to the floor, the material of his trousers stretched tautly over his muscular thigh; the other leg was bent beneath him so as not to crowd out his small patient, a thin boy of around two years old.

'This lady is a doctor like me, Sammy. She's come to see how we're doing.'

Sammy didn't react. Instead, he lowered his head and remained silent, looking at the fresh plaster cast on his leg. Brodie sent him a quizzical glance. He silently indicated to Caitlin to take a seat by the bedside.

'His mother's with the nurse at the moment,' he said quietly. 'She's talking to her about the break in his leg bone and advising her on painkillers and so on.'

Caitlin nodded and went to sit down. She felt sorry

for the little boy. With that injury perhaps it was no wonder the poor child didn't feel like responding.

Brodie turned his attention back to Sammy. 'Do you want to see my stethoscope?' he asked, showing it to the infant, letting him hold the instrument. 'If I put the disc on my chest, like this, I can hear noises through these earpieces...see?' He demonstrated, undoing a couple of buttons on his shirt and slipping the diaphragm through the opening. The little boy watched, his curiosity piqued in spite of his anxieties.

'Oh,' Brodie said, feigning surprise, 'I can hear a bump, bump, bump. Do you want to listen?'

The boy nodded, leaning forward to allow Brodie carefully to place the earpieces in his ears.

His eyes widened. Brodie moved the diaphragm around and said, 'Squeaks and gurgles, gurgles and squeaks. Do you want to listen to your chest?'

Sammy nodded slowly and, when Brodie carefully placed the disc on the boy's chest, the child listened, open-mouthed. He still wasn't talking but clearly he was intrigued.

'Do you think I could have a listen?' Brodie asked and he nodded.

Brodie ran the stethoscope over Sammy's chest once more. 'Hmm. Just like me, lots of funny squeaks and crackles,' he said after a while, folding the stethoscope and putting it in his pocket. 'Thanks, Sammy.' He picked up the boy's chart from the end of the bed and wrote something on it, getting to his feet and handing the folder to the nurse who was assisting.

A moment later, he glanced back at the child. 'The nurse will help you to put your shirt back on and then you can lie back and try to get some rest. Your mummy will be back soon. Okay?'

Sammy nodded.

Caitlin followed as Brodie walked away from the bed and spoke quietly to the nurse. 'There's some infection there, I think, so we'll start him on a broad-spectrum antibiotic and get an X-ray done. He's very thin and pale,' he added. 'I'm a bit concerned about his general health as well as the injury to his leg—I think we'll keep him in here under observation for a few days.'

'Okay.'

He left the room with Caitlin but at the door she turned and said quietly, 'Bye, Sammy.'

The infant looked at her shyly, not answering, and as they walked out into the corridor Brodie commented briefly, 'He seems to be very withdrawn. No one's been able to get a natural response from him.'

'How did he come to break his leg?'

'His parents said he fell from a climbing frame in the back garden. He'll be in plaster for a few weeks.' He frowned. 'The worry is, there was evidence of earlier fractures when we did X-rays. He was treated at another hospital for those, but the consultant there brought in a social worker.'

She looked at him in shock. 'Do you think it might be child abuse?'

'It's a possibility, and the fact that he's so quiet and withdrawn doesn't help. I'd prefer to make some more checks, though, before involving the police.'

She shook her head. 'I just can't imagine why anyone would hurt a child. It's unbearable.'

'Yes, it is. But Sammy's parents do seem caring, if a little naive, and at least he'll be safe here in the meantime.'

They went back to the main reception area and she tried to push the boy's plight to the back of her mind as Brodie began showing her around the unit. Each ward was set out in a series of small bays that clustered around a central point housing the nursing station. He stopped to check up on various patients as they went along.

'It's a beautifully designed children's unit,' she remarked some time later as they stopped off at the cafeteria to take a break for coffee.

'That's true,' he agreed, 'But I think there are things we can do to make it even better for the patients and their families. There are some children—like Sammy, perhaps—who need more than medicine and good nursing care to help them to get well. I want to do what I can to help them feel good about themselves.'

She sent him an oblique glance. 'That's a tall order,' she murmured, but perhaps if anyone could do it he could. He certainly seemed to have the determination to set things in motion. But then, he'd always had boundless energy and drive, even though he might have used it to the wrong ends years ago when he was a teenager.

'Well, if I'm to be any good at my job, I need to feel I'm making a difference,' he said. 'It's important to me.'

She studied him thoughtfully. He was an enigma—so focused, so different from the restless, cynical young man she had known before. 'That must be why you've come so far in such a short time. Your career obviously means a lot to you.'

'Yes, it does…very much so. I've always aimed at getting as far as I can up the ladder. I try to make all the improvements I can to a place where I work and then move on—at least, that's how it's been up to now.'

So he probably wouldn't be staying around here once he'd made his mark. She frowned. But this time he'd bought a house and he planned to do it up—would that make a difference to his plans? Probably not. Houses could be sold just as easily as they'd been bought.

He finished his coffee and then glanced at the watch on his wrist. 'I must go and look in on another young patient,' he murmured in a faintly apologetic tone.

'That's okay. I've enjoyed shadowing you, seeing how you work.'

He looked at her steadily. 'So, do you think you might want to work with us?'

She nodded. 'Yes—but only on a part-time basis to

begin with, if that's possible. I'll need to be close at hand for my mother when she's back at home.'

He smiled. 'I can arrange that.'

'Good.' Her phone rang just then, and after listening for a while, she told him, 'My mother's in the recovery ward. I need to go and see how she's doing.'

'Of course.' He sent her a concerned glance. 'I hope she's all right. I know how worried you must be about her.' He went with her to the door of the recovery ward. 'Perhaps I'll see you later on, back at home?'

'I expect so.' She wasn't planning ahead, just taking one step at a time. It seemed like the best way to proceed at the moment. 'Thanks for showing me around, Brodie,' she said. 'Your children's unit is a really wonderful place and everyone involved with it is so dedicated. If children have to be in hospital, I think they're lucky to be here rather than in any other unit.'

'I'm glad you think so.' He smiled at her, pressing the buzzer to alert a nurse to release the door lock. 'It's been good meeting up with you again, Caitlin.' Somehow they had ended up standing close together, his arm brushing hers, and her whole body began to tingle in response. She didn't know how to cope with the strange feelings that suddenly overwhelmed her. It was bewildering, this effect he had on her. She loved Matt. How could she be experiencing these sensations around another man?

As soon as the door swung open she moved away from him, going into the ward. 'Thanks for coming with me and showing me the way,' she murmured, sending him a last, quick glance.

At last she could breathe more easily… But she hadn't been the only one to be affected by their momentary closeness to one another; she was sure of it. His awareness was heightened too. She'd seen it in his slight hesitation, the way his glance had lingered on her, and now she felt his gaze burning into her as she walked away from him.

How was it going to be, having Brodie living nearby? Part of her was apprehensive, worried about how things might turn out. After all, it was one thing to contemplate working with him, but having him as a neighbour could end up being much more than she'd bargained for.

She couldn't quite get a handle on what it was that bothered her about the situation, exactly. Over the last few weeks her world had been shaken to its foundations by the way Matt had behaved. She was unsettled, off-balance, totally out of sync. In her experience having Brodie close by could only add to her feelings of uncertainty. He was a spanner in the works, an unknown quantity.

She frowned. Perhaps the neighbour dilemma would only last for a short time, while her mother recovered from surgery. After that she could find a place of her own, away from Brodie, but near enough so that she could keep an eye on her mother and at the same time maintain her independence.

The nurse in charge of the recovery ward showed her to her mother's bedside. 'She's very drowsy, and unfortunately she's feeling nauseous, so it might be best for you to keep the visit short. She'll probably be more up to talking to you in the morning.'

Caitlin nodded. 'Okay.' She asked cautiously, 'Did the operation go well?'

'It did. The surgeon placed screws across the site of the fracture to hold everything in place and that all went quite satisfactorily. Your mother will need to stay in hospital for a few days, as you probably know, but we'll try to get her walking a few steps tomorrow. It seems very soon to get her on her feet, I know, but it's the best thing to do to get her on the mend.'

'All right. Thanks.' It was a relief to know that the major hurdle was over. Now the hard work of rehabilitation would begin.

Caitlin went to sit by her mother's bedside for a while but, as the nurse had said, she was very sleepy, feeling sick and wasn't up to saying very much. 'I'll leave you to get some rest, Mum,' Caitlin said after a while. 'I'll come back to see you tomorrow.'

She took a deep breath and left the hospital. At least her mother had come through the operation all right. That was a huge relief. She could relax a little, now, knowing that she was being well looked after.

On the way home she called in at the vet's surgery to pick up the lotion that her mother had mentioned earlier.

'It's a mite infection,' the veterinary nurse told her after looking at the notes on the computer. 'You can't see the mites on the rabbit's skin, they're so tiny, but you might see dander being moved about.' She made a wry face. 'That's why the condition's sometimes known as "walking dandruff".'

Caitlin pulled a comical face at that, accepting the box containing the lotion that the nurse gave her.

'The vet gave Ruffles an injection,' the nurse said. 'But you need to put a few drops of the lotion on the back of his neck to get rid of any mites that are left. I think Mrs Braemar forgot to take it with her when she came here yesterday. He'll need another injection in eight days' time. Meanwhile, you could comb him to get rid of any loose fur and dander.'

'I'll do that. Thanks.'

Caitlin drove home through lanes lined with hedge-rows, eventually passing over the bridge across the lock where brightly painted narrowboats were moored by the water's edge. Soon after that she came to a sleepy, picturesque village, a cluster of white-painted cottages with russet tiled roofs and adorned with vibrant hanging baskets spilling over with masses of flowers.

Her former family home was about half a mile further on, a rambling old house set back from the road, protected by an ancient low brick wall. There was one neighbouring property—Brodie's—but otherwise the two houses were surrounded by open countryside, giving them a magnificent view of the rolling hills of the beautiful Chilterns.

Trees and flowering shrubs surrounded the front and sides of her mother's house, adding glorious touches of colour around a lush, green lawn. Caitlin gave a gentle sigh of satisfaction. She always felt good when she returned home. Here was one place where she felt safe, sheltered.

Her old bedroom was just as she'd left it the last time she'd been here, about three weeks ago, except that her mother had laid a couple of books on her bedside table in readiness for her homecoming. Caitlin's mouth flattened a little. That had been unexpectedly brought forward by her mother's fall. She'd talked to her boss about it and he'd said she could take compassionate leave instead of working out her notice. It was a relief to know she had no worries there, at least.

She went into the farmhouse kitchen and made herself a snack of homemade soup from a tureen she found in the fridge, eating it with buttered bread rolls. The soup was made from fresh vegetables that her mother grew in the large kitchen garden out the back, and as she ate it Caitlin was filled with nostalgia. She had loved growing up here, having her friends to stay and her cousins to visit.

It was sad, then, that her cousin Jenny should be the one to steal the man she loved. Her fingers clenched on the handle of her spoon. How could things have turned out this way, leaving all her hopes and dreams cruelly shattered?

She pushed away her soup bowl and started to clear the table. Keeping busy was probably the best thing she could do right now. She made a start on various chores around the house, seeing to the laundry and collecting a few clothes and necessities to take into hospital for her mother. When she had done all she could in the house, she went outside to water the crops, and after that she made a start on the animal feeds.

True to form, as with everything that had happened so far today, she discovered from the outset things weren't going quite to plan. As she approached the hen house there was a sudden honking sound, an awful shrieking that made her cover her ears and look around to see what on earth was going on.

A trio of buff-coloured geese came rushing towards her, flapping their wings and cackling loudly. The male bird—she assumed he was male, from his aggressive manner—hissed at her and made angry, threatening gestures with his beak, while the other two kept up a noisy squawking.

'Go away! Shoo!' Her counter-attack made them stop for a second or two, but then the threats started all over again and she looked around in vain for a stick of some sort that she could wave at them. The way things were going, they weren't going to let her anywhere near the hen house.

'Get back! Shoo!' She tried again, frantically trying to keep them at bay for the next few minutes.

'Are you having trouble?' To her relief, she saw Brodie striding rapidly down the path towards her. Perhaps he would know how to stop the birds from attacking. 'I heard the racket they were making, so I came to see what's happening.'

'I don't think they want me around,' she said, concentrating her efforts on warding off the gander. 'In fact, I know they don't.'

'They're protecting their territory. Flap your arms at them and hiss back… You need to show them who's boss.'

She did as he suggested, waving her arms about and making a lot of noise. Brodie joined in, and to her amazement the geese began to back off. The gander—the male bird—was the last to give way, but eventually he too, saw that she meant business.

'Well done!' Brodie said approvingly when the birds had retreated. 'They're not usually an aggressive breed, but the males can be bullies sometimes, and you have to show them you're bigger and more fierce than they are. I'd say you've won that one!'

'Well, let's hope I don't have to go through that palaver every time I want to feed the hens. At least I'll be prepared next time.' She was breathing fast after her exertions and she was sure her cheeks must have a pink glow to them. 'I'd no idea Mum had bought some new birds.'

'She liked the idea of having goose eggs and thought the geese might sound a warning if any foxes came sniffing around.'

'Ah. I guess they're doing what she wanted, then. They're guarding the place.'

Perhaps he saw that she'd had enough of trouble for one day because he came up close to her and gently laid an arm around her shoulders. 'It hasn't been the best homecoming for you, has it? How about you finish up here and then come over to my place for a cold drink?'

'I…I don't know…' She was suddenly flustered, very conscious of his long body next to hers, yet at the same time strangely grateful for the warm comfort of his embrace.

He'd changed into casual chinos and a short-sleeved cotton shirt that revealed his strong biceps. The shirt was undone at the neck, giving a glimpse of his tanned throat.

'I…um…there's a lot to do; I still have to find the quail and clip his claws.' She pushed back the curls that clung damply to her forehead and cheek. 'I've never done it before, so it could take me a while to sort things out—once I manage to catch him, that is.'

'I can do that for you. He's in with the hens; your mother pointed him out to me a few days ago. She said wherever he came from, he hadn't been able to run around and scratch to keep his claws down, so that's why they need doing. It's not a problem. I know where she keeps the clippers.'

'Oh.' That would be a terrific help, one less problem for her to manage. 'Okay, then, if you're sure you don't mind?' Her excuses obviously weren't going to pass muster with him. Anyway, a cold drink was really, really tempting right now when she was all hot and bothered. She wiped her brow with the back of her hand.

'Good, that's settled, then. I do a great watermelon and apple blend. I remember you used to like that.' He released her, but her skin flushed with heat all over again at the memory of hot summer days spent with her friends in flower-filled meadows.

Brodie and his brother had often come with them as they'd wandered aimlessly through the fields and by the river. They would stop to share sandwiches and drink juice or pop they'd brought with them. They had been fun days, days of laughter and innocent, stolen kisses in the time before Brodie had unexpectedly, disastrously, gone off the rails.

Together, they finished off the feeding then she watched as Brodie deftly caught the quail and carefully set about trimming the tip of each claw. 'These little birds get stressed easily,' he said, 'So it's best to get them used to being handled.' He placed him back down in the pen and the bird scampered off as fast as he could. 'He'll be all right now. I doubt he'll need clipping again now that he has a solid floor to run on and plenty of scratching litter.'

'Thanks for that.' Finished with all the chores for now, Caitlin locked up the pen and together they

walked over to his house. It was a lovely big old property with a large, white-painted Georgian extension
built on to an original Tudor dwelling. The walls were
covered with rambling roses and at the side of the house
there was an overgrown tree badly in need of pruning.
The front lawn was dotted about with daisies and un-
kempt shrubs sprawled over the borders.

'I need to get the garden in order,' Brodie said ruefully, 'But I've had other priorities up to now, at work
and back here.' He led the way along the path to the
back of the house. 'In estate agent jargon, "in need of
some renovation"; that can be interpreted in lots of
ways,' he said with a wry smile.

She nodded, sharing the joke. 'I've always loved
this house,' she said, glancing around. 'I expect it will
need a lot of care and attention to restore it to its former glory, but it'll be worth it in the end.'

He nodded. 'I think so too. That's why I was so
pleased when it came on to the market. I took to this
house from a very early age. When I was about ten my
friends and I used to climb over the wall and steal the
apples from the orchard, until one day old Mr Martin caught us. We thought we were in big trouble, but
he surprised us. He invited us into the house, gave us
cookies and milk, then sent us on our way with a basket full of fruit.'

'He was a kind old man.'

'Yes, he was.' He showed her into the kitchen and
she looked around in wonder.

'You've obviously been busy in here,' she said admiringly. 'This is all new, isn't it?'

'It is. It's the first room I worked on. I looked into different types of kitchen design and decided I wanted one where there was room for a table and chairs along with an island bar. This way, I can sit down for a meal and look out of the window at the garden; or if I'm feeling in a more casual mood, I can sit at the bar over there and have a cold drink or a coffee or whatever.'

She smiled. 'I like it, especially the cream colour scheme. You have really good taste.' She studied him afresh, surprised by the understated elegance of the room.

'Good taste for a rebel whose idea of fun was to spray graffiti on any accessible wall?' He laughed. 'I'll never forget that day you let rip at me for painting fire-breathing dragons on your mother's old barn. You handed me a brush and a pot of fence paint and told me to clean it up.'

'And you told me to forget it because the barn was old and rotting and ready to fall down—but later that night you came back and painted the lot.'

His brow lifted in mock incredulity. 'You mean, you've known all along who did it?'

She laughed. 'I never thought you were as bad as people said. I knew there was a good person struggling to get out from under all that bravado.' She'd understood him, up to a point, knowing how much it hurt to lose a parent. She'd turned her feelings inwards but back then Brodie had become more confrontational and forcefully masculine.

Smiling, he filled a blender with slices of apple and watermelon and added ice cubes to the mix. He topped that with the juice of a lime and then whizzed it up. 'That looks ready to me,' he said, eyeing the resulting juice with satisfaction. 'We'll take this outside, shall we?'

She nodded and followed him through the open French doors on to a paved terrace where they sat at a white wrought-iron table looking out on to a sweeping lawn. This was part of the garden that he had tended to, with established borders crowded out with flowering perennials, gorgeous pink blossoms of thrift with spiky green leaves alongside purple astilbe and bearded yellow iris.

He poured juice into a tall glass and handed it to her. 'I hope you still like this as much as you used to.'

She put the glass to her lips and sipped. 'Mmm… It's delicious,' she said. 'Thanks. I needed that.'

'So, what's been happening with you over the last few years?' he asked, leaning back in his chair and stretching out his long legs. He glanced at her ringless left hand. 'I heard you were dating my friend, Matt, until recently.'

She pulled a face, bracing herself to answer him. 'Yes, that's right. We were going to get engaged,' she said ruefully. 'But then things went wrong. Disastrously wrong.'

It was still difficult for her to talk about it but at the hospital where she had worked with Matt everyone knew the situation and it had been virtually impossible to escape from the questions and the sympathy.

He frowned. 'I'm sorry. Do you want to tell me what happened? Do you mind talking about it?'

'It still upsets me, yes.' She hesitated. 'He met someone else.'

Brodie studied her, his eyes darkening. 'I knew about that but I never understood how it came about. Matt and I haven't seen each other for quite a while. Was he looking to get out of the relationship?'

'No...at least, I don't think so.' She thought about it and then took a deep breath. 'It started about a year and a half ago. My cousin Jenny's car broke down one day and when Matt heard about it he offered to go and pick her up. Apparently she was in a bit of a state—she'd missed an appointment, everything had gone wrong and she was feeling pretty desperate. So he took her along to the nearest pub for a meal and a drink to give her time to calm down. Things just went on from there—he was hooked from that meeting. It was what you might call a whirlwind courtship.' She frowned. 'You knew Matt from school, didn't you? I suppose you know they're getting married soon?'

He sent her a cautious glance. 'I received an invitation to their wedding this morning.'

'Yes, so did I.'

'It was short notice, I thought. They must be in

a hurry.' A line creased his brow. 'How do you feel about it?'

She exhaled slowly. 'Pretty awful, all things considered.' She picked up her glass and took a long swallow. The cold liquid was soothing, and she pressed the glass to her forehead to cool her down even more. 'They wanted to get married before the summer ends and the vicar managed to fit them in.'

He was thoughtful for a while. 'How are you going to cope with the wedding? Will you go to it? Yours has always been a tight-knit family, hasn't it? So I can see there might be problems if you stay away.'

'I don't know what to do. I feel hurt and upset. The thought of it makes me angry but, like you say, my family has always been close and if I don't go there could be all sorts of repercussions. I keep thinking maybe I'll develop a convenient stomach bug or something on the day.'

He winced. 'I doubt you'll get away with that.'

'No.' She pulled a face. 'You're probably right.' She sighed. 'My mother's already upset because she might not be well enough to attend. Jenny's her sister's child. My mother and my aunt have always been very close. I suppose it all depends how well her recovery goes.'

'Let's hope it all goes smoothly for her.' On a cautious note, he asked quietly, 'Did Jenny know about you and Matt—about you being a couple? If she did, she must have known it would cause problems with your family.'

She shook her head. 'Not until it was too late. I was upset, devastated, but I tried to keep the peace for my aunt's sake and my mother's. But it's been hard, keeping up a pretence. I'm not sure how I'll get through the wedding without breaking down.'

She didn't know why she was opening up to him this way. It was embarrassing; she'd been humiliated and her pride had taken a huge blow. But Brodie was a good listener. He seemed to understand how she felt and she was pretty sure he wouldn't judge her and find her wanting.

'We could go to the wedding together,' he said unexpectedly. 'I'd be there to support you and we can put up a united front—show them that you don't care, that you're doing fine without him.'

'Do you think so? That would be good if it worked,' she said, giving him a faint smile. 'I'm not sure I could pull it off, though.'

'Sure you can. I'll help you. We'll make a good team, you and I, you'll see.'

She might have answered him, but just then a noise disturbed the quiet of the afternoon—the sound of footsteps on pavement—and a moment later Brodie's brother appeared around the back of the house.

'Hey there. I've been ringing the front doorbell but no one answered. I felt sure you were around somewhere because I saw the car.' He glanced at Caitlin and did a double take. 'Hi, babe,' he said, his voice brimming over with enthusiasm. 'It's good to see you, Caitlin. It's been a long time.'

'Yes, it has.' She was almost glad of the interruption. Anything and anyone that could take her mind off Matt was welcome. 'Hi, David. How are you doing?'

He was a good-looking young man in his late twenties with dark hair, brown eyes and a lively expression. 'I didn't know you were living in our part of the world,' she said. 'I thought you were settled in London.'

'I am, mostly, but we're doing some filming down here for the latest episode in the TV drama series *Murder Mysteries*—I'll bet you've seen it, haven't you? It's been on the screens for over a year. It's turned out to be really popular, much more so than we expected.'

She nodded. 'I've seen it. It's good—you've certainly found yourselves a winner there.' She studied him briefly. He too had come a long way in just a few years. 'I see your name on the credits quite often. So, am I right in thinking you write the screenplay?'

'I do.'

Brodie pulled out a chair for him and David sat down. 'Do you want a drink?' Brodie asked, lifting the jug of juice.

'Sure.' He glanced at the pink liquid in the jug. 'It looks great, but is there a drop of something stronger you could put in it?'

'I can get you something from the bar if that's what you want.' Brodie sent him a thoughtful glance. 'Do I take it you're not planning on driving anywhere after this, then?'

David shook his head and sent Brodie a hopeful look. 'I was wondering if I might be able to stay here for the duration—while the research and the filming is going on.' He frowned, thinking it through. 'It could take several weeks, depending on what properties we need to rent, though the actual filming won't take more than a few days. Would that be all right?'

'Of course.' Brodie sent him a fleeting glance. 'You don't want to stay with Dad, then, at the Mill House?'

David sobered. 'Well, you know how it is. I love the old fellow but he's not much fun to be around lately. At least, not since…' He trailed off, his voice dwindling away as he thought better of what he was going to say.

'Not since he heard I was back in the village…is that what you were going to say?' Brodie made a wry smile. 'It's okay. I know how it is.' He pressed his lips together in a flat line. 'Things are still not right with us after all this time…' He shrugged. 'What can I do?' It was a rhetorical question. Caitlin sensed he didn't expect an answer. 'I've tried making my peace with him over the years, and again these last few weeks, but he doesn't seem to want to know. That's okay; I accept things as they are.'

Caitlin watched the emotions play across his face. Things had gone badly wrong between Brodie and his father and no one had ever known why. It had been the start of Brodie's resentment and rebellion; nothing had gone right for him for a long time after that.

'I'm sorry, Brodie,' David said. 'I'm sure he'll come around eventually.'

'Do you really think that's going to happen after all these years?' Brodie gave a short laugh. 'I wouldn't bet on it.'

'Maybe he'll get a knock on the head and develop amnesia. You'll be able to start over.' David grinned and Brodie's mouth curved at the absurdity of the situation.

'I guess we can see how you came to be a screenwriter, brother. You have a vivid imagination.'

David chuckled and turned his attention back to Caitlin. 'I'm sorry about that. You don't want to have to listen to our family goings-on. I can't tell you how great it is to see you again.' He looked her over appreciatively. 'You're absolutely gorgeous, even more so than I remember, and you were stunning back then. Are you going to be staying around here for long? That's your mother's place next door, isn't it?'

She nodded. 'I'm coming back to the village permanently. I'll be living with Mum until I can find a place of my own…for a few months, at least. That should give me time to find somewhere suitable.'

'Wow, that's fantastic.' He moved his chair closer to hers. 'We could perhaps get together, you and I— go for a meal, have a drink, drive out to a nightclub in town. It'll be fun; what do you say—?'

'Don't even think about it, David,' Brodie cut in sharply, perhaps with more force than he'd intended. His eyes narrowed on his brother. 'I saw her first—way back when we were teenagers and now since she's come back to the village. Besides, she deserves someone with more integrity and staying power than you possess.'

'Oh yeah?' David's dark brows shot up. 'And since when were you the man to offer those things? You—the man who never settles with one woman for more than a few months at a time. I don't think so, bro. Get ready to move aside, man. Brother or no brother, this is a fair fight and Caity's a jewel worth fighting for. This is war.'

'Uh…do you two mind? Have you quite finished?' Caitlin looked from one to the other, deciding it was time to butt in before things got out of hand. 'I'll decide what happens where I'm concerned, and right now neither of you is in the running. From my point of view, you're probably both as bad as each other. So back off, both of you!'

David stared at her, looking reasonably chastened. 'Sorry, Caity.'

He soon recovered, shaking himself down and saying cheerfully, 'I think I'll go and hunt out a bottle of something from Brodie's bar, if that's okay?' He glanced enquiringly at his brother.

'That's fine.'

David left them, taking himself off into the house.

Brodie looked back at Caitlin, a trace of amusement in his expression.

'You were always one to speak your mind,' he said. 'I like that about you, Caitlin. It's the barn incident all over again. You've never been prepared to put up with things you're not happy about.'

His smile was crooked as he added softly, 'Years ago, you told me we were a pair of hooligans on the rampage, David and me, not to be trusted. You weren't ever going to date either one of us…me especially, you said.' His face took on a sober expression. 'No matter how hard I tried, you'd never let me persuade you otherwise.'

'So the message was received and understood.' She smiled at him as she took a long swallow of her drink.

'Perfectly.' He returned her gaze, his blue eyes glinting. 'Of course, it's always been out there between us as something of a challenge. I know you like me and there were times when you might have been tempted to go against your better judgement. You do realise, don't you, that my feelings towards you have never changed?'

'Oh, you can't be sure about that,' she said. Even as she tried to make less of it, a tingle of excitement ran through her. 'It's been a long time… Perhaps you only want what you can't have.'

'I don't know, Caity. Perhaps you're right. Things happened when I was a teenager, things that made me question who I am and what I could expect out of life.

I always wanted you, that's for sure. I just wasn't certain that I deserved you. I still have doubts, but seeing you again has brought all those feelings back to the surface.'

The breath caught in her throat but she ran her finger idly around the rim of her glass to give herself time to think. Why would he feel he didn't deserve her? Was it because of his behaviour back then, because it had been out of control?

Surely now, more than ever, she had to guard her heart against being hurt?

She said slowly, cautiously, 'It isn't going to happen, I'm afraid. I think we both know that. I'm totally off men right now. They're far too fickle for my liking.'

'Hmm.' He studied her, taking in the faint droop of her soft, pink lips. 'We'll have to see about that.'

CHAPTER THREE

'I KNOW IT's going to be terribly difficult for you this afternoon,' Caitlin's mother said worriedly. She was sitting in a chair by her hospital bed; now she shifted uncomfortably, wincing at a twinge of pain in her hip.

'Yes.' Caitlin's answer was brief. The day of the wedding had come around all too soon for her liking. Her emotions were all churned up inside her, though it wasn't only the forthcoming nuptials that bothered her. A fortnight had gone by since her mother had first come into hospital and after a brief spell at home she had been readmitted. It was distressing.

'Your aunt's desperate for everything to go off smoothly. She's been stressed about one thing and another for some time now.' Her mother's grey-blue eyes were troubled. She winced again, moving carefully as she tried to get comfortable. Small beads of perspiration had formed on her brow. 'She keeps saying how you and Jenny used to be so close.' She frowned. 'I wish I could be there to give you some support.'

Caitlin nodded, acknowledging her anxieties. 'I

know.' Soothingly, she dabbed her mother's brow with a damp cloth. There was no way she could leave hospital, let alone go to her niece's wedding.

Instead of making good progress in the last couple of weeks, a nasty infection had set in around the site of the surgical incision, causing her mother a lot of pain and discomfort. Caitlin was worried about her. The consultant had inserted tubes in the wound to try to drain away the infected matter but it was turning out to be a slow process. No one knew how the infection had started but Caitlin suspected it had crept in when the dressing was changed.

'I'm pretty sure Jenny hasn't told her family that Matt and I were already a couple when they met,' she commented softly.

Her mother's brows rose in startled disbelief. 'Oh, you don't think so? Heavens, that hadn't occurred to me. It's probably the general stress of the wedding that's getting to her.'

Of course, if Caitlin didn't turn up for the celebrations this afternoon, her aunt would soon realise something was badly amiss and would want to know what was going on, wouldn't she? Caitlin felt more despondent than ever. Even more reason why she should go along to the event—yet all her instincts were clamouring for her to stay away.

She pushed her own problems to one side and sent her mother a quick, sympathetic look. 'It's rotten for you to be stuck in hospital today of all days. I know you were looking forward to seeing Aunty Anne and having a good chat—but she did say she would come and see you as soon as she could get away.'

'Yes, I'll look forward to that.' Distracted momentarily, her mother patted the magazines that littered the bed. 'At least I have plenty of reading material to keep me occupied in the meantime. Thank you for these.' She smiled. 'So how's the new job going? It was good of Brodie to set you on, wasn't it?'

'It was…' He'd been nothing but kind and helpful so far, but Caitlin couldn't help but think he had an ulterior motive. Hadn't he more or less said so that afternoon in his garden? He wanted to change her mind about men—and about him in particular. Could he do that? A tingle of alarm ran through her at the prospect. Of course he couldn't. That would be unthinkable. Talk about jumping from the frying pan into the fire. When he'd left the village years ago, she'd tried to forget about him, put him from her mind. It had been far too upsetting to dwell on what might have been.

'It's going all right so far, I think,' she said. 'The unit runs very smoothly—everyone knows their job and we all seem to work well together. I'm sure a lot of it's down to Brodie being in charge. He's very organised and efficient, and extremely good with people. Somehow, he always manages to get them to do what he wants.' It was remarkable how people responded to his innate charm.

Her mother nodded agreement. 'I'm amazed how

well he's doing. Whoever would have guessed he'd turn his life around like that? I mean, I always liked him, but when he went so completely off the rails as a teenager it was upsetting. His poor mother didn't know where to turn.'

'Hmm.' Brodie's problems had started some time before his mother's death and Caitlin had never been able to find out the root cause. 'Maybe leaving the village was the making of him. He had no choice but to fend for himself, and I suppose that was bound to make a man of him. Of course,' she added with a wry inflection, 'Discovering he had an inheritance must have been a huge boost.'

Her mother nodded. 'True, but he could have gone the other way, you know, and squandered it. Instead, he put it to good use. I think he turned out all right. He seems to be a good man, now, anyway.' She frowned. 'Though I have heard he's still restless, still can't settle.' She sighed then hesitated, sending Caitlin a quick look. 'Does he mind that you keep coming up here to see me in the middle of your work?'

Caitlin shook her head. 'No, not at all…in fact, he's encouraged me to come to see you. He wants to know how you are. He's very fond of you. Anyway, I use my break times to slip away from the unit, so there's no real problem.' She glanced at her watch and gave her mother a rueful smile. 'In fact, I should be heading back there right now. I've a couple of small patients I need to see before I can go home.'

'All right, love. You take care. I'll see you later.'

'Yes. Try to get some rest.' Caitlin gave her a hug and hurriedly left the room.

Brodie was checking X-ray films on the computer when she returned to the children's unit a few minutes later. He shot her a quick glance as she came over to the desk to pick up her patient's file. 'How is your mother?'

'She's not feeling too good at the moment, I'm afraid…though she'll never complain.' She pulled a face. 'The site of the incision's still infected and she's feverish. The doctor's prescribed a different course of antibiotics and some stronger painkillers, so all we can do now is wait and see how she goes on. This setback isn't helping with her rehabilitation.' She sighed. 'It's all been a bit of a blow. We were hoping she'd be able to come home in a couple of days' time but that's definitely not on the cards now.'

'I imagine she's upset about missing the wedding?'

'Oh yes, that too.' Her mouth made a crooked line. 'I think she's secretly hoping I'll be her eyes and ears there. I imagine she'll want to see a video of the highlights on my phone—though she won't come out and ask.'

He smiled. 'It would probably help her to feel better about not being there, but I'm sure she's more concerned about your feelings.'

'Mmm. Maybe.' Even at this late stage Caitlin was desperately looking for a way out. Perhaps she could manufacture a sudden headache that would incapacitate her? Or maybe her car would develop an imaginary mechanical fault at the last minute?

Matt and Jenny were being married mid-afternoon, so as to accommodate relatives who were travelling from some distance away, and Caitlin was becoming more and more twitchy as the morning wore on. In a way, she was glad she'd chosen to come into work for a few hours to keep her from thinking too deeply about the situation. From when she'd woken earlier today, her whole body had been in a state of nervous tension.

She skim-read the notes in her four-year-old patient's file. 'I have to go and look in on the little boy who has pneumonia,' she told Brodie. 'I sent him for an X-ray before I went to see Mum and I'm hoping the results are back by now. He's not at all well: breathing fast, high temperature… He's on antibiotics and supplemental oxygen as well as steroid medication. Hopefully, it should all start to have an effect soon.'

'You're talking about Jason Miles?' Brodie brought up the boy's details on the computer. 'Here we are. Radiology have sent the films through.'

Laying the file down on the table, she studied the images on screen and frowned. 'That looks like an air-filled cyst on his lung, doesn't it? No wonder he's uncomfortable, poor little thing.'

'It does. What do you plan to do?'

'I'll leave it alone for now—it's best to avoid surgical intervention, I think. I'll put him on intravenous cefuroxime and see if that will do the trick. As the pneumonia improves, the cyst should start to disappear.'

He nodded. 'Good. I think you're right. That's probably the best course for now.' He sent her a sideways glance. 'Is he your last patient for today?'

'I just want to look in on Sammy to see how his fractured bone is healing. He went home for a while, didn't he, with a social worker overseeing things… but he's back in today for a check-up?' She frowned. 'Do you still think the other earlier fractures are suspicious? I know the social worker pushed for police action and Sammy's parents are distraught… They're overwhelmed by all the accusations being laid at their door. They're due to appear in court soon —he could be taken into foster care. Yet they do seem to be a genuine couple to me.'

He was silent for a moment or two, thinking it through. 'You could be right about the parents. I've spoken to them about taking extra precautions with him, though they insisted they were already being really careful.' His brow creased. 'I'm beginning to wonder if we aren't dealing with some underlying disease that could cause the bones to fracture more easily than most. I think we should get a blood sample for DNA testing along with a small skin biopsy and send them off to the lab. We'll need to keep an eye on the boy in the meantime—have him seen in the clinic on a regular basis.'

'Okay. I can set that up before I leave.'

'Good.' He leaned back in his chair and studied her. 'So, I'll come and pick you up after lunch, shall I— around two-thirty? Then we'll head off to the church?'

'Um…' She ought to have been expecting it but the reminder still caught her off guard. 'I…um…well, you know, I was thinking… It might be embarrassing for Jenny to have me there. I know her mother dealt with a lot of the invitations, so I'm not necessarily Jenny's choice as a guest.'

She wriggled her shoulders slightly. 'Perhaps it would be for the best if I were to send a message to say something's cropped up—an emergency at the hospital or some such. I mean, it's true, isn't it? Jason's very poorly—maybe I should come back here to keep an eye on him?'

He shook his head, his mouth quirking a fraction. 'You know that won't work, Caitlin, don't you? You're not an emergency doctor and we have people here who will take excellent care of him. You're trying to find excuses, when instead perhaps you should be facing up to things. You need to deal with this, once and for all, instead of running away.'

Her grey eyes narrowed on him. Coming on top of all her worry and apprehension, his comment seemed a bit like a reprimand.

'Are you saying I'm a coward?' After everything she'd been through, the thought irritated her, and she reacted in self-defence. 'Why should I be the one who has to suffer? *They're* in the wrong. Why do *I* have to pay the price for what *they* did?'

'Because you won't be able to live with yourself if you don't,' he said in a matter-of-fact tone. 'Sooner or later, you have to face up to the fact that it's over between you and Matt. He's in love with someone else. See it and believe it. Isn't that what you're running away from? The truth?'

'How can you be so heartless?' Her voice broke and she stared at him, frustration welling up inside her. 'Do you have no feelings? Is that all relationships are to you—off with the old and on with the new?' A muscle flicked in his jaw but he remained silent and she went on. 'What about the aftermath? It's so easy for you to shrug things off, isn't it?'

Resentment grew in her and all her past dealings with him came bubbling up to the surface. 'No wonder Beth was so hurt when you finished things with her. You didn't care too much, though, did you? Not deep down. As far as you were concerned it was just one of those things that happened from time to time. You changed your mind about her, didn't like getting in too deep, and decided to call a halt. It didn't matter to you how she felt, did it? You were ready to move on and you weren't about to look back.' She stared at him. 'How could I ever have believed you might have changed?'

'So this is all about me, now, is it?' His dark brows lifted. 'I don't think you can get out of it that easily,

Caitlin, by turning everything around. You're the one who has the problem and the best way you can deal with it is to put on a brave face and go to the wedding.' His voice softened a little. 'I'll be there with you,' he said coaxingly. 'Show Matt you've found someone else, that it doesn't matter what he's done—that you and I are a couple, if that will make you feel any better.'

She looked at him aghast. 'You think I can do that with you—pretend that we're together, that we care about each other?' She gritted the words out between her teeth. 'I don't think so, Brodie. I'm not that much of an actress.'

To her surprise, he flinched, his head going back a fraction at her sharp retort. Obviously her dart had struck home.

'Is it such an alien concept? I'm sorry you feel that way,' he said quietly. 'Finding you after all this time, I was hoping we might be able to put the past behind us and move on, get to know one another all over again. I've always had feelings for you, Caitlin, and I thought this might be a chance for us to get together.'

Still upset, she said tautly, 'Did you? That's unfortunate, because it isn't very likely to happen. We're all out of fairy godmothers right now.'

She picked up Jason's file from the table and walked away from him. For her own peace of mind, she needed to put some distance between them. Her nerves were stretched to the limit. Deep down, though, she knew she'd gone too far, knew she'd said too much.

As she drove home some time later, she warred with herself over the way she'd behaved, over what she ought to do. Through it all she was still trying to find ways out of the mess she was in. How could she get out of going to this wretched wedding?

Back at home, it was some time before she could bring herself to admit that maybe Brodie was right. She couldn't keep running forever, could she?

She fed the hens and tried to think things through as she scattered corn and dropped a couple of carrots into the rabbit's run. By now the geese had learned to accept her and were grateful for a bucket of greens and a bowl of food pellets.

Why was she so convinced she could bury her feelings by pushing them aside, by hiding them away? Matt was marrying someone else. He didn't love her any more. Perhaps he'd never truly loved her because, if he had, surely this would never have happened? What was it Brodie had said? *Was he looking to get out of the relationship?* Perhaps Matt hadn't been consciously looking but somewhere a chink had opened up in the wall and opportunity had crept in.

She went back inside the house. She had to face up to this once and for all: go along to the wedding or berate herself for her weakness for the rest of her days.

Besides, no matter how bad she felt for Caitlin's dilemma, her mother would be desperate for pictures... She rolled her eyes, looking briefly heavenward. Then she took a deep breath and went upstairs to get ready.

She'd burnt her boats with Brodie but somehow, when she met up with him at the church later on, she would have to do her best to put things right.

She'd bought her dress especially for the occasion, hoping it might help to boost her confidence. It was knee-length with a ruched bodice and a cross-over draped skirt that fell in soft folds over her hips. A small scattering of spangles embellished the thin straps at the shoulders.

She pinned up her hair so that a few errant curls softened the line of her oval face then carefully applied her make-up, adding a touch of lipstick to her full mouth. A final spray of perfume and she was ready.

The doorbell rang as she came down the stairs. Her eyes widened as she opened the door to find Brodie standing on the doorstep.

He whistled softly. 'Wow!' he said in a breathless kind of way. 'You look beautiful. Are you quite sure there isn't a fairy godmother lurking around?' He peered into the hallway as if searching for the mythical figure. 'How else could you have made such a stunning transformation in such a short time?'

'Well, maybe she turns out for the odd emergency.' She smiled at him. 'You look terrific,' she murmured, giving him an appreciative glance. His grey suit was immaculate, finished off with a silk waistcoat and matching grey silk tie. 'I didn't really expect to see you here this afternoon after what I said to you earlier.'

He made a vague gesture with his shoulders. 'I

guessed you were under a bit of a strain. We all say things we regret sometimes. Anyway, I was pretty sure you would change your mind about going.'

'What gave you that idea?'

'Keeping the family peace is important to you. Besides, I knew you wouldn't let your mother down, not when she's in hospital wanting to know what's going on.'

She laughed. 'You're right about that. Thanks for turning up.'

He gave her a crooked smile. 'We'll put in an appearance, then, if only to eat the canapés and drink the wine?'

'That sounds okay to me.'

'Good. The taxi's here already.'

She collected her bag and a light jacket then went with him to the waiting cab. 'Will your brother be coming to the wedding?' she asked. 'I haven't seen him around.'

He nodded. 'He's at the studios going over the screenplay for *Murder Mysteries* but he'll come straight from there.'

They arrived at the church in time to be seated by the ushers; in the hushed atmosphere, Caitlin's gremlins came back in full force. She had to steel herself against a rising tide of panic. She would not faint, she would not be sick, she wouldn't make a fool of herself by breaking out in a sweat… No way…this couldn't be happening…

Brodie reached out to her, covering her fingers with his palm. 'It's okay, you're doing fine,' he said softly. His voice and that reassuring touch of his hand on hers helped to calm her. 'Just think how many generations of families have married in this church. Weren't your parents married here?'

She nodded. 'Were yours?'

'Yes.' He looked around, frowning at something, and she saw that his brother had entered the church. The usher was showing Brodie's father and him to a seat a few rows behind theirs. She felt Brodie stiffen.

'You still haven't managed to make up with your father?' she asked in a whisper.

'No.'

'I'm sorry. I thought you might have had a chance to talk by now. Maybe you could have another go at the reception? A family occasion like this might be the ideal time for you to get together and patch things up.'

'Maybe, though I think it'll take more than a patch to mend things between us.'

The wedding service passed in a blur for Caitlin. Jenny looked beautiful in ivory silk, and Matt was tall and elegant in his tailored grey suit and silver cravat. Watching them, she felt a lump form in her throat, a sadness welling up in her for what might have been. A sick feeling burgeoned inside her.

Brodie clasped her hand firmly as they stood to sing the hymns. He wasn't about to let her sway or lose control and she would be eternally grateful to him for that.

At last the service was over and they went outside
to pose for photographs. She gulped in a lungful of
fresh air. Brodie's arm went around her waist and she
glanced up at him briefly, reading the intent, unmis-
takeable message in his gaze. He would be there for her.
She was safe. She gave him a faint, answering smile
and, when she looked away a moment or two later,
feeling calmer, she saw that Matt was watching her, a
bemused, quizzical expression on his face.

Yes, it was perfectly true, she was safe…for now,
at least.

They went on from the church to a hotel where a
wedding banquet had been prepared for them. Everything was beautifully set out with lovely flower arrangements as centrepieces on the dressed tables and
soft floor-length drapes at the windows reflecting the
silver-and-lilac colour scheme.

'Have something to eat…you'll feel better for it.'
Brodie wasn't listening to any excuses about not
being hungry as they sat down at their allotted table.
He tempted her with delicate morsels of crispy confit
duck and delicious forkfuls of beetroot carpaccio fla-
voured with lemon, dill and finely chopped red onion.
He held them teasingly to her lips until she capitulated.

'All right, all right,' she laughed. 'I'll eat.' She
glanced at all that was on offer. 'It looks wonderful,'
she admitted.

David and Brodie's father were seated close by but,
although the brothers spoke to one another in a relaxed

fashion, the tension between Brodie and his father was noticeable. The older man was straight-backed, uncomfortable, speaking in monosyllabic tones, while Brodie for his part seemed guarded. He tried several times to open up a conversation with his father but the result was stilted and went nowhere. Caitlin watched them cautiously, slowly sipping her red wine.

Eventually, to her relief, the dinner and the speeches were over and it was time for music and dancing. Matt and Jenny started things off with the first waltz then Brodie took Caitlin's hand in his and led her on to the dance floor.

He drew her into his arms and held her close. 'I've been wanting to do this, it seems, like for ever,' he murmured. 'You're gorgeous, Caity, irresistible. And you've been so brave—I wanted to hold you tight and tell you everything was going to be fine. You're doing really well.'

She was glad of his embrace just then. It saved her from thinking about Matt and Jenny whirling around the dance floor locked in each other's arms. 'I couldn't have done any of this without you,' she said with a rueful frown. 'I think I'd still be at the hospital with Jason, if it wasn't for you.'

He made a wry smile. 'I'm sorry if I upset you back then. Matt's a fool for going off with someone else. I can't imagine why he would behave that way—you're beautiful and fun to be with and I can't think what went wrong between you to make him do that. I hate to see you hurting, Caitlin, but I wanted to shake you out of your negative state of mind. You wouldn't have felt right if you'd backed off.'

'Maybe not.' She gave in to the flow of the music and succumbed to the lure of his arms as he swept her around the dance floor. He held her easily, close but not too close, their bodies brushing tantalisingly as they moved to the rhythm of the band.

Perhaps it was the warming effect of the wine but it wasn't long before she found herself relaxing, wanting more, wanting to lean in to him and feel the safety of his arms wrapped even more securely around her.

'I think you should let me take a turn around the floor with Caity,' David said, coming over to them as the musicians took a break. He looked his brother in the eye. 'You've had her to yourself for long enough.' He glanced back at the seating area. 'Besides, it's time you had another go at talking to Dad.'

Brodie frowned, giving way reluctantly to his younger brother. 'Two minutes,' he said. 'That's all you're getting.'

'As if.' David's retort was short and to the point.

'Wow, what it is to be popular,' Caitlin said with a smile as David took her hand in his. The music changed to disco style and they moved in time to the beat opposite one another. She shot a quick look to where Brodie and his father stood side by side. 'I don't understand what went wrong between them. They were always uneasy with one another, I know that, but it was so much worse when he turned fifteen. And then, after your mother died, the animosity spiralled out of control.' She shook her head in bewilderment. 'Do you think they'll ever sort things out?'

'I suppose it's possible, now that Brodie's come back to the village to stay—at least for a while. He's never been one for putting down roots, has he? But that's probably down to the way things were back when he was a teenager. In a way, he's out of sync with the world and he can't seem to find his place in it. He can't settle but he can't move on because nothing feels right.'

She shook her head. 'None of that makes any sense to me.'

'No, well, it's up to Brodie to explain, I think. I wouldn't want to step in and cause even more chaos by trying to fathom what goes on in his mind. All I know is things won't be right with Brodie until he and Dad find some kind of closure.'

They danced for a while then David offered to go and get her a glass of wine from the bar. A late-evening buffet had been set out and there was a mouth-watering selection of food on display. Suddenly hungry, she chose a selection of West Country beef, mixed salad and warm, buttered new potatoes.

'You're feeling better, I see,' Brodie murmured, coming to stand alongside her and filling his plate with savoury tart, a charcuterie of meats, prosciutto, duck liver pâté and sausage, along with ricotta cheese.

'Yes, much better,' she said, surprised at herself. 'It's all down to wine, good food and the company, I expect.'

His gaze moved over her. 'Especially the company, I hope?'

She smiled. 'Of course.' She dipped her fork into a summer-berry meringue and revelled in the combination of sweet and tart flavours as the dessert melted on her tongue. They chatted for a while, enjoying the food, drinking wine and sharing reminiscences with David when he returned to the buffet table.

'I'm supposed to go and dance with the brides-maids,' David said, draining his glass and placing it down on a tray. 'Jenny's orders. I think the blonde has the hots for me…except it could be simply that she's hoping to get a part in *Murder Mysteries*.' He squared his shoulders. 'Ah, well; a man has to do what a man has to do…'

They laughed and watched him go. 'Shall we go out-side and get some air in the garden?' Brodie suggested when they had finished eating. 'I've been to a function here before—the terrace is lovely at this time of night. You can wander along the pathways and breathe in the night-scented flowers.'

'Okay, that sounds good.' She walked with him to the open doors that led out on to the balustraded ter-race. It was, as he said, lovely, with soft, golden lighting and the fragrance of wisteria that bloomed in profu-sion against the wall. Further away from the building, alongside the pathways, were occasional trellises covered with honeysuckle and flowerbeds where sprawling nicotiana gave up its perfume.

As they walked, he put his arm around her and she loved the feeling of closeness. The night air was warm and full of promise. It would be all too easy to fall for Brodie, she conceded. He was attentive, supportive and he had the knack of boosting her confidence when she needed it most. But he wasn't the staying kind, was he? He'd never been one for commitment.

'How did you get on with your father?' she asked. 'I saw you talking to him. He seemed to have lightened up a bit.'

'He's had a drink or two. I guess that's the key to loosening him up and getting him to overlook my shortcomings, although he's never going to feel for me the same way he feels for David. He always favoured him.' He said it without rancour, as a statement of fact. 'When David came along the world was a brighter place and my father expected me to watch over him and keep him safe.'

She sent him a quick look. 'You didn't seem to mind doing that.'

'I didn't, not at all. We fought sometimes, we got into scrapes, but we were brothers. I think the world of him and I'd do anything for him.' His expression became sombre. 'My one regret was that I had to leave him behind when I left home. David didn't forgive me for a long time. He hated that I'd left.'

'I liked the way you took it on yourself to watch out for him. I'm sure he knew you weren't left with much of a choice but to go away, back then.'

She looked up at him as they stopped in the shade of a spreading oak tree. Moonlight filtered through its branches, casting them in a silvery glow. She leaned back against the broad trunk of the tree and he stood in front of her, sliding one arm around her waist.

She'd always liked him—wanted him, even—but always there had been this wariness whenever she was with him. Perhaps it was her youth that had held her back from him in those far-away days, the knowledge that he was at odds with the world, always in trouble, yet he didn't seem to care… There had been that element of danger about him. There still was. Being with him set her on a path of uncertainty—a path that could surely only lead to heartbreak because she still yearned for him. Even as she gazed up into his eyes and read the desire glittering in their fiery depths she recognised the folly of what she was contemplating.

'Caity,' he murmured, lifting a hand to brush her cheek gently. 'You're so lovely. You take my breath away.'

He bent his head towards her, his face so close to her that his lips were just a whisper away from hers. She longed to have him kiss her but she was confused, her emotions a maelstrom of doubt and insecurity. This day had started off with so many echoes of unhappy feelings, she didn't know how she could have come so far to wanting this…

A soft sound drifted on the night air, a footfall on the path just a short distance away, and as she looked out into the shadows she became aware of Jenny and Matt walking along the path, talking quietly to one another. They paused and stopped to gaze up at the moon.

Caitlin closed her eyes to shut out the image and then looked back at Brodie. His gaze was dark with yearning, smoky with desire; in that instant she lost herself, caught up in the flow of that heated current. She needed his strength right then, his powerful arms around her, everything that meant shelter and protection from the outside world. She ran her fingers up over his chest, lacing them around the strong column of his neck.

His kiss was gentle, coaxing, a slow, glorious exploration of everything she had to offer. His lips brushed hers, the tip of his tongue lightly, briefly, tracing the full curve of her mouth, seeking her response. She kissed him in return and in a feverish surge of passion he drew her close, easing her into the welcoming warmth of his taut, muscular thighs.

Her soft curves meshed with his hard, masculine frame and a ragged sigh escaped her, breaking in her throat. He kissed her thoroughly, desperately, his hands moving over her in an awed, almost reverent journey of discovery.

'Brodie…' She didn't know what she wanted to

say…just his name was enough. She wanted him, needed him, longed for him to make her his.

And yet…wasn't he too strong, too male, too much of a driving force that would sweep her up and carry her along with him until he had done with her and was ready to move on? Perhaps she had always cared too much… She'd cared for Matt and he'd walked all over her; she cared for Brodie and he would eventually push her away. Could she handle that rejection, that awful nothingness that was bound to come?

But, then again, why shouldn't she experience once and for all the joy that was his to give, theirs to share, a memory to cherish for all time? She needed him, craved his touch. Somehow in these last few heated moments she had lost all sense of caution, thrown inhibition to waft on the night breeze.

'Caitlin?' He spoke softly, urgently. 'I want you; you know that, don't you?'

She nodded, her gaze fixed on him, intent. 'Yes. I want you too.' It was a whisper.

A soft gasp escaped him. 'I don't want you to regret anything that happens between us… Do you understand what I'm saying?'

'Of course.' Her eyes widened, becoming luminous with unshed tears. 'Of course I understand. But why are you saying this?' Why was he bringing it out into the open, making her think about what she wanted to keep back?

'I know you only kissed me because Matt was there

on the path with Jenny,' he said. 'I know why you did it and that's all right. I'm okay with that. I can handle it—at least, I think I can.'

He cupped her face lightly in his hands. 'And I know that you want me too, if only for the moment. But I need you to be sure about what you're doing. I have feelings too, you know. You mean too much to me, and I don't want to ruin what we have by sweeping you off your feet and then having you regret it.'

'I didn't set out to do this.' Her hands were trembling as she drew them back down his chest. 'I didn't mean for it to happen. I'm sorry,' she whispered brokenly. Tears trickled down her cheeks. 'Have…have they gone?'

He nodded. 'They've gone.'

'I'm sorry,' she said again. 'I don't know what I was thinking. I'm so sorry, Brodie.'

'Maybe there's a chance you could change your mind?' His dark eyes were brooding.

'No, there isn't.' She looked up at him, her whole body shaking. 'I can't do this.'

He pulled in a deep breath and seemed to steel himself. 'It's okay. Come on, then. I'll take you home.'

CHAPTER FOUR

THE KNOCK AT the door came as Caitlin was getting on with some chores upstairs before getting ready for work on Monday morning. She wasn't due to start her shift until later that day so up till now she'd been taking things at a fairly relaxed pace. Now, though, as the knocking came again, she frowned. It couldn't be Brodie wanting to see her, could it?

She wasn't ready to face him yet. She was still in shock from the way things had turned out on Saturday evening at the wedding reception. How could she have let things get out of hand that way? But wasn't she secretly, deep down, wishing she'd made a different decision? Why couldn't she have let things take their course, see where they led? The longing haunted her.

She hurried downstairs to answer the door. She would have to see him and try to work with him once more as if nothing had happened. How was she going to do that?

It would be so difficult...though how much worse

would it have been if she'd given in to her feelings for him? Would she have regretted it the next morning?

Maybe not. A wave of heat surged through her. The more she thought about it, the more she had to admit that she really had wanted him for himself and not just because Matt had been there to muddle her thinking. Brodie had been wrong when he'd thought that; in truth it was Brodie who had managed to turn her world upside down, not Matt.

And how could that be? Matt was the one she was supposed to care for. He'd been the love of her life, hadn't he? Or had he? The truth was beginning to dawn on her and it was much harder to handle than she might have expected.

Could it be that Matt had been the consolation prize, the runner-up, the one she'd turned to because wanting Brodie all those years ago had been an impossible dream? She groaned softly in frustration. Why did Brodie have to come back into her life and confuse her this way?

The knocking came again, getting louder, and she called out, 'Okay, I'm coming.'

She opened the door, half-expecting to see Brodie standing in the porch, but instead she looked down to see a young girl of around ten years old. She recognised her from the village.

'Hello, Rosie. What can I do for you? Is everything all right?' Rosie didn't look all right. She was breathing fast, as though she'd been running, and her expression was anxious.

'Oh!' Rosie seemed put out. 'I thought you'd be Mrs Braemar.' The girl shook her head at her mistake. 'Hi. It's just—she always looks after the animals.' Rosie frowned and tried to gather her thoughts. 'We found a dog, see, a girl dog—along the lane—my friend and me. She stayed with it, Mandy did. We were playing in the fields, looking for wild flowers on our way to school—there are some summer activities going on there. I think the dog might be hurt.' She pulled a face. 'She doesn't want to move. Will you come and look at her?'

Caitlin thought quickly. The best place for an injured dog would be at the vet's surgery but that was way across town and she had to be at work this morning. Even so, if the animal was injured…

'Give me a minute, Rosie. I'd better call on the doctor next door and see if we can borrow his pick-up truck to go and fetch her.' Old Mr Martin had left the truck behind when he'd sold the house to Brodie and from what she'd heard it was still in working order. Brodie had used it to take unwanted bits and pieces of furniture from the house when he'd moved in.

'Okay.' Rosie prepared to wait patiently.

Caitlin rang Brodie's doorbell, more than a little apprehensive about meeting up with him once more. She'd not seen sight nor heard sound of him since the early hours of Sunday morning when the taxi cab had dropped them both off at home. It had been a moment fraught with tension and Brodie had acknowledged that, reaching for her, wanting to hold her once more. To her everlasting regret, she'd made an excuse and turned from him in a panic.

Now, though, he wasn't answering his door, so she pressed the bell again more firmly until eventually she heard him padding down the stairs.

'Hi there.' Brodie was frowning as he opened the door, concentrating on rubbing at his damp hair with a towel. 'What's the problem?' Caitlin guessed he'd hastily pulled on trousers and a shirt after his shower. His black hair glistened and his skin was faintly damp where his shirt was open at the neck. He looked… He was breathtaking… She swallowed hard.

'Um…I…I wondered if…'

'Oh…hi, Caitlin.' He blinked, collecting himself, as if seeing her clearly for the first time. He straightened, suddenly alert, heat glimmering in his blue eyes. 'Come in.' He stood back to allow her access but frowned when she hesitated. 'Is something wrong? Is it your mother?'

'No…no, it's not Mum.' Though that was a worry in itself. She'd spent some time with her mother at the hospital yesterday and she'd not seemed well at all.

He looked beyond her, saw Rosie and frowned again. 'Has something happened?'

'Rosie's found a dog. She thinks it's hurt; I wondered if I could borrow the pick-up truck to go and get it. I don't know how badly it's injured.'

'Sure. Uh—give me a minute and I'll come with you. You may need a hand to lift it.' Brodie went along the hallway to dispose of the towel and grab his keys from a hook in the kitchen. Almost as an afterthought, he said, 'I'll get a blanket,' and took the stairs two at a time. A moment later he was back, saying, 'Okay, let's go, shall we?'

He smiled at Rosie and helped her into the cab of the truck, waiting while Caitlin climbed into the cab alongside the girl. 'Away we go, then. Show us where you found the dog, Rosie.'

'It's along the lane, near a lay-by,' Rosie said. 'We were playing by the stile. I don't think the dog belongs to anyone in the village—at least, I've never seen it before.'

They drove the short distance to the lay-by then they all piled out of the truck to go and see where the dog lay on its side in a wild-flower meadow by the stile. Rosie's friend was sitting down beside the animal, a golden-haired terrier, gently stroking its head.

'Hi, Mandy,' Caitlin said, going to sit beside her on the dew-misted grass. 'How's she doing?'

Mandy shook her head. 'She hasn't moved.'

'Poor thing, she looks exhausted.' Caitlin checked the dog over. 'Heavens, she's pregnant. Quite heavily pregnant, I'd say.'

Brodie knelt down beside them, lightly running his

hand along the terrier's flank. 'She's very cold,' he said. He carefully examined the skin at the back of her neck, adding, 'And from the way her skin reacts she's dehydrated as well.'

Caitlin frowned. 'There's no name tag or anything to identify her. I wonder if she was abandoned in the lay-by last night? She must have wandered around for a while before settling down here.'

'More than likely. Of course, she may be micro-chipped—the vet will be able to tell us that. We'll get her home and warm her up—see if she'll take a drink—and then decide what to do from there. I can't see any injuries anywhere but she'll need to see the vet as soon as possible.'

He lifted the dog on to the back of the pick-up truck and Caitlin clambered up beside her, wrapping her in the blanket and doing her best to soothe the pant-ing, distressed dog. 'Good girl,' she murmured softly. 'You're doing okay. We'll look after you.'

Rosie and Mandy were standing by, watching ev-erything and looking worried. 'Will she be all right?' Mandy asked.

'I think so,' Brodie answered. 'She's cold and worn out—very stressed, I imagine—but we'll take good care of her.'

'Thanks for letting us know about her,' Caitlin said with a smile, preparing to jump down from the back of the truck. Brodie held out a hand to her, helping her to the ground, and for a lightning moment as their bodies meshed a spark of stunning awareness flashed between them. Caitlin caught her breath and tried not to show that she'd been affected by his touch… Not easy, when she was tingling from head to foot. Did Brodie feel the same way? His smoke-blue gaze lingered for an instant longer on the pink flush of her cheeks before he reluctantly let go of her hand and turned back to the girls.

'Perhaps you should get yourselves off to school now,' he suggested quietly. 'You did well, both of you.'

'Okay. Can we come and see her later on?' Rosie's glance went to the back of the truck.

'Of course. Any time—though she might have to stay at the vet's surgery for a while.' Caitlin smiled. 'You saved her—you're bound to want to know how she's doing.'

The girls went on their way at last, chatting animatedly, and Caitlin climbed into the cab beside Brodie. 'I ought to stay with her until she shows signs of getting better,' she said. 'I don't know if she could cope with the journey to the vet right now. Will you be able to get someone to cover for me at the hospital if I'm a bit late?'

'Yes, don't worry about it. We need to be sure she's all right.'

'I can't imagine how anyone could abandon a dog like that. It's bad enough if it's a strong and healthy animal but a pregnant bitch… It's unbelievably cruel.'

'Yeah.' He was silent for a moment or two, deep in thought as he drove back along the lane towards the house. Caitlin noticed he drove slowly, carefully, so as to make a smooth journey for the ailing dog.

'You've always loved animals, haven't you?' she said now, thinking back to when he was a teenager. 'I remember once you found a rabbit that had been caught up in a snare and you nursed it back to health. You kept it in an outbuilding, didn't you, until it was time to set it free?'

'That's right.' He gave a wry smile as he pulled the truck into the driveway of his house and cut off the engine. 'It never did want to leave. I ended up taking it with me to medical school.'

She laughed. 'You're making it up.'

He gave her an exaggeratedly earnest look. 'Am not. He listened to so many of my tutorials on the computer he could have taken the exam for me.'

They both chuckled then she said thoughtfully, 'There were other animals too: a stray kitten…and you kept pigeons in a shed at one time, didn't you?'

He nodded briefly. 'Until my father made me send them away. It was after my mother died. I don't think he would have done it before then because she always encouraged me in whatever I wanted to do. He said they were too messy, too noisy and there were too many of them.' He pulled a face as he sprang down from the cab. 'I suppose that last was true, in the end. More and more birds wanted to join the flock.'

'You must have found some comfort in looking after animals,' she said musingly. 'Perhaps it was because, when everything else was going wrong in your life, you always had them to turn to.'

He gave her a quick, half-amused look from under his lashes. 'You noticed that, huh?'

She nodded, being serious. 'Well, you used to come to my mother for advice on how to care for them. I could see how different you were around them. You were gentle, relaxed... Not the angry, hot-headed young man that everyone else saw.'

He smiled. 'Pets can be very calming. I was thinking of introducing pet therapy on the long-stay children's ward. It could do wonders for morale—if we bring in the right kind of animal, of course. They would have to be vetted for temperament.'

'Wow!' She stared at him. 'You amaze me, sometimes. I'd never have thought of it. But you could be right...'

He unclamped the back of the pick-up. 'We'll have to think of a name for this one. We can't keep calling her Dog or Girl, can we?'

She gave it some thought. 'How about Daisy, since we found her in a field full of them?'

He moved his head slightly, mulling it over. 'Okay,' he said at last then lifted the lethargic dog into his arms. 'Where shall I put her?'

'There's a kennel round the back...a proper one, with purpose-made quarters. I'll show you.'

She led the way to the kennel and he carefully laid Daisy down in a rigid plastic bed with half the blanket tucked under her for warmth. She didn't stir, but her brown eyes followed him and then flicked to Caitlin. 'You're safe now, Daisy,' she told her.

'I'll get another blanket,' Brodie said. 'Maybe she'll take some water.'

Caitlin stayed with her while he went to get what he needed. 'You'll be all right,' she murmured soothingly, stroking the dog. 'Good girl. I'm sorry you're in this state, but you'll be fine. Good girl.'

Brodie returned with the second blanket and gently laid it over the dog, tucking it in around her. She wouldn't take any water from the bowl he brought, and all they could do was stay with her and wait for her to warm up. Eventually, she accepted sips of water from Caitlin's hand.

After a while, Brodie glanced at his watch. 'I have to get to the hospital,' he said. 'I'm sorry to leave you, but at least she's a bit more responsive than she was half an hour ago. She's starting to look around a bit. Maybe she'll be strong enough for the journey to the vet now.'

'Yes. I'll take her. I'll give the vet a ring and warn him that I'm on my way.'

Brodie stood up and handed her the keys to the pick-up. 'She might as well stay in the bed. I'll carry it out to the truck.'

He made sure that Daisy was settled in the back of the pick-up once more and then glanced at his watch. 'I must go. I'll see you later. Good luck.'

'Thanks.'

She drove carefully into town, unused to the truck, and very conscious of the ailing dog in the back. It wasn't just one dog she had to worry about: the welfare of the unborn puppies was paramount too. Who could tell when Daisy had last eaten, and surely her blood pressure must be way down?

'Ah, we'll keep her warm and get her on a drip right away to replace the lost fluids and electrolytes,' the vet said, examining Daisy a short time later and giving Caitlin a friendly smile. 'She's young—around a year old, I'd say—so that's in her favour. There's no microchip, unfortunately, so we don't know who she belongs to. Anyway, leave her with us for a few hours and we'll see if we can get her to eat something. The pups seem to be okay—I can hear their heartbeats. I'd say she has a few days before she's due to give birth. I'll give you a call later to let you know how she's doing.'

'Thanks. It's such a relief to know that she's in safe hands.' Caitlin stroked Daisy once more and said softly, 'I'll come back for you later. You'll be okay, I promise.'

She went from the vet's surgery straight to the hospital, keen to get started on her day's work. Luckily, she wasn't late, so she wouldn't feel guilty later at taking a break to go and look in on her mother.

'We've admitted an infant, three months old,' the staff nurse told her when she went over to the desk. 'He's feverish, with a swollen jaw and bouts of irritability and crying. I've spoken to the mother, and she's obviously distressed, so I'm going to get her a cuppa, calm her down and talk to her in the privacy of the waiting room.'

'That's great, thanks, Cathy. I'll go and take a look at him now.' It wasn't surprising that the mother was upset. Babies couldn't tell you what was wrong with them and it was heart-breaking to see such tiny little things miserable and in pain.

Caitlin held the baby in her arms and rocked him gently, trying to comfort him, and gradually he seemed to settle. 'I'll give him a quick examination—listen to his chest, check his ears and so on,' she told the nurse who was assisting her. 'But I'm going to need to do blood tests and get an X-ray to make a proper diagnosis.'

She worked as quickly and efficiently as she could, holding the child once more when she had finished, soothing him. 'I'll send these samples off to the lab,' she said. 'We should get the results back fairly soon.'

After that, she looked in on all her small patients, checking their progress and making sure they were comfortable and cheerful. Youngsters were resilient, she found, and recovery could come about sooner than expected. Four-year-old Jason, suffering from pneumonia, was sitting up in bed watching a DVD. She smiled, pleased he'd found the strength to take an interest.

'You should go and take a break,' Brodie said, coming over to her at the desk mid-afternoon. 'You haven't stopped since you got here.'

'I wanted to make sure I pulled everything in,' she

told him. 'Working part-time gives me room to manoeuvre, but I worry about fitting it all in. The wards are at full capacity right now. We're very busy.'

'You're not on your own here,' he said. 'Don't try so hard. You're doing great.'

'I hope so.'

He nodded. 'Is there any news from the vet?'

She nodded. 'He rang to say I can pick Daisy up on my way home. She's a lot better in herself now—still a bit lethargic, but at least she's taking a little food and responding to people.'

He smiled. 'That's good. I'll look in on her later, back home, if that's okay with you?'

'Of course it is.' She glanced at him, a little anxious, uncertain how they would go on together. He'd made no mention of what had happened between them at the weekend but that kiss was seared on her memory for ever... The feel of his hands on her body was imprinted on her consciousness for all time.

He placed a file in a tray on the desk and she looked at those hands—strong, capable, yet at the same time gentle, seeking, magical...

'I...um...I'll grab a sandwich and go and find out how Mum's doing,' she said hurriedly, needing to distract herself. 'She seemed to have some kind of lung problem coming on this morning, so I'm hoping they've managed to sort it out.'

'Uh-huh.' His glance moved over her, slowly, considering, but she couldn't tell what he was thinking.

Had he been able to read her thoughts? Surely not? Her cheeks flushed with heat. She was in enough of a quandary already, with her emotions all over the place.

Then he said softly, 'Maybe we'll find some time to talk things over…sort things out between us…? I care about you, Caity—I always have done—more than I can say.' He pulled in a sharp breath. 'Things were super-charged for you on Saturday—I knew that—and I should have taken heed. I shouldn't have let things get out of hand. It was my fault. But maybe we can move on from there?'

'Maybe.' The word came out as a whisper, but immediately she was filled with self-doubt. What was she doing even contemplating getting together with him? 'I don't know… I don't know what I was thinking…' She'd been hurt before—she wasn't about to put herself through that heartache all over again, was she? In the cold light of day it seemed like sheer folly to go from a broken relationship straight into Brodie's arms. What was she, some kind of masochist? 'I should go…'

She hurried along to her mother's ward and sat with her for a while, calming herself down, slowing the churning in her stomach by eating one of the sandwiches from the pack she'd bought.

'You seem stressed,' her mother said, watching her from her bedside chair. 'Is…everything all…right?' She reached for a paper hanky. She sounded as though she was out of breath and Caitlin's head went back a little in alarm.

'I'm fine.' She frowned. 'Mum, what is it? Are you…?' She stood up quickly as her mother began to cough and small flecks of blood appeared on the tissue.

Swiftly, Caitlin drew the curtains around the bed and called for a nurse. 'My mother's not well,' she told her as soon as she hurried forward. She quickly explained what had happened. 'I'm concerned this is a new development. Will you ask the consultant to look in on her, please? I understand he's still here in the department.'

The girl nodded. 'He ordered scans—they were done earlier this afternoon. I'll page him right away. He's on the next ward, doing a round of his patients.'

'Thanks.' Caitlin turned back to her mother, doing her best to make her comfortable. 'It could be a chest infection,' she told her, though she thought that unlikely with all the antibiotics she'd been given for her hip problem. A stronger possibility was that a blood clot had formed in her thigh because of her mother's enforced lack of regular activity. That clot could have broken up and spread to her lungs, where an embolus would cause a blockage. That could be very bad news, depending on how large it was.

The consultant appeared at her mother's bedside within a few minutes. 'I was going to look in on you very shortly, Mrs Braemar,' he said, 'but it looks like things are taking a bit of a turn. We'll get you started on some supplemental oxygen right away.' He indicated to the nurse to set that up then continued, 'I've had a look at your scans and I'm afraid there are a few small blood clots in your lungs. That's what's causing the pain in your chest and it's why you're having difficulty breathing.'

'Is it bad?' Her mother took short, gasping breaths, clearly worried.

'Not at the moment, my dear—not as bad as it might have been. The clots are small, you see, so we can start you on medication rather than having to do any more surgery.'

'Tablets, you mean?'

'Well, we'll give you intravenous heparin to start with, because that acts quickly. It will stop the clots from getting any bigger and will prevent any more from forming. At the same time I want to start you on warfarin tablets. They take two or three days to work and once they've kicked in we can stop the heparin.'

'So the clots won't get any…bigger but they'll… stay in my lungs?' Her mother looked bewildered and Caitlin hurried to explain.

'Your body will dissolve the clots gradually,' she said. 'You should start to feel better soon.'

The consultant patted her mother's hand. 'At least your hip infection is clearing up,' he said with a reassuring smile. 'That's one blessing.'

'True.' She made a weak smile. 'Bring on the rest.'

Caitlin stayed with her while the medication was

started but left a little later when she saw her mother needed to sleep. The consultant had put a light slant on things but it was one more thing that Caitlin would worry about. Her mother had always been so active and healthy prior to these setbacks. It was upsetting to see her like this.

She was subdued as she went back to the children's unit. Her mother would be all right, she told herself; the clots weren't huge and although she was uncomfortable she was in no immediate life-threatening danger.

Brodie was tending a small patient with feeding difficulties when she went to check up on the lab results for the baby she'd seen earlier. He was in a nearby bay, setting up a drip feed so that the infant would receive nourishment after an abdominal operation. The baby cooed gently, enjoying the attention as Brodie made funny faces and wiggled his fingers.

Caitlin watched them for a moment or two, her heart full. He was a natural with children. Why, oh why, did he make her care for him so much?

He, in turn, glanced at her; he must have sensed that something was wrong because his expression was quizzical.

'Something wrong with your mother?' he asked.

She nodded, not wanting to talk about it right now. She needed to keep a firm grip of herself so that she could do her job properly. Instead of saying anything more, she turned away and went to look through the lab reports.

'How is your little fellow doing?' Brodie asked later on as she went to check on the baby she'd seen earlier. He looked down at the crying infant in the cot and held out a hand to him. The baby grabbed one of his fingers and pulled, wriggling his legs. Brodie smiled.

'He's not too happy right now,' she answered. 'He's been on indomethacin to alleviate the pain and try to reduce the swelling in his jaw but I think I'll add a corticosteroid to get things working a bit better.'

'Sounds good. Have you had the test results back yet?'

She nodded. 'They showed an elevated erythrocyte sedimentation rate and raised alkaline phosphatase among other things. After seeing the X-ray films, I think we're dealing with Caffey's disease.' She grimaced faintly. 'There are changes in the bones of his jaw and his thigh bones are wider than you would expect.'

'That was well spotted, Caitlin.' He looked at her with renewed respect. 'From what I know of it, it's a rare, not very well-understood disease—with a genetic basis, I believe?'

She nodded. 'It may be passed down through a parent, or it could be through a gene mutation. Of course, it may be rare simply because a lot of cases go undiagnosed in infancy.'

'Yes—they tend to resolve themselves in early child-hood.'

'True. At least I can tell his parents that the disease is generally self-limiting and the bones should remodel themselves in a few months.'

She organised the new drug regime and then checked her watch. Her shift was coming to an end and she needed to go and collect Daisy and get her settled at home. She would need to buy tins of dog meat, kibble and maybe supplements to sustain the pregnant dog—hopefully the vet would be able to advise her on what to get. A comfy, padded base for the dog bed would come in handy too.

'You're off home?' Brodie walked with her to the exit doors.

'Yes, in a few minutes. I have to drop these lab forms off in pathology first. I thought I would take a shortcut through the quadrangle.'

He walked with her, stopping by the bench seat in the dappled shade of a silver birch. 'I'm due a break,' he said. 'Do you have time to sit for a minute and tell me what's going on with your mother? I've been to see her, but she always says she's fine, and I know she isn't.'

'Oh…of course, I'm sorry. You must be worried about her too. I keep forgetting how close you were back when…' Her voice trailed away. He wouldn't want to keep being reminded of the time when his life had taken a nosedive. 'She has some pulmonary emboli that are causing her problems—they're not too large, and the consultant's starting her on anti-coagulation therapy, so that should help things to get better.' They sat down beside one another on the bench.

'I'm sorry, Caity.' He wrapped an arm around her shoulders. 'I could see you were upset when you came back down to the unit. If there's anything I can do to help you, tell me—it must be a shock, everything that's happening.'

She nodded wearily. 'Things seem to be going from bad to worse. I thought I'd have her at home by now, Brodie.' She gazed up at him in despair. 'She was always so active, into everything; it feels so strange, seeing her the way she is now.'

'Her consultant's a good man. I'm sure he'll soon have her on the mend.' He ran his palm down her back in a comforting gesture. 'She'll be back home with you before too long, you'll see. She's a fighter, your mum. Things will soon be back to how they were.' He smiled. 'You were always such a loving family unit—you, your mum and your dad.'

'Yes, we were.'

He sighed. 'I'm almost ashamed to say I envied you back then—you seemed to have everything I was missing out on.'

She looked at him in surprise. 'I'm sorry.'

'There was always something not quite right between me and my dad.' He shrugged. 'I think your mother recognised that and that's why she took me under her wing—David too, of course, after Mum died, though somehow he seemed to cope a bit better than I did. Yet your mother must have gone through agonies when your dad passed away.'

'Yes, it was bad. It was very sudden, a heart attack that took him before we could realise what was happening. But she managed to hold things together. I think she felt she had to, for my sake…and yours. David's too.' She glanced at him. 'My father's death helped bring you and I closer together, didn't it? It gave us a stronger bond…and my mother sensed that. I think she was pleased that we talked a lot because she knew we could be good for each other. She knew you were deeply troubled—not just about your mother—and she wanted to help.'

'We needed all the support we could get. She's a lovely woman. She was like a mother to me after my mum passed away. I always felt I could talk to her. She listened—she didn't always offer advice, but she was there for me whenever I was wound up, wanting to hit out, needing to offload because of some new quarrel with my dad. She usually managed to calm me down somehow.'

Caitlin frowned. 'What did you argue about, you and your dad? I never understood it. You were the oldest child, the firstborn—I'd have expected things to be very different. But, like you said, you and your father never seemed to get on.'

His mouth flattened. 'No, we didn't. I was never sure why, but nothing I did was ever good enough for him. The one, constant feeling he showed towards me was…irritation. In the end I learned to be guarded around him, I suppose. I tried to toe the line…until, one day, we had a terrible argument and everything came to a head and boiled over. I'd had enough at that point and I decided I wasn't going to put up with his hassle any more.'

She studied him, her grey eyes troubled. 'What happened? I wish I could help, Brodie. You never spoke about it, so it must have been something major. Can you talk to me about it? Whatever it is, I promise, I'll keep it to myself.'

'I know.' He idly caressed her shoulder, drawing her to him. He moved his head so that his temple brushed her cheek and the breath caught in her lungs. She wanted to hold him to her. He said quietly, 'I trust you, where I wouldn't trust anyone else—except my brother.'

She loved the closeness, the warmth, that came from him but after a moment or two he straightened and she felt the loss acutely. Pulling herself together, remembering their surroundings, she said cautiously, 'What was the argument about?'

He gave a wry smile. 'Actually, it was about David… or, at least, me looking after him. Dad was at work on the Saturday morning—Mum had a bad headache and was lying down. I was supposed to take David to a football training session but it was damp and drizzly and on the way there he said he didn't want to go.

He was never that much into football. He said he was
going to hang out with a girl instead, someone we met
up with along the way. He said he didn't want me tag-
ging along—he was barely twelve and they were just
pals from school, nothing more. She wanted to listen
to music back at her house, so I said it was okay.'

'But it didn't work out like that?'

He shook his head. 'A bit later on they apparently
decided to go for a walk by the brook. Like I said, it had
been raining earlier. David was a bit overambitious—
showing off, I expect—and managed to slide down a
steep slope, straight into the water. It wasn't deep but he
fell in and finished up soaked through and muddy. Dad
caught him before he had time to change his clothes.
After that it was all hell let loose. I was the one in
trouble because I hadn't been with him to watch out
for him.'

Caitlin was puzzled. 'But that's the kind of thing
most youngsters get up to. Why would it cause such
a big problem, one that lasted for years to come? Did
you both overreact?'

'We certainly did—big time. Dad said I was totally
irresponsible…couldn't be trusted to keep my brother
out of trouble. Of course I became defensive and argued
back, asked why was it all down to me…why was he
putting his job on to me? He was the father, wasn't he?
Not that he'd ever been a decent father to me like he
had to David, the favoured one… Et cetera, et cetera;
I expect you know how it goes.'

'So you went too far?'

'Oh, yes…and he lost it completely. Said I wasn't his son so why would he care about me? He didn't give two hoots about me, just put up with me for my mother's sake.'

Caitlin gasped. 'Oh, Brodie… I'm so sorry. Was it true, what he said, or had he made it up on the spur of the moment?'

Brodie moved his arm from around her and brought his hands together in his lap, clasping his fingers together. It was as though he was totally alone in that moment; she wanted to reach out, wrap her arms around him and comfort him. He was rigid, though, his whole manner isolating himself from everyone and everything.

'Oh, yes. It was true. I asked my mother and she eventually admitted it to me. She was pregnant with me when she married my father, she said. He knew… He didn't like it, because she was having someone else's child, but he married her all the same. He just never wanted me and when I came along he couldn't bring himself to make a bond.'

Caitlin reached out and laid her hand over his. 'Did your mother tell you who your real father was?'

He shook his head. 'She didn't want to talk about him; said it was a fleeting thing—she made a mistake with a man who was never going to stay around for long. He was ambitious, wanted to go back to the city where he lived, wanted to make something of himself.

She was a home bird, a country girl, and she didn't think she would ever be part of his world.'

'No wonder you went off the rails. You must have been so bewildered.'

'I was angry… Not with my mother—I could understand how she might have fallen for someone and how she turned to my dad when this man went away. She was always loving towards me, and there were endless rows between her and Dad over the way he treated me. He loved her, I'm sure, but he couldn't get beyond the other man who had figured in her life and things were never easy between them. We weren't what you'd call a contented family.'

She ran her hands lightly over his forearms. 'I wish I'd known at the time. Perhaps I could have helped, instead of being mad at you for the way you behaved. I knew there was a reason but I couldn't fathom it and I didn't know how to reach you…the real you.'

He gave a crooked smile. 'That's because he went missing for a while.' His expression was sombre. 'Perhaps part of him is still beyond reach.'

She shook her head. 'You don't mean that.'

He looked at her, taking in the vulnerable curve of her cheek and the soft fullness of her pink lips. 'I don't know—I'm still unsure about a lot of things— but it makes me feel good to know that you wanted to reach out to me.'

'I'm glad about that.' She wanted to say more—to

go on talking with him, get him to open up to her—
but someone stepped out into the quadrangle and they
moved apart. 'I should go,' she said and he nodded.

'Me too.'

CHAPTER FIVE

'YOU'VE BEEN BUSY.' Caitlin's mother looked at the basket of fruit Caitlin had brought for her. 'That's not all come from home, has it?'

'It has, actually.' Caitlin was proud of the amount of fruit she'd managed to harvest. It was mostly being sold at the local market but she'd gathered together an assortment for the gift basket. There were early fruiting James Grieve apples, a few pears, pink-skinned Victoria plums and some of the later varieties of strawberries. 'I thought it might help to cheer you up.'

It had also given her something to do, had helped keep her occupied outside of work. It gave her less time to dwell on situations that were fast running out of her control. Brodie had given her a lot to think about with his revelations about his father. His background meant that he probably still had a lot of self-doubt and she wondered if he would ever be able to make a proper commitment to her. She was falling for him all over again but for her own self-preservation she knew she should guard against losing her heart to him.

'Bless you, it's wonderful; a real treat.' Her mother smiled. 'Oh, it makes me long to be back home. I can't wait to get back there and see how everything's going on.'

'I'm sure it won't be too long now,' Caitlin agreed, trying to give her some encouragement. 'You're certainly looking a bit brighter. There's colour in your cheeks and you seem to be breathing a little easier.'

'I am. I'm managing to get a bit further with the walking frame now before the lack of breath stops me.'

'That's good to know.' Caitlin smiled. 'And there's a bit of news I thought you'd want to know about—David has asked if the film unit can use the smallholding as one of their sets for an episode of *Murder Mysteries*. He said they would pay well, so I said I'd ask you. I didn't really think you'd have any objection. They promise they won't leave a mess, and the filming will all be done over two or three days. I think they especially want to use the barn and the area around the hen hut.'

'Oh, how exciting! Yes, of course that's okay. It'll be so interesting to see our home on the television, won't it? I wonder what they'll make of it? Oh, I can't wait!'

Caitlin chuckled. 'I thought you'd be all right with it. David's asked if we'll be extras and take part in the filming—Brodie and me—along with some of the villagers. Brodie's a bit wary but apparently the villagers are all really keen to get in on the act.'

'I'll bet they are…' Her mother started to cough, overcome with anticipation, and Caitlin frowned. She was looking better and it was all too easy to forget how ill her mother had been.

'Don't try to talk,' she said now. 'Just rest. I'll fill you in on what's been going on.'

'Yes…' Interested to know what was going on, her mother ignored her suggestion not to speak. 'Tell me about the dog you found. How is she?'

'She's doing fine. Rosie's mother drops by whenever she can while I'm at work to make sure she's okay. She and Rosie are helping to take her for walks.'

'Isn't she about due to give birth?'

Caitlin nodded. 'Could be today, according to the vet, so Rosie said she'd keep a special eye on her. I'm not sure what to look for, except the vet said something about temperature changes—she'll get a rise in temperature and then it will drop when she's about to go into labour.'

'You'll know when she's ready.' Her mother paused, getting her breath. 'She'll probably be restless.'

'I'll look out for that. I hope she's okay.' She glanced at her mother, making sure she was all right. 'She's such a sweet-natured dog. Here, I took a picture of her on my phone…' She showed her the photo of the shaggy, golden-haired terrier and told her how the vet had said to feed her on puppy food because it was higher in nutrients and therefore good for her while she was pregnant.

'Brodie comes over every day to see her and she follows him everywhere. At least, I think it's Daisy he comes to see.' She couldn't be altogether sure. They'd taken to sharing the occasional snack supper together of an evening, alternating between the two houses. He'd not pushed anything when it came to starting any kind of relationship with her but she had the feeling he was finding it hard to stay away. She was glad about that. She liked having him around.

A wave of heat ran through her at the direction her thoughts were taking and she quickly forced her mind back to the dog.

'She's fixated on him ever since he tucked the blanket around her and offered her a pull toy and a biscuit. I think she would up sticks and go and live with him if she could.' She made a mock-peeved expression. 'I'm not certain how I feel about that—I think I'm quite put out about it.'

Her mother laughed. 'He always did have a way with the girls.'

'True.' Caitlin didn't want to go too deeply into that. Despite her misgivings she'd come closer to him in these last few days than ever before and it invoked all sorts of exhilarating and tummy-tingling sensations inside her that she'd never experienced before—not even with Matt. But falling for Brodie was definitely not on the cards, was it?

'Are you and he getting on all right?' her mother asked.

'Yes, fine.' She sent her a guarded look. 'Why wouldn't we?'

Her mother shrugged lightly. 'I know how he used to look at you and how you kept putting up barriers—you didn't want to get involved with someone who kicked against the establishment and who seemed happy to play the field. I doubt he's changed that much. He doesn't go with the crowd or let the grass grow under his feet. He has his own ideas and likes to follow through.'

She paused, pulling air into her lungs. 'As to the rest, I've seen him with the nurses when he's come to visit me… They all think the world of him and the single ones are ripe for the picking. I really like him but I don't want to see you get hurt.'

A quick stab of jealousy lanced through Caitlin at the mention of the nurses, but just then a bout of coughing caught her mother out. Caitlin stood up and quickly handed her the oxygen mask that was connected to the wall-mounted delivery system close by.

'Here, breathe in slowly, steadily. Take your time.'

After a few minutes her mother was feeling better and she put the mask aside. 'I'm fine now,' she said. 'I just need to rest for a bit.'

Caitlin nodded, giving her an assessing look. 'Okay. I should be getting back to work, anyway. I've a new patient coming in and I need to look her over.' She gently squeezed her hand. 'I'll be back to see you later.'

She went back to the children's unit, pleased to see that a trio of small children who were able to get out of bed for short periods had gathered around the brand-new aquarium tank that Brodie had introduced to the ward. They were pointing, talking and smiling a lot.

'I see your tropical fish tank is a hit with the youngsters,' she told Brodie at the desk as she read through her patient's file.

He smiled. 'Yes, I noticed one or two of them going up to the glass and watching what was going on. They seem to like the shipwreck and submerged treasure chest, and the fish are colourful.' He brought up some CT scans on the computer screen. 'The next step for me, I think, is to develop a rehab garden outside so that children like Jason and maybe Sammy, who are recovering, can get their strength back by walking about outside on good days.'

'That sounds like an interesting idea.' She looked at him curiously. 'What did you have in mind?'

'Different levels. Nothing too high but raised flower beds, pathways, short flights of wide steps—providing the children have physiotherapists or parents with them to help them negotiate the obstacles. I thought maybe scented flowers and herbs, or different colours and textures, would go down well.'

'Something to attract wildlife, like birds and squirrels, would be good,' she said. 'So maybe you could put up a bird table and plant a variety of shrubs that have the right kind of berries.' She broke off, studying him once more. 'I think you have some great ideas, but where's the funding coming from?'

'There are hospital charities keen on helping out,'

he answered. 'And I'll think about putting some of my own money into it. It all depends if I decide to stay here for the long term.'

She frowned at that. Was he really thinking of moving on?

He brought up X-ray films on to the screen of his computer then he frowned and pointed to the images. 'Have you seen these?'

'No. Whose are they?'

'They're films we had done recently to check Sammy's progress. Along with the results of his DNA and collagen tests, I think we finally have an answer. We're dealing with a specific bone disease—*osteogenesis imperfecta*.'

She winced. 'Poor Sammy,' she said softly. The diagnosis, otherwise known as brittle bone disease, meant that his body didn't make enough collagen—the main protein building block of bone—so his bones and connective tissue, such as tendons and ligaments would suffer as a result. 'So his bones are thin and liable to break more easily than others.' She studied the films on screen carefully. 'It's difficult to detect from the X-rays alone.'

'But the bones are definitely thinner than normal—perhaps his case is mild and he's been unfortunate up to now.'

'Well, let's hope so. The physiotherapist is working with him because of the fracture but it'll be good for him to have ongoing therapy to help him regain his strength and mobility—safe exercise and activity to develop his muscle control.'

He nodded. 'His parents will need advice on nutrition—we can't replace the collagen, but we can make sure his muscles and bones are as strong as possible. Bisphosphonates are the mainstay of drug treatment as far as that goes.'

'I'll get things organised.' She gave a faint smile. 'The one good thing to come out of the diagnosis is that it means the parents are off the hook. It's going to be difficult for them to take it on board—a bittersweet experience.'

'But they'll have an answer at last and so will Social Services and the police.'

'Yes.' Caitlin hurried away to make several phone calls and to get the next phase of Sammy's treatment started. This was a case where she didn't want to waste any time. The parents had been weighed down by doubt, uncertainty and recriminations for long enough; perhaps now Sammy would truly start to make a recovery. It was hardly any wonder the child was quiet and withdrawn.

The rest of the day passed quickly. A little girl, Janine, was admitted with an infection and Caitlin ordered tests to find out what they were dealing with. 'I'll prescribe a broad-spectrum antibiotic,' she told the staff nurse. 'But when we get the results back from the lab we can prescribe a more specific drug.'

'Okay, I'll see to it,' the staff nurse said.

'Thanks.'

When her shift ended Caitlin was more anxious than usual to get home. Brodie came out of one of the bays where he had been examining a child and sent her a quick glance as she went to collect her jacket. 'You're off home, then? You look anxious. Are you worried about Daisy?'

She nodded. 'I am, a bit. Rosie's mother phoned to say Daisy was quite restless, so I'm expecting things to kick off any time soon.'

'I'll come and join you as soon as I finish here. I could pick up a Chinese takeaway on my way home, if you want? I know you like it and that'll be one less chore.'

'Ah, my favourite food...' she said with a smile. 'Beef and green peppers in black bean sauce—yum— and sweet-and-sour chicken. Oh, I'm hungry already at the thought of it.'

'Me too.' He said it softly, his gaze moving over her, lingering; somehow she had the feeling his mind wasn't simply dwelling on the prospect of food.

It was only after she'd left the hospital and was driving home along the country lanes that she wondered about the wisdom of spending too many of her evenings with him, especially this evening, when they were planning to share a mutual treat. It was one thing to throw a sandwich together out of expediency— quite another to make a date. Because that was what it seemed like, all at once. Things were moving too fast.

It wasn't too long ago that she'd been looking forward to spending her free time with Matt and look where that had left her. She frowned. What was it about Matt that had made her think he was the one for her, when he so obviously wasn't?

Brodie turned up at the house a couple of hours later as dusk was falling. Caitlin had been watering the plants in the kitchen garden but now she turned off the tap and put the hose away.

'How is Daisy?' Brodie asked. 'Is anything happening with her?'

Caitlin nodded. 'She's definitely not herself. She's a bit agitated, so I brought her into the house—she's in the utility room. Her bed fits in there nicely under the worktop, and it's shaded from the sun during the daytime. She seems to like it there, anyway, so I'll probably let her stay. I left her rearranging her blanket. Come and see.'

She led the way into the house and Brodie put his packages down on the kitchen table. The appetising smell of Chinese food wafted on the air.

She hastily set plates to warm in the oven and then they looked in on Daisy. She looked up at them from her bed, panting, her tongue lolling eagerly.

'She looks happy enough, anyway,' Brodie commented, stroking the dog's head then heading back towards the kitchen. He washed his hands at the sink then helped Caitlin to set out the food.

'Has David said anything more about the filming?' Caitlin asked a while later as she nibbled on a hot spring roll.

He nodded. 'It's all going to start in a couple of days—they have the weekend marked up for it. He's even roped Dad in. Heaven knows how he managed it, but he's going to be kitted out as a farm worker, by all accounts.'

'You're kidding?' It was hard to believe that Colin Driscoll would ever have agreed to it. 'How do you feel about that?'

He lifted his shoulders briefly. 'I'm not sure. I suppose anything that gets us together is a good thing. We're both adults now and it's about time we sorted out our differences. He may not have wanted me around, but he brought me up from when I was a baby, so you'd think he'd have found some feelings for me along the way.'

He frowned. 'But then things happened... I started acting up, and after I turned eighteen I stayed away, just coming back to see David whenever I could. It seemed for the best.' He raised his dark brows a fraction. 'Maybe, after all this time, Dad might be able to come to terms with the circumstances and finally find acceptance, though I think that's a tall order—for both of us.'

Caitlin mused on that. 'He was never the easiest man to get along with. Not in later years, anyway. He'd come over here to buy produce from my mother, but he was often brusque, and wouldn't want to stay and chat.'

She dipped her fork into delicious fried rice and said thoughtfully, 'Have you tried to find your real father?'

He nodded. 'There's no father named on my birth certificate. Dad said he was a Londoner, someone who was setting up his own business, but he didn't know his surname or very much about him. I think he and Mum made some kind of pact not to talk about him. So finding him has always seemed like a non-starter.'

'I'm sorry. I can't imagine what that must be like, not knowing your parents.'

'You learn to live with it.' He speared a tender shoot of broccoli and rolled it around in the spicy sauce. 'There's always a part of you that's missing; when you do something or think something odd or slightly different from usual, you wonder if that's come from your absent parent. Genetics suddenly seem ultra-important, but there's not a thing you can do to find out the truth, so you have no choice but to bury the frustration inside.'

'David says you can't settle and you can't move on— perhaps, like your dad, you need to find acceptance of some sort.'

He gave a short laugh. 'That's easy to say but not so easy to do in practice. David knows who he is, where he comes from. He's content with his life as it is. It's reasonably orderly and he doesn't need to think too deeply about what he wants from life. He assumes he'll have a great time now and settle down when he finds the right person. He seems to be fairly certain that will happen some day; I'm glad for him.'

'But you're not so clear about that for yourself?'

He shook his head. 'I've seen how people mess things up—I'm a direct result of that—and I don't want to be part of causing it to happen to anyone else. Perhaps I don't believe in the happy-ever-after. I wish I did. I wish it was possible.' He sent her a quick, almost regretful glance. 'For myself, I think I prefer to live in the here and now, and take things as I find them. If I can have fun along the way, that's great, but I don't make any long-term plans because I don't know what's around the corner.'

'That's what you were trying to tell me the other day, isn't it? I shouldn't look for anything more from you.' She studied him, her grey eyes solemn. 'I'm sorry about that—I can't help thinking it's a pity you can't put as much meaning into your personal life as you do into your work.'

He gave her a rueful smile. 'You're right. I do concentrate most of my energy in my work. That's important to me.' He frowned. 'I can't seem to help myself, Caitlin. Maybe I don't want to think too deeply about anything else.'

'I thought that might be the reason.' Her mouth turned downwards briefly. 'But I suppose all the hard work is paying dividends. I've seen what you've managed to achieve at the hospital. The patients are well looked after, the parents are fully involved in their care and the staff are focused. I'm not surprised you've become head of a unit so early in your career.' She sent him a quizzical glance. 'This won't be your last stop, will it? You'll do what you need to do here and then move on to improve things at some other hospital.'

His blue gaze meshed with hers. 'I don't know about that. Right now I'm concentrating on the job here.'

They finished their meal and went to check on Daisy. There had been no sound coming from the utility room but now, as they looked in on the dog, they heard soft licking noises.

'Oh, my word, look at that!' Caitlin gasped as she saw two wriggling, sleek little puppies suckling at their mother's teats. Too busy to notice that she had visitors, Daisy was intent on licking them clean and only stopped when a third pup began to put in an appearance.

'Well, who's a clever girl?' Brodie grinned as he knelt down beside the dog bed. 'Look at you—you've managed it all by yourself.' Caitlin crouched down beside him and he put his arm around her, drawing her close. 'She's a natural,' he said. 'And there was me thinking we might have to help out, or call the vet if she got into difficulties.'

Caitlin was overwhelmed as she watched Daisy deliver a fourth then a fifth puppy, all perfect, all hungry and vying for a place where they could suckle. 'It's wonderful,' she said, thrilled to bits to see that they were all healthy and strong looking. She turned her head to look at Brodie and he smiled back at her.

'It is,' he agreed. He moved closer to her so that his lips were just a breath away from hers—then he kissed her, hard and fast, a thorough, satisfying kiss. She was so taken by surprise and caught up in the joy of everything that was going on that she kissed him back, loving the feel of his arms around her, loving the fact that they'd shared this momentous occasion together.

They kissed and held on to each other for what seemed like a blissful eternity, until there was a sharp rapping at the kitchen door and David was calling out, 'Anyone at home? Caitlin? Brodie?'

They broke away from one another as they heard the outer door open; David stepped inside the kitchen and came looking for them. Sure that her cheeks were flushed with heat, Caitlin looked back at the dog and her wriggling pups.

'We're in here,' Brodie said. 'We've had some new additions to the family.'

'Hey, that's great.' David came to look at the proud mother, kneeling down to stroke her gently and admire her offspring. 'Well done, Daisy. Are you all done, now? Is that it…five altogether? Wow!'

They watched the tableau for a while and then David asked, 'Is that Chinese food going spare in the kitchen? Only, I haven't eaten for hours.'

'Help yourself.' Caitlin stood up. 'I'll get you a plate.'

'Cheers. You're an angel,' David murmured. 'Oh,

and at the weekend, I thought you might want to play the part of a farm girl feeding the hens—Brodie can be hoeing the kitchen garden. I talked it over with the producer and he's okay with that. You don't have to say anything, just do the actions.'

Brodie followed them into the kitchen, frowning. 'So what's the scene all about?'

David took a seat at the table and helped himself to stir-fried noodles and chicken. 'It'll be mostly centred around the barn—the detective is looking for a suspect and asks the farmer if anyone's been hiding out in the barn overnight. The farmer says no, but then they find a bloodstain in the straw and after that the forensic team is brought in.'

'That's it?' Brodie raised his brows expressively.

'Yeah. It's an essential part of the drama. Someone was there, see, but the body has been moved.'

'The plot thickens.' Caitlin chuckled. 'What does your father have to do in the scene?'

'He'll be delivering foodstuff for the animals—unloading it off a lorry. I suppose Brodie could go and give him a hand—yeah, that would be good. It'll fit in with the red herring we planned: he looks like the man who drove the getaway car—our prime suspect.'

Caitlin smiled. 'What a pity the drama spans the TV watershed; the youngsters in the children's unit will be missing a treat—their favourite doctor on TV. Unless, of course, their parents let them stay up for the first half.'

Brodie's eyes narrowed on her. 'Please don't tell them. I'll never hear the last of it.'

She chuckled, but David said quickly, 'I think most people roundabout will know, sooner or later. The press will be on hand for the filming—you know the sort of thing: "*Murder Mysteries* will be back on your screens for the autumn. Filming is taking place now in the peaceful, picturesque village of Ashley Vale, Buckinghamshire. Local doctors have given over their properties for the recording…"'

Brodie groaned. 'Why did I ever agree to this? We'll have the local newshounds all over us as well as the national.'

Caitlin lightly patted his shoulder. 'Look on the bright side: you'll be out at work most of the time. Unless they follow you and find you there, of course…'

He groaned again, louder this time, and they laughed.

The film crew arrived early in the morning on Saturday to allow time for costume, make-up and setting the scene. David had the bright idea of putting Daisy and her puppies in a wooden feed trough in the barn. They would be written into the scene, he said—a means whereby the victim of the story was drawn to the barn. 'It'll be a sweet moment in the drama,' he said, 'Seeing them all golden-haired and snuggled together.' They were certainly thriving, getting bigger every day.

Dressed in jeans and a T-shirt, Caitlin duly went

out to scatter corn for the hens. There was a moment of aggravation when the geese decided they needed to ward off the visitors, but after a few minutes of chasing about, she and Brodie managed to grab hold of them and shut them in one of the outhouses.

'I'll give them a feed of leftover vegetables and pellets to keep them happy,' Caitlin said, breathless after her exertions. 'I hope we haven't disrupted the filming too much.'

'I think they're used to happenings like that on set,' Brodie murmured. 'Besides, it's given you quite a glow—you'll look great on camera.'

So she was flushed and harassed already—not a good start. One of the extras was wheezing heavily as he walked by the barn to the lorry but she decided perhaps that was the part he was meant to play. Anyway, Brodie was with him, unloading sacks of grain, his shirt sleeves rolled up, biceps bulging.

She looked away, her own lungs unexpectedly dysfunctional all of a sudden. She began to spread corn over the ground, trying not to show that she'd been affected in any way by his sheer animal magnetism.

For his part, Brodie's father stood by the lorry and helped to unload the sacks. He and Brodie spoke briefly to one another in undertones as they worked, but their expressions were taut, businesslike. Brodie heaved another sack from the lorry and walked with it on his shoulder to the barn.

'Okay, thanks, everyone. That's a wrap on this

scene!' the director said after a while. He went over to the film crew. 'We'll move on down the lane in half an hour and do the accident scene. David, you need to come along with us—I'm not sure the script works too well where the policewoman finds the overturned car with the woman at the wheel. She's on her way to meet her daughter at the farm but I'm not sure her feelings of anxiety are fully shown. Maybe you can tighten it up a bit.'

'Okay.' David winced briefly but he didn't seem too bothered by the request and Caitlin guessed he was used to being asked to make last-minute changes.

'An overturned car?' Brodie shot David a piercing look. 'You didn't mention that part of the script when you told me about the episode.'

David pulled a face. 'It was something the producer wanted written in to heighten the drama. There are only the main members of the cast involved, so I didn't think you'd need to know the details.'

Brodie's expression was taut. 'Don't you have any problem with it?'

David's mouth flattened. 'Of course I do—but it's my job, Brodie. I don't have a choice but to go along with things. You understand that, don't you?'

Brodie didn't answer. His jaw flexed and his eyes glittered, bleak and as hard as flint.

Caitlin watched them, two brothers deep in earnest conversation, and knew something was badly wrong. A car accident had featured heavily in their young lives—it had been the cause of major tragedy for both of them. Was that what was causing the tension between them now?

David glanced at her. 'I should have said something before this,' he murmured. 'It was bound to come as a shock…a reminder of what happened. I've had time to get used to it because I've been working on the original script for some weeks.' The director was on the move, briskly calling for the crew to follow him, and David looked back at his brother. 'I have to go. Will you be all right?'

'Of course.' Brodie's answer was curt but David clearly wasn't convinced. Once more, he looked at Caitlin and made a helpless gesture with his hands.

She gave an imperceptible nod. 'Brodie, let's go and get a coffee, shall we? And I need to let the geese out of prison as soon as the crew have gone.'

'They're all packing up and moving out along the lane. It shouldn't take them too long. I imagine it will be safe soon enough.' He walked over to the barn, calling out, 'I'll get Daisy and her brood.'

His father had already left, Caitlin noticed, and she wondered if that bothered him too. She'd invited Colin to stay behind for coffee and a snack earlier, but he'd declined the offer, saying he had to get back to Mill House. He was having problems with his roof.

Brodie installed Daisy and the puppies—three male, two female—back in their new home in the utility room and then came into the kitchen. Caitlin poured coffee into a mug and slid it across the table towards him. 'I see you let the geese out,' she murmured, glancing through the kitchen window. 'They've taken up position by the gate, just in case anyone tries to come back.'

He made a faint smile at that. 'It's good to know we don't need a guard dog. I'm not sure Daisy would be up to the job right now.'

'I don't know about that. Wait till the pups are wandering about. I expect she'll be very protective of them—the mothering instinct will take over.'

Brodie's expression tautened and she quickly sat down opposite him at the table, placing her hand over his in a comforting gesture. 'What's wrong, Brodie? Do you want to tell me about it?'

'Nothing's wrong.' He stiffened, sitting straight backed, his gaze dark.

'Your mood changed as soon as you heard about the car scene. Perhaps it will help to talk about it.'

'I don't see how. Anyway, it was all a long time ago. It shouldn't…' His voice trailed off and Caitlin gently ran her hand over his.

'Did you ever talk about what happened? This is about your mother, isn't it? Why don't you bring it out into the open once and for all? Tell me what you're thinking. It might help.'

Angry sparks flared in his eyes. 'Don't you think David suffered just as much as I did? He lost her too, you know, and he was younger than me. She was a huge loss to all of us.'

'I know. But there's something that's been burning inside you ever since it happened. I saw it in your face after the accident. I knew there was something you weren't telling me...something you kept locked up inside. What is it, Brodie? Why can't you tell me what's wrong?'

He wrapped his hands around his coffee cup and pulled in a deep breath, bending his head so that she wouldn't see his face. When he spoke, finally, it was almost a whisper. 'It was my fault,' he said.

She frowned. 'How could it be your fault? You weren't there. It was dark and there was a rainstorm—the roads were treacherous. She went into a skid on a bend in a country lane and the car overturned. How was that your fault? How could you even think it?'

'I was sixteen. I'd stayed out too long in town—way past when I was supposed to be home—and the buses weren't running. I didn't have the money for a taxi, so I phoned home and asked for a lift.'

His voice was low so she strained to hear what he was saying. He took a shuddery breath and went on, 'Dad answered the phone. He was furious because I'd been irresponsible and he told me to walk home in the rain. It was twelve miles, and I argued with him, kicked up a fuss, which made him worse. He was going to put the phone down on me but my mother came on the line and wanted to know where I was. She came out to fetch me because he refused.'

His hands clenched into fists. 'It was my fault she died,' he said. 'I should have walked home. In the end, the police came and found me and told me what had happened. My dad didn't speak to me for days.'

A small gasp escaped her. 'I didn't know…about the row, I mean. I'm so sorry, Brodie.' She stood up and put her arms around him. 'It was an awful thing to happen, but it wasn't your fault. Lots of teenagers get into scrapes and cause their parents hassle. You can't go on blaming yourself.'

'But I do.' He pulled a face. 'Logically, I know all the reasoning, the explanations—but in my heart I feel the guilt all the time. I don't feel I have the right to be happy. I didn't know how to handle it when I was younger, but later I decided to try to make some kind of reparation by going into medicine. It doesn't appease my guilt but it helps, a bit.'

'Believe me, you've done everything you can. And now you have to put it behind you. Your mother wouldn't want you to go on blaming yourself. She wouldn't want you to waste your life feeling guilty.'

His brow creased. 'No, perhaps not.'

'Definitely not. She was always there for you, Brodie. She loved you. She would want you to be happy. And I think she would have wanted you to make up with your dad.'

She rested her cheek against his. 'She would

have hated the way your father reacted afterwards, not speaking to you, but have you ever thought that maybe, once he was over the initial shock, that he felt guilty too? You asked him to come and get you and he refused—maybe, if he'd been driving, he'd have handled the road conditions differently. Perhaps that's why you and he can't get on—you both feel that you're equally to blame for what happened.'

He sighed heavily. 'I know… I know…you're probably right. I've been over and over it in my mind. But I don't see how we can resolve things after all this time. I stayed away because I wasn't wanted but now I've come back here to work, he does his best to avoid me.'

'Does he? Are you sure about that?' She straightened, letting her arms fall to her sides. 'Why did he take part in the filming today? He didn't have to do it. He could have found an excuse and stayed away. But he didn't, Brodie. He came along, knowing you would be here. It isn't much, but it's a start. Don't you agree?'

'I suppose so.' His mouth made a crooked, awkward line. 'The truth is, I'm not actually sure I want to make up with my dad. He treated me harshly and it left a scar.'

'You've both been scarred. It's time to start the healing process.'

He gave her a long, assessing look. 'When all's said and done, I think that's what I like about you, Caity. You've always made me look at the big picture, made me face up to what I'm doing with my life; shown me what a mess I'm making…even if it's not what I want to know at the time.'

'Maybe I do it because I care about you,' she said softly. 'I don't think you're making a mess of things—you're doing the best you can in the circumstances. I want to help you. I don't want to see you hurting.'

And maybe she did it because she loved him… because she'd always loved him, though she hadn't always recognised it.

His revelations had shocked her to the core, but now she understood why he had so many doubts about himself. Perhaps this tragedy of his childhood, together with the uncertainty of his parentage and the difficult relationship with his father, were all part of the reason why he couldn't commit to love.

For herself, she had come to realise that her feelings for him went very deep, far more than she had allowed herself to acknowledge until this moment. He might not feel the same way about her, didn't even know what he wanted right now, but she would look out for him all the same. She couldn't help herself.

CHAPTER SIX

'I HAVE TO go over to the hospital to deal with a couple of things that have cropped up,' Brodie said. It was Sunday morning; he'd surprised Caitlin by appearing on her doorstep some time after breakfast.

She was dressed casually in a short-sleeved shirt and pencil-line skirt that faithfully outlined her curves. She was inwardly thrilled that he appeared totally distracted for a moment as he looked at her, until he shook his head, as though to clear it.

'Uh, something…something's happened with one of your patients—a reaction to the medication she was prescribed—and I wondered if you want to come with me. It's Janine, the five-year-old with the chest infection.'

'Heavens, yes, of course I'll come with you.' She was appalled by the news and immediately on the alert. 'Is she all right?'

'I believe so. It looks as though she's allergic to the penicillin she was given this morning. Her throat swelled up, she was wheezing and she has an all-over rash. The registrar acted quickly to put things right, but obviously the parents are upset, so I want to go and talk to them.'

'Okay.' She made sure Daisy and the puppies were safely ensconced in the utility room and grabbed her jacket, going out with him to his car.

The roads were fairly clear of traffic but Brodie drove carefully as usual and appeared to be deep in thought. 'You're very quiet,' she commented. 'Are you worried about the situation at the hospital?'

He shook his head. 'These things happen. It's no one's fault, and the little girl is all right.'

'Okay.' She glanced at him, noting the straight line of his mouth. Was he dwelling on what they'd talked about yesterday, about his problems with his father? 'Is it your dad, then? Are you going to try to sort things out with him this afternoon when the film crew set up again?'

He shrugged. 'I haven't given it much thought. I prefer not to think about it.'

It was clear he wasn't going to talk about it and she was disappointed. Maybe that was selfish on her part, but she couldn't help feeling that sorting out the problems from his past was the key to his chance of true happiness for the future.

Would that future include her? Something in her desperately wanted to keep him in her life but, at this point in time, who could tell if it would come about? More importantly, would any relationship last? He had more than enough problems to overcome and, as for herself, she'd been through a lot of heartache; she didn't want to put herself through any more. Caring had been her downfall. Somehow, she had to be strong, put up defences and guard herself against being hurt.

And right now they both had more pressing matters to deal with. Of course he was right to stay focused.

At the hospital, Brodie showed Janine's distraught parents into his office and invited them to make themselves comfortable in the upholstered chairs. The room was designed to put people at ease—carpeted underfoot and fitted out with pale gold beechwood furniture.

'Unfortunately, Janine had an allergic reaction to the penicillin,' he told them. 'It's fairly unusual, but luckily the doctor on duty caught it quickly and gave her an injection of adrenaline. We'll give her steroid medication as well for a short time, and obviously she needs to have a different antibiotic.' He frowned. 'The allergy wasn't noted before this on her records, so I'm assuming this is the first time she's had a reaction like that?' He looked at the parents for confirmation.

The girl's mother nodded. 'She's always been healthy up to now and not needed penicillin. We were just so shocked when we saw what was happening to her.'

'That's understandable.' Brodie was sympathetic.

'I'm so sorry this happened to her,' Caitlin said. 'We hoped that the penicillin would resolve the problem of her infection but clearly she'll need to avoid it in any form from now on.'

'We'll inform her GP,' Brodie said. 'And a note will be made in the records. This shouldn't happen again but you'll need to tell any medical practitioner of the allergy if they plan on prescribing antibiotics for her.'

'We'll do that,' the father said. 'Thank you both for taking the trouble to come and talk to us. It's been a worrying time.'

'I know it must have been very distressing for you,' Brodie said. 'But I've spoken to the registrar and you can be reassured that Janine is all right. She won't suffer any long-lasting effects and the rash will fade in a couple or so days.'

They spoke for a little while longer then, as they were leaving the office, the staff nurse took Caitlin to one side. 'I have a mother here who is worried about her baby,' she said quietly. 'Seeing that you're here, would you have a word with her?'

'Of course.'

'You might as well use my office,' Brodie said. He lightly touched her arm in a gesture of reassurance. 'I expect this thing with the mother is something you can sort out easily enough.'

Caitlin hoped so too.

'I have to go and meet up with my animal therapy volunteer,' Brodie said. 'She rang me earlier to say she'd like to come in—but I'll catch up with you later.'

'Okay.'

The nurse handed her the baby's thin file and she skimmed the notes quickly. By the time the young mother arrived at the office with the infant in her arms, she was fully prepared.

'How can I help you?' she asked with a smile, inviting her to sit down in a comfy armchair.

'It's just that the surgeon tried to explain things to me, but I don't really understand what's happening to my baby.' The young mother held her baby close to her, wrapping her more firmly in her shawl and looking anxiously at Caitlin. 'Olivia's only five weeks old— she keeps being sick and she's losing weight. I'm really worried about her. Why can't she keep her milk down?'

'I know this is upsetting for you, but really, it's a simple, straightforward operation,' Caitlin answered kindly. 'I'll get some paper and a pen and see if I can draw it for you.'

Swiftly, she drew the outline of a baby's stomach, showing the opening into the intestine. 'Usually, see, the opening is wide enough to let the milk pass through—but sometimes the muscle here is thick and causes a blockage. When that happens, the milk can't get from the stomach to the intestine and the baby brings it back up. It's a forceful, projectile vomiting, as you've discovered, rather than a gentle regurgitation of excess milk.'

'How will the surgeon put it right? Is it a big operation? Will it leave a scar?'

'The incision will be very small, near the belly button, and there shouldn't be much of a scar at all, once it's all healed up. The surgeon will cut the muscle and that will cause the opening to be wider.'

'Okay, I get that, I think.' The young woman frowned. 'The doctor said she would be admitted to hospital today but they wouldn't operate until tomorrow. What does it mean? Will you be doing tests and so on?'

'Mainly for the next few hours we'll be making sure that she's not dehydrated—that's our biggest concern, so she'll have a fluid line inserted in a vein. It won't hurt her, but the repeated vomiting means she's lost a lot of fluid and it needs to be put right, along with minute traces of sodium and potassium and so on that might be out of balance. We'll need to do some blood tests to check that all's well.'

'All right.' The woman nodded, seemingly reassured. 'Thanks for explaining it to me.' She gently rocked the baby in her arms, soothing her. 'How long will she need to be in hospital?'

'Until about two or three days after the surgery to make sure she's feeding properly and that her temperature and blood pressure and so on are normal.'

The girl looked troubled. 'Will I be able to stay with her?'

'Yes, we have a room where you can sleep and still be close to Olivia. The nurse will show you where you can put your things—and if you think of any more questions, just ask. We're all happy to help.'

'Thanks.'

A nurse came to show her where the baby would be looked after and Caitlin, relieved that she'd been able to help, went in search of Brodie. He was in one of the patients' bays.

He smiled as Caitlin entered the room. A woman was with him, a slim, middle-aged woman with a kindly face, and she had a calm-looking yellow Labrador on a lead by her side.

Caitlin watched as the woman introduced the dog to the children. They patted and stroked him and Brodie was smiling, looking totally relaxed. Maybe a dog was good therapy for Brodie too, she mused.

'He's like a giant, cuddly teddy bear,' Jason said, laughing in delight. The four-year-old was getting on well now, off the oxygen for the most part, but having brief sessions with the nebuliser every few hours. He was sitting in the chair by his bed with his parents looking on.

The other little boy, Sammy, two years old and still with his leg in a cast, was much more reticent. He was in hospital briefly for further tests. He too was seated; now he cautiously reached out to touch the dog's head but pulled his hand back when the dog turned to look at him with big, brown eyes.

'It's all right, he won't hurt you,' the dog's owner told him. 'He loves children and he likes being stroked.' She crouched down to his level and demonstrated.

Sammy seemed to take to her. 'What's his name?' he asked in a timid voice.

'Well, we call him Toffee, because he's such a gorgeous toffee colour. I think it suits him, don't you?'

Sammy giggled. 'Toffee,' he said and giggled again. 'Toffee…' He bent over, laughing, as if he found that hilariously funny. Recovering himself, he looked at the Labrador once more and tentatively reached out to stroke him. 'Toffee's a sweetie, what you eat,' he said, chuckling.

Toffee's owner smiled and Sammy's mother said cheerfully, 'Well, he is a bit of a sweetie, isn't he? He's lovely.' She looked at the woman and then at Brodie. 'I'm so glad you brought him in to see us. It's been the best thing for Sammy—for Jason too, from the looks of things.'

Both boys were patting the dog now, their troubles forgotten for the time being. Caitlin relaxed, seeing her young charges happy and on the mend.

'That worked out really well,' she commented to Brodie when they went for lunch in the cafeteria. 'I'm glad we came in this morning.'

'So am I. Anyway, I wanted to be here when the dog was brought in. I think he'll be a great hit with the children. He certainly brought Sammy out of his shell.'

'He did. We'll have to try the dog with children who are in wheelchairs—there won't be any danger of them being accidentally nudged and he'll cheer them up no end.' They filled their trays with a Sunday roast dinner—beef, Yorkshire puddings with roast potatoes and an assortment of vegetables—and went to sit at a table in the far corner of the room.

Brodie glanced at Caitlin as he started to eat. 'I meant to tell you, I heard from Matt the other day.' His gaze was thoughtful, pondering. 'He phoned.'

'Oh yes?' She stared at him, suddenly very still.

'He's been back at work for a while now and he was asking about you. He wondered how you were doing.' She nodded slowly, taking that in, and he went on, 'He said to tell you the little boy you were treating—the one with the infection in his knee—is completely better now and fully mobile. He came to the outpatients' clinic the other day.'

'I'm glad about that.' Molly must have told him she wanted to follow up on the boy. She looked at Brodie guardedly. Matt hadn't phoned only to update her, had he? 'What did you say to him?'

He lifted a dark brow in query. 'About how you were doing?'

She nodded, not trusting herself to speak. She hadn't thought about Matt recently but now, at the mention of him, her palms were clammy and her mouth was dry. Her hand trembled a little so she laid down her fork and rested her fingers beside her plate. Brodie's blue eyes followed the action.

'I told him you were doing fine—no thanks to him, since he'd treated you so badly.'

She gave a small gasp. 'You said that? But Brodie, he's your friend…'

He shrugged. 'I couldn't say too much to him about it at the wedding—it was the wrong time—but I wanted him to know that I didn't like the way he'd behaved towards you.'

She shook her head. 'You shouldn't have done that—it was between me and him.'

His blue gaze was steady. 'He was my friend, yes, my best friend, so I could be straight with him. I didn't like it in the first place when I heard he'd started dating you; all kinds of bad feelings swept over me… jealousy, for the most part…but when he took up with Jenny I had mixed feelings. I was glad it was over between you because it meant you were free—but I was concerned for you.'

Her eyes widened a fraction. He'd been jealous? 'I'd no idea you were keeping tabs on me.'

'I've often enquired after you—talked to people I know, kept in touch with your mother from time to time.' His mouth flattened. 'Anyway, I told Matt you were getting on well in your new job, that it was great living next door to you and I wished I'd moved in sooner. It's all true, of course.' His gaze meshed with hers.

She smiled faintly at his admission. It made her feel better, knowing he liked being near to her, and she expelled her breath in a soft sigh. 'I thought I was in love with him, that we would get married, but I had it all wrong, didn't I? How is it possible to make a mistake like that? It's left me so that I don't know if I can trust my feelings any more.'

'Yes, I know. But you could have ended up in a bad marriage. So maybe you had a lucky escape.'

She tried a smile. 'Then again, we could have been okay. Marriage is what you make it. It depends what you put into it.'

He shook his head. 'You'd both have had to work at it, and Matt obviously wasn't prepared to do that. Something must have been out of sync for him to go off with Jenny the way he did.'

'Yes, you pointed that out once before.' She pressed her lips together, trying not to let her emotions show. After all this time she was still on fragile ground, and she sensed that Brodie was pushing things, testing her to see if she would stumble.

'Have you given it any thought?'

She nodded. 'I have but I'm still not exactly sure what happened,' she said cautiously. 'All I can think is…' She took a deep breath. 'I've always tried to handle situations by myself the best way I can. Ever since my dad died, I've tried to be independent, to make sure Mum was all right. But Jenny was never like that. She needed help—with her car, with her state of mind. Things had gone wrong for her and she was a damsel in distress. She's often needy and I think that must have appealed to Matt. Perhaps he needs to be with someone who will rely on him for support. She brings out the protector in him, whereas I… Perhaps I don't have that same vulnerability.'

Brodie mulled it over as he slid his fork into green beans. 'I don't know about that—the vulnerability thing. I'd want to make sure you were okay, no matter what.' He ate thoughtfully for a second or two. 'You could be right, though. Matt does tend to want to take control.' He studied her as she picked up her own fork once more and began to eat. 'He's a fool, if he doesn't see what he let go.'

'Thanks for that. But perhaps it was for the best. I suppose it wouldn't have worked out for us in the end. I wouldn't want to be in a bad marriage. My parents were always good together, and their kind of relationship is what I want for myself.'

'I can understand that. That's probably why I've never felt the urge to try it. I don't want to make a mistake like my mother did with my real, my natural, father and then again with my dad. If it had been a good marriage, he would have handled things differently.'

'Perhaps…but they stayed together, so they must have had something pretty strong going for them.'

He seemed to be mulling that over. 'I suppose so. I've been looking at things from a different angle.'

She tasted the medium-rare roast beef, savouring it for a moment on her tongue. His troubled background would always affect the way he felt about relationships. 'Obviously, when it comes to marriage, you're afraid,' she said eventually. 'That's why you flit from woman to woman without making any commitments.'

His eyes narrowed in mock jest. 'Who's been talking?'

She gave a wry smile. 'My mother, for one, and the hospital grapevine is rife with rumour as usual.'

He laid down his fork. 'Your mother I can't account for, and I won't argue with her because I'm really very fond of her. But I can tell you now that whatever you've heard on the grapevine is pure conjecture. I haven't dated anyone since I came back to Ashley Vale.'

She looked at him steadily. 'Maybe you've been too busy.'

He gave a short laugh, returning her gaze with a penetrating blue glance. 'Yes, maybe. Perhaps I've found someone special…someone who cares about me and makes me feel I might actually be worthy.'

The breath caught in her throat as she met his gaze. If only she could believe what he was saying. 'That sounds…wonderful…something to be working on.'

'I'm glad you think so.' Smiling, he returned his attention to his meal.

Caitlin finished her main course and reached for her dessert, a Bramley apple pie topped with creamy custard. She didn't know what to think. He was making out he was perfectly innocent but she knew him of old. He was a wolf in sheep's clothing. He would lure her into a false sense of security then when she was completely ensnared he would devour her and move on in search of new prey. Didn't she know better than to fall for his charm? She'd already been hurt badly by Matt. She was feeling stronger now but surely she shouldn't make herself vulnerable again if she could help it? All the same, she was so, so tempted.

'Hey, you two, have you seen the pictures in the papers? You've even made the nationals—look.'

Cathy, the staff nurse from the children's unit, came over to their table. 'Am I interrupting?'

'No, of course not,' Caitlin said. 'Are these the pictures from *Murder Mysteries*?'

Cathy nodded. 'Yes, look. I bought the local paper and the *Tribune*. You're both splashed over the TV feature pages—it's mostly the main characters they're showing, but you two are there as well. I can't wait to see the series when it comes out. I'll be watching out for your scenes all the way through.'

Caitlin and Brodie glanced through the papers. 'Oh,' Caitlin said, 'They filmed the geese when they ran up to the camera!' Brodie was in the shot, smiling as he looked at the startled cameraman. 'I thought they would edit those shots.'

'They probably have in the TV version—but the press will choose whatever appeals, I suppose.' Brodie was amused. 'Thanks for showing us these, Cathy.'

'You're welcome. I expect they're in all the papers. All the nurses are talking about them.'

She went off to join her friends, leaving Caitlin and

Brodie to finish their lunch. Afterwards, they went to spend some time with Caitlin's mother.

'The doctor says I should be well enough to leave here in a few days,' her mother said, looking happy. Her cheeks were flushed with anticipation. 'I'm so pleased. I can't wait.'

'It'll be good to have you home,' Caitlin said, giving her a hug.

They stayed for half an hour then left to meet up with the film crew once more back at the smallholding. David was already there, organising things. Caitlin had given him access to the house and grounds.

'I thought Daisy and her puppies would like to be out in the sunshine for a bit,' he said, coming over to greet them, 'so I've put them on the lawn. They won't be going anywhere,' he added with a rueful grin. 'The geese are keeping an eye on them. At least they're leaving the camera crew alone today. They're too busy guarding the newcomers.'

Caitlin smiled, seeing the geese gently nudging the puppies back on to the grass whenever they wandered near the edge of the lawn. They were just beginning to find their feet, but Daisy seemed happy to let the birds shepherd her flock while she simply lazed in the sunshine and gathered her strength. Thanks to good food and plenty of love and care, she was thriving, and her shaggy coat was beginning to take on a healthy glow.

The film crew spent some time working around the house and outbuildings, and then moved off to concentrate their attention on the wooded area around the smallholding. A couple of villagers acted as extras, wandering along the footpath that led from Brodie's property to the copse beyond. The same man who'd been wheezing the day before was there. Caitlin stood and watched them go.

'I think they've finished with us for now,' Brodie said as he walked with her to the back of her house. He gave her a long, appreciative look. 'It looks as though I have you all to myself at last.'

'Is that what you want?' she murmured.

'Oh yes,' he said. They came to a halt on the terrace overlooking the lawn and in the privacy of a jasmine-covered arbour he leaned towards her.

'I never seem to get you alone, what with David being around, the film crew and whoever else decides on a whim to drop by.' He slid his arm around her waist and tugged her towards him. 'You've had all sorts of creatures demanding your attention: a rabbit, the quail, Daisy and the pups, three terrifying geese— and for all I know a motherless kitten could turn up at any minute to distract you. I'm all for moving in on you while I can.'

She smiled and lifted her face to him, rewarded instantly when he bent his head to hers and claimed her lips. She was ready for his kiss, wanting it, needing it, craving the feel of his arms around her. He eased her against the rustic trellis, supporting her with his fore-arm, raining kisses over her cheek and throat, nuzzling the creamy velvet of her shoulder beneath the loose collar of her shirt. 'Do you think we could be together, you and I?' he murmured. 'A couple? Could we give it a go?'

The sweet fragrance of white jasmine filled the air as she moved against him, pressing her soft curves into his muscular frame. 'Oh, yes…yes.'

She heard his gasp, revelled in his strength, and lost herself in his kisses, running her hands up over his chest, delighting in the swift intake of his breath as his body tautened against her.

'Ah, Caity…you've made me so happy. I want you so badly. You know it, don't you?' His voice was roughened, the words thick against her cheek, her lips. 'When I saw you first thing this morning, it took all I had to keep my hands off you.' He kissed her again, hungrily. 'You're so lovely, so perfect, Caity. You're everything I could ever want.'

'Mmm… I want you too, Brodie,' she murmured. She snuggled up against him, loving the way he needed her, exhilarated by the feel of him, by the delicious stroking of his hands as they moved over her curves, filling her with feverish excitement. If only it was true, what he was saying. Could she really be everything he could ever want? 'I want you so much…'

She was seduced by him, by the heady perfume of jasmine that wafted on the air, the warmth of the sun on her bare arms and legs and by his wonderful, coaxing hands that seemed to know instinctively how to make her body yearn for more. Why shouldn't she accept what he was offering, let him take her on that tantalising, breathtaking voyage of discovery?

'Let's go inside the house…' His voice was husky, urgent, ragged with passion; she was more than willing to go along with him.

'Okay.' She didn't want to break away from him and neither, it seemed, did he want to move away from her. He kept his arm around her as they walked the short distance to the kitchen door.

But before they made it as far as the kitchen, they heard David's voice calling to them from across the garden. 'Are you there, bro? I need to talk to you. Brodie?'

The geese started cackling at the intrusion and Caitlin gave a slow, heavy sigh, her fizzing, shooting senses coming back down to earth with a bump. Beside her, Brodie stiffened.

'One of these days…' Brodie said, gritting his teeth. 'He's my brother,' he said under his breath, 'and I'm very attached to him, but there are times, I swear, I could…' He didn't finish what he was saying.

David came around the back of the house. 'There you are. I thought I saw you both in the garden a minute ago. There's a problem with the look of the back of the house—your house, Brodie. It's too neat. The director wants to know if we can put some plants there in place of yours—shrubs and so on—to make it look straggly and overgrown. We'll put everything back how it was afterwards.'

'Sure. That's fine.' Brodie's answer was brisk and to the point. 'Why don't you go and see to it right away?'

'Hmm. Am I sensing something here?' David looked from one to the other. 'The thing is, I would go away…but you need to come and talk to the director and see what he wants to do. There are papers you need to sign.'

'You can sign them for me.' Brodie's impatience was showing and David studied him thoughtfully.

'Sorry, no can do. Anyway, you did say you'd be available to deal with any queries that came up today.'

His glance went to Caitlin, who was waiting edgily through this back-and-forth chitchat. She was coming to realise how very close she'd come to burning her boats with Brodie.

'He seems anxious to be rid of me,' David commented. He raised his brows in a silent question that she decided to ignore. 'I'm hugely jealous,' he said, his dark eyes glinting with mischief. 'You know that, don't you? You always said you wouldn't lose your heart to either of us because we would trample all over it.'

'Leave it off, David,' Brodie warned, his whole body tense. But David merely smiled, for all his worth playing the part of the irritating younger brother. He glanced at Caitlin, as though expecting an answer.

'Did I say that?' She sounded breathless, even to her own ears. 'That was a long time ago.'

'Yes, well, nothing much has changed. Except I'm the one you should go for.' Again, that imp of devilment appeared in his eyes. 'I'd make you happy.'

'You're right,' she agreed. 'Nothing's changed, has it? I ought to know better than to listen to either of you. My father used to warn me about you two. "Pair of young rascals," he said. "Full of testosterone, looking for conquests and moving on."'

She'd been very young when her father had died—fifteen years old and emotionally insecure. But her father had loved and cherished her; she knew that. He'd wanted the best for her and she'd missed him so much after he died. Perhaps his loss was the reason she'd tried so hard not to fall for Brodie…then and now. It hurt so much to lose someone you loved. Was she making the biggest mistake of her life?

David smiled. 'Your father had a point. We were very young and immature.' He started to move away across the terrace. 'See you in a minute or two, bro.'

Caitlin turned to Brodie with a rueful smile. 'Perhaps you should go and sign your papers. I think that motherless kitten has arrived.'

'I guess he has.' Brodie gave her a long, steady look. 'Another time, then,' he said quietly. 'I've already waited a lifetime…what does a little longer matter?'

'I don't know about that, Brodie,' she said equally softly. 'I don't know if I'm making a mistake.'

'He was just teasing you.'

'I know. But perhaps it's a good thing that I have

time to think. I've just finished one relationship. Maybe this is the wrong time to be stepping back into the fray.'

'And, then again, it might be the perfect time. Sometimes you need to follow your instincts.'

She nodded. 'Okay,' she said softly, still troubled.

'We'll be fine,' he said. 'I promise.' He gently brushed her mouth with his and then went off in the direction of the camera crew.

She watched him go, the memory of his kiss imprinted on her lips. David's comments played over in her mind, though. He had given her food for thought and taken her right back to when this had all started. Brodie had pursued her since they were teenagers. He'd never faltered, taking up where he'd left off as soon as they'd met up again. He couldn't resist a challenge.

Perhaps to him she was simply the one that got away and that was why he persisted in going after her.

CHAPTER SEVEN

CAITLIN WAS NEARING the end of her shift on Monday afternoon when the staff nurse asked her to look in on baby Olivia. 'Her mum's worried—she had her operation first thing this morning, and she started taking small feeds six hours later, but the poor little thing's still vomiting.'

'Okay, Cathy. Bless her—I'll go and see her now. She's still on a fluid drip until her full feeding regime is restored, so there aren't any worries on that score.'

She hurried away to go and look in on the mother and baby. She and Brodie had been busy all day and hadn't really had a chance to talk. Even at lunchtime he'd been involved in meetings with chiefs from the local health authority.

Now she went to see Olivia, checking the heart and respiration monitor, glad to find that all was well there. The infant looked reasonably content, squirming a little in her mother's arms; every now and again her pink rosebud mouth made little sucking movements.

'Hi,' Caitlin said, going to sit down beside them. 'I hear she's having a bit of a problem?'

'That's right.' The mother's brow creased with anxiety. 'She keeps being sick. Does it mean the operation hasn't worked?'

'Not at all. The surgeon reported that everything went very well. This type of surgery is very low risk.' She stroked the baby's palm and felt the infant's fingers close around hers. 'She's lovely, isn't she?' A quiver of unforeseen, overwhelming maternal instinct ran through her, melting her insides.

The mother nodded and smiled. 'Yes, she is. She's so precious to us and this is all very upsetting.'

'It *is* upsetting, but it's quite usual for a baby to be sick after this kind of surgery. It happens because there's often a bit of swelling after the operation, but that will soon go down and she should be able to feed normally after that. I'll ask the nurse to check how often she's being fed and how much, and to work with you on that. Things should soon settle. She just needs tiny feeds for the time being. I'm sure she'll be fine.'

'Thanks.' The girl looked relieved. 'I'm sorry to be such a pain…'

'No, you're not being a pain at all. I'm sure all new mums worry. It's natural.'

Maybe one day she would be holding her own child in her arms, looking down at him or her with such love and tenderness. She already knew how good Brodie was with children; she'd seen him in action with children and animals and he was wonderful with them all. Did he want to have a family of his own? Would he ever contemplate taking that step? She'd dearly love to have children with him. He'd be a fantastic father.

A rush of heat rippled through her. She'd never once contemplated having a family with Matt, even when they'd talked about getting engaged. It was very odd but it simply hadn't occurred to her.

She met up with Brodie as he was getting ready to leave the hospital for the day. 'They're filming at the village pub this evening,' he told her. 'David said he hoped we would both be there.'

'Yes, he mentioned it to me.'

'How do you feel about it? Do you fancy going along? We don't have to do anything—the camera crew will be filming the actors and we'll be in the background somewhere with the rest of the pub's customers.'

'Yes, okay. I'd like to go.'

He smiled. 'Good. It's a date, then. He said to come early—he wants me to meet someone, something to do with one of the photos that appeared in the papers. He says it's important, but he didn't go into details. I can't imagine what that's about.'

'Perhaps a talent scout saw you on camera and wants you to do a hero doctor drama series,' she said with a smile.

He laughed. 'Of course, why didn't I think of that?'

She walked with him to the car park and her expression sobered. 'Are you and David getting on all right now? I was a bit concerned after the way you were sniping at one another yesterday afternoon.'

'We're fine. It's just banter—on his part, especially.' He gave a wry smile. 'David was a demon for trying to wind me up when we were younger…you probably remember that?'

She nodded. 'He hasn't changed much, has he?' she said with a smile.

He shook his head, sending her a sidelong glance. 'Though I suspect yesterday's comments came about because he has a big crush on you.'

She shook her head. 'No, he doesn't. He may have fancied his chances years ago, but now it's all bravado—designed to get a response from you, I think. He only makes a play for me when you're around. That's a definite hangover from the old days.'

'Maybe.' They parted company as they reached their cars. 'I'll call for you in about an hour and a half,' he said. 'And we'll stroll down to the pub together…is that okay?'

She nodded. 'It's the last of the filming sessions today, isn't it? I heard they'd arranged a celebratory buffet meal for everyone in the lounge bar for when it's all over.'

'Sounds good to me.'

Caitlin rushed through her chores as soon as she arrived back at the house, feeding the animals and making sure Daisy and the pups had a run outside before quickly getting ready for the evening. She showered and dressed in slim-fit jeans and a layered top. Leaving her hair loose to flow in burnished chestnut curls to her shoulders, she applied a swift dab of make-up to her face, finishing off with a light spray of perfume.

Brodie sucked in his breath when he called for her a short time later. 'You look beautiful,' he said, his eyes darkening with appreciation. He stepped inside the house and moved towards her. 'Shall we give the pub a miss and stay in?'

'Behave yourself,' she admonished him with a laugh. 'Anyway, you know David will only come and find you if you don't turn up—or else the director will decide it's a good idea to do a final scene outside your house.'

'I don't care. I'm prepared to risk it,' he murmured, walking further into the hallway and sliding his arms around her. As an afterthought he pushed the front door shut with his foot to give them some privacy then he lowered his head and stole a kiss.

Instantly, in an intuitive, innate response, her lips softened beneath his and she kissed him tenderly, wanting him, loving him, yet at the same time warring with herself about what she was doing. It had hurt so badly to be rejected when she'd been with Matt; she couldn't help feeling she was storing up trouble for the future by getting ever more deeply involved with Brodie. The trouble was, she couldn't help herself.

Brodie deepened the kiss, tugging her closer to him

so that she could feel the passion burning in him. There was no mistaking his desire for her. His hands moved over her, making sweeping forays over all the curves and planes of her body, shaping her, tantalising her with his gentle, knowing expertise; all the while his lips teased the softness of her mouth and made gentle trails over the silken skin of her throat.

His fingers slid beneath the flowing hem of her top, slowly gliding upwards until he found the soft swell of her silk-clad breasts and lingered there. A shuddery, satisfied sigh escaped him. 'Ah, Caity, you're so lovely...'

A muffled gasp caught in her throat. His touch was heavenly, sensual, luring her into a state of feverish euphoria. It was pure seduction, taking her to heights of ecstasy she'd never known before, making her want ever more. She groaned softly, heat intensifying inside her as he moved against her. She felt the brush of his thigh against hers, his hard, muscular body driving her to distraction.

And then came the jarring, insistent bleep of a mobile phone and she blinked in bewilderment, her body recoiling in a spasm of shock.

'What is it? Who can it be...?' She stared up at him, dazed, uncomprehending. Her whole being was in a state of traumatic distress.

He shook his head. Perhaps he managed to recover his equilibrium faster than she did because he said cautiously, 'It's not my phone. It must be yours.'

'Oh…are you sure?'

He nodded.

Befuddled, she searched in her jeans pocket with shaking hands and drew out her phone. It was the hospital calling and immediately she was on alert, worried. Was something wrong with her mother? Had she taken a turn for the worse?

She listened carefully to what the nurse had to say. 'Thank you. Thanks for letting me know,' she said quietly at last.

She cut the call and looked up at Brodie. 'My mother can come home tomorrow—if her blood pressure, pulse and so on are okay. Her blood oxygen level is fine now, apparently. The consultant just paid her a quick visit while he was there to see another patient.' She gave a rueful smile. 'I think, actually, she probably badgered him into it.'

'That sounds like your mother—she likes to get things sorted. She must be feeling a lot better.'

She nodded, looking at him, not knowing quite what to say. The mood had been totally disrupted. Now that she was thinking clearly again, making love right now didn't seem like such a good idea. She might love him and want children with him but she wanted the whole package: love, marriage and a vow of eternal devotion. Was he even capable of that?

'I guess we ought to head for the pub,' he said reluctantly, gauging her reaction. 'I suppose you were right earlier. David's quite likely to come looking for me. He seemed particularly anxious for me to meet this person.'

'A man?'

'A woman, I believe.'

She frowned. 'Do I need to be jealous?'

'Would you be?' He sounded almost hopeful and that surprised her a little. Didn't he know how she felt about him?

'Oh yes, very much so. I want you all to myself.'

'Good. I'm glad about that.' He opened the door and she stepped out onto the porch with him.

'The trouble is, I never quite feel safe with you, Brodie…emotionally, I mean. I'm never sure if you'll decide to look around and see if the grass is greener somewhere else.'

They started to walk along the country lane. 'Have I ever given you any reason to doubt me?' he asked. 'Nowadays, I mean…since I came back here?' He studied her, his expression suddenly brooding. 'Surely I'm the one who needs to be on his guard? After all, you're still hankering after Matt, aren't you? How do I compete with him?'

She shook her head. 'You're wrong about that. I don't even think about him any more. It's over.'

He made a short, dismissive sound. 'I don't believe that's true. His name came up the other day when we were having lunch and your hands were shaking. I don't think you're over him at all.'

She sent him a troubled look. 'It was a shock, that's

all: what he did; the way he finished with me… Everything in my life changed overnight. It was just a reaction to what had been a harrowing episode in my life.'

'Well, when you can be with him or think about him without trembling, maybe then I'll believe you. Till then, it's all up in the air.'

Caitlin pressed her lips together briefly. No matter what she said, she had the feeling he wouldn't believe her right now. Yet, deep inside, she truly wondered why she'd ever thought she was in love with Matt. He was a good man—pleasant company, supportive—but he'd never made her feel the way she did when she was with Brodie.

'You don't need to worry about Matt,' she said.

He reached for her, holding her briefly, his hands cupping her arms. 'I want you, Caity. I want you all to myself, and I'll do whatever I can to drive him from your mind. I'll prove to you that I'm good enough for you, that I won't let you down.'

Brodie made her insides tingle with longing, he made her blood fizz with excitement, and he made her yearn for him when he wasn't around. If she explained that to him it would more than likely incite him to launch a full-scale, bone-melting sensual assault on her body and mind, no holds barred, right here in the lane. Much as she'd love that, she wasn't at all sure she could handle the consequences.

She loved everything about him: the way he helped out around the smallholding without a care; the way he was there for her before she even knew she needed him; even the way he accepted her for what she was, without wanting to change her.

'Ah, you made it. Good.' David looked pleased to see both of them when they walked into the pub's lounge bar and several of the villagers who were seated nearby or standing by the bar nodded acknowledgement. In the background the camera crew were setting up, getting ready for filming, and the actors were going over their scene in readiness.

'Heard you're doing good things up at the hospital,' one of the men at the bar said to Brodie. 'My sister's little girl had to stay there for a day or so—they were very impressed.'

'I'm glad to hear it, Frank. We aim to please.'

Frank Brennan had been one of Brodie's arch accusers way back when Brodie had been an annoying teenager. He'd been subjected to trespass and minor vandalism and he'd borne the brunt of Brodie's talents as a graffiti artist on his various outbuildings. Caitlin looked on and smiled at how things had turned full circle.

'Also heard you had the offer of another job in London,' Frank went on. Caitlin frowned at that, sending Brodie a quick, sharp glance. He returned her gaze fleetingly, looking slightly uncomfortable.

This was the first she'd heard about any forthcoming new job. If it was true, it meant Brodie had kept his cards very close to his chest, and it seemed as though all her fears were coming to fruition. She felt a painful, involuntary clenching of muscle in her abdomen. He wasn't going to be staying around, was he? He was prepared to go all out after her, make her care for him beyond reason, then he would calmly leave as though it didn't matter at all. Being with her was simply a ripple on a pool.

She looked at him once more. Perhaps it was just a rumour. Ought she not at least give him the benefit of the doubt?

Brodie sent Frank a quizzical glance. 'News travels fast around here. How did you come to know about it?'

He wasn't denying it, then. Caitlin let out a slow, fraught breath. Her nerves were in shreds.

'Through my father-in-law. He works in admin at the hospital. Said the bosses at the local health authority were well taken with the way you'd changed things and wanted you to do the same thing at one of the London hospitals.' He gave Brodie an assessing look. 'So, what are you thinking? Will you be taking them up on the offer?'

So that was why he'd been involved in meetings at lunchtime. They must have been discussing the new role and the opportunities it presented.

'I don't know yet, Frank,' Brodie said. 'I've only been at this hospital for a short time and the new contract isn't due to start for a few months. I'm still thinking about it.'

'Well, whatever you decide, from the sound of

things you'll go far.' Frank laughed. 'I never thought I'd hear myself saying that.'

'Likewise.'

Brodie went to the bar and bought drinks, sending Caitlin a cautious glance as he handed her a glass of sparkling wine. 'I was going to tell you,' he said, reading her thoughts accurately. 'I was just waiting for the time to be right.'

'When would that have been, I wonder?' In the background, she was conscious of the filming taking place, but at least the cameras weren't pointed her way.

He shrugged awkwardly. 'I knew you would be concerned about me moving on—but the offer came out of the blue very recently and out of respect for the bosses I have to give it some thought.'

She was distressed, certainly, and she might have said more, but Brodie's father came and stood next to them, looking uneasy.

He nodded towards Caitlin and then turned his narrowed gaze on Brodie. 'I couldn't help hearing what you and Frank were saying. So you're thinking of going away again in a few months? You don't like to stay still, do you? You've only just come back here.' There was almost a hint of accusation in his tone.

'It's more that I like to feel I'm achieving something,' Brodie answered carefully. 'I didn't go looking for the job offer. They came to me with it.'

'You'd call it being headhunted, I suppose?' His father's manner was gruff.

'I suppose.' Brodie took a swallow of his drink. He sent his father an odd, questioning look. 'I didn't think you'd be bothered.'

Caitlin nudged him. Despite her unhappy mood right now she felt she ought to remind him of the conversation they'd had a while ago. 'Remember what we talked about?' she said in an undertone.

His father might well care more for Brodie than he liked to admit. He could be carrying a burden of guilt that he hid from everyone. She only hoped Brodie would cotton on to what she was getting at. 'You don't always see things the way others do,' she murmured.

'No, that's true.'

David decided to join in. 'If Brodie took the job in London he'd get to see more of me, most likely,' he said, giving an exaggerated smile and showing his teeth. 'What better reason could he have for going there?'

'Like I said, I haven't made a decision yet.' Brodie looked at Caitlin then back at his father. 'Anyway, if I did make up my mind to accept it, it's only an hour and a half by car. I could easily get back here, the same as David does.'

'Sure. I get back here often enough,' David agreed. He was about to expand on that when he saw someone heading towards the bar and excused himself. 'I have to go—I'll be back in a minute or two.'

Brodie's father shifted awkwardly. 'I know you well enough, Brodie. You'll do what you want, I don't doubt.

You always did.' He turned away to take a long gulp from his drink; Frank Brennan took him to one side to talk to him about the repairs going on at Mill House.

'I hear you're thinking of having the roof fixed,' Frank said. 'I can match up the slates for you, if you want. I know they're special—a particular kind.'

Caitlin didn't hear Colin Driscoll's muffled reply. She was uneasy.

'An hour and a half may sound like nothing at all,' she told Brodie, 'But it's a three-hour commute in the day and he knows it wouldn't be too long before it turned into a long-distance relationship.' She blurted out what was on her mind then took refuge in sipping her drink.

'You're not just talking about my father and me, are you?' Brodie asked, his gaze moving over her curiously. 'You're thinking about the way it might affect our relationship—yours and mine?'

'It applies equally well to both—though, yes, I'm thinking about you and me. It's hopeless, though, isn't it? If you're planning on going away it looks as though it's even more unlikely that you and I will ever get together in any meaningful way, doesn't it?'

'You could always come with me.' His blue eyes were suddenly dark and impenetrable like the sea.

'Could I?' She looked at him and inside her heart wept. 'You don't really think that's a possibility, do you? You know I wouldn't want to be too far from Mum now that she's had a fall. I couldn't leave her to fend for herself. I'd always be worrying about her.'

Besides, it would take more than a casual offer of 'why don't you tag along with me?' to make her go with him, wouldn't it? Where was the love, the cherishing, the for-ever promise that she desperately needed?

'It doesn't have to be a major problem,' Brodie insisted. 'We could work something out.'

Her heart lurched at the prospect. Could they? Was it possible?

He took a step back from her as David came over to them, bringing with him an attractive girl who looked to be in her late twenties. Caitlin knew the chance of pursuing the conversation was lost for now, and she resigned herself to putting it on the back burner.

'This is the young woman I wanted you to meet.' David introduced the woman to both of them. 'This is Deanna.' To Deanna, he said, 'This lovely girl is Caitlin, and this is my brother, Brodie.'

Deanna smiled at both of them. She had mid-length dark hair and grey eyes; she looked at Brodie as though she was especially thrilled to be meeting him.

'I just had to come and see you,' she said, gazing up at him eagerly, her eyes shining. 'I saw your picture in the paper and I knew I had to get in touch with the film company.' She hesitated. 'I hope you don't mind?'

'I don't think I mind,' Brodie said, smiling at her enthusiasm. 'Is there any reason why I should?'

'It's this picture, you see.' She pulled a sheet of

newspaper from her jacket pocket and opened it out. Brodie was in the picture, looking straight into the camera as he attempted to rescue the cameraman from the goose intent on pecking his leg.

'Okay…' he said slowly. 'That's me.' He looked at her questioningly.

'There's another picture you should see.' This time she opened up her handbag and carefully took out an envelope. 'Take a look at this.'

She waited with bated breath. Brodie gave her a puzzled look but opened up the envelope and drew out a glossy photograph. He stared at the photograph for several seconds and then looked back at Deanna. He passed the photo to Caitlin. When he spoke, his voice was cracked, almost a whisper, as though he was in shock.

'Who is this?' he asked.

Deanna pulled in a deep breath. 'He's my father,' she said. 'That photo was taken when he was a young man. When I put the two pictures together, I knew I had to come and find you. You're exactly alike, aren't you?'

Caitlin looked at the photo and sucked in her breath, her mind racing, while Brodie appeared to be struggling to find words. 'Is he…does he…does he know about me…about the picture in the paper?'

Deanna shook her head. 'He's not seen it yet. He's been busy lately—he had to go out to Sweden to sort out a new order for his company.' She glanced at her watch. 'He was flying back today—in fact he should have landed at the airport a couple of hours ago. Anyway, I wanted to talk to you before I showed him.' She hesitated. 'It's a bit awkward. He never mentioned having a son—apart from my younger brother, Ben, I mean. But there's such a strong likeness between the two of you, I can't help thinking there's a connection between you. I had to come and find out if there's any history, any kind of background that we didn't know about—'

She broke off, floundering a bit. 'Do you understand what I'm trying to say? I don't know if my father had a relationship with a woman before he met and married my mother, but if he did…I think you could be my half-brother.'

Brodie dragged in a deep breath and Caitlin wanted to wrap her arms around him and hug him. This must be an incredible moment for him. Instead, being in a public place, she reined in her instincts and contented herself with sliding an arm around his waist, trying to show him some silent, unobtrusive support.

He looked at her fleetingly and a wealth of understanding passed between them. Then he braced himself.

'You've obviously spoken to David, about this,' he said, glancing at David for confirmation, then back to Deanna. 'So you must know something of my background.' David acknowledged that with a slight movement of his head.

'Yes, I have,' Deanna said excitedly. 'That's what

made me think there could be something in it. David told me your mother's maiden name—I want to ask my father if he ever knew her.' She looked at him searchingly. 'How do you feel about that?'

Brodie was silent for a moment or two. Then he said guardedly, 'It depends… Obviously I want to know the truth, but I'm not sure how he might react, or whether his response is going to cause trouble for your family—for your mother and your brother. They're bound to have strong feelings about this—and in the end they might have more to lose than I do. I've always wanted to know who my father is but I don't want to cause heartache for his family.'

Deanna relaxed. 'My father's an easy-going kind of man, a very fair-minded person. And I've already sounded my mother out about any previous relationships. She said there was a woman in Dad's life before they were married but it was over when she met him.' She gave Brodie a steady, assessing look. 'I'd really like your permission to ask my father about this.'

Brodie exhaled slowly. 'You don't need my permission. But you have it anyway. Go ahead and ask him.'

Deanna still seemed to have something on her mind. 'What is it?' Brodie asked.

'Um… I could phone him right now?' She said it in a questioning way.

Brodie nodded, taking a deep breath. 'Okay. Go ahead.'

'Perhaps it'll be better if I go outside, into the garden to make the call. Why don't you come with me? It will be quieter out there and we can find a more private place to call him.'

'Okay. But I want David and Caitlin to come along.'

'All right.'

Caitlin had been afraid she would be left out of this major event but her spirits soared when Brodie included her. He put his arm around her waist and led her to the paved seating area outside.

They sat at a bench table in a far corner, brightened by a golden pool of light that spilled out from an overhead lamp. Deanna phoned her father and, after chatting to him briefly about his trip abroad and his flight home, she told him about the item of news featured in the paper and gently sounded him out about his life before he met her mother.

'Did you ever know a woman called Sarah Marchant?' Deanna asked.

Caitlin didn't hear what he said but Deanna listened, glanced at Brodie and then said, 'So you were involved with her for a while?' The conversation continued and after a while Deanna said, 'Dad, I think there's something you should know…someone you should meet.'

It was a fairly lengthy conversation; when it eventually came to a close, Deanna put down her phone and looked at Brodie. 'He'd like to see you. He suggested that either he could come here or you could meet in London?'

Brodie gave it some thought. 'I'll go to London,' he

said. 'After all, it isn't just my father I have to meet. It looks as though I have to catch up with a whole new family I knew nothing about until now.'

Deanna hugged him. 'I'm so glad I saw that picture in the paper,' she said. 'I can't describe to you what a shock it was. I was certain you must be related to me in some way.'

Brodie hugged her in return then after a few minutes they all trooped back into the bar. The filming was finished and the landlord was busy setting out the food the production company had asked him to provide.

It was a wonderful buffet, colourful, tasty and beautifully presented; Caitlin duly tucked in alongside Brodie, his brother and newfound half-sister. They were all in a happy mood, smiling and cheerful.

She couldn't help thinking, though, as she let Brodie tempt her with filo prawns with sweet chilli dip. and mozzarella and sunblush-tomato bruschetta, that this celebratory meal was the exact opposite of what she was feeling.

She didn't feel like making merry, because Brodie was going to London to meet his new family—what were the chances he would be tempted to stay there with them? He was more than keen to go and it didn't call for a lot of working out to know that the prospect of taking up a new job there would absolutely complete the picture for him.

'I could go over there next weekend,' Brodie said to

her, smiling as he helped himself to a selection from the cheese board. 'Will you come with me?'

'I'd love to,' she said, but frowned, thinking about the practicalities. 'But I don't know if I should leave Mum alone so soon after she's home from hospital. And there are the animals to see to: she won't be up to it for quite a while, with her mobility problems. It'll be some time before she's walking unaided.'

'I'm sure we could find somebody to help out, if only for a short time.'

'I suppose so,' she agreed. 'She has friends in the village who would be glad to help.'

'But something else is bothering you, isn't it?' He studied her, his gaze shifting over her thoughtfully. 'I can read you, Caitlin. What is it?'

'Nothing.' She smiled at him, not wanting to spoil the moment for him. 'I'm really, really happy for you, Brodie. This is what you've wanted for so many years and it's wonderful that you have the chance of some kind of closure.'

'But? There is a *but*, isn't there?'

Clearly, he wasn't going to leave it alone. She lifted her hands in a helpless gesture.

'I'm just worried about how things will work out in the long term—for us, I mean. I can see you wanting to move away now that you've found your family. It's natural you'll want to be with them and, with the job offer, how could it have worked out better? It's bound to affect us, though.'

She looked at him unhappily, taking in a deep breath. 'I want to be with you, Brodie, but I came back to Ashley Vale to make my home here—I don't think I want to uproot myself again.'

He frowned. 'The truth is, you came back here because Matt was getting married to Jenny.'

'Initially, that was the reason, yes, but then things changed. My mother had an accident. That made things different.' He had her on the defensive now and she didn't like it. She was confused—about him, about everything. Her emotions were tangled and for the life of her she couldn't sift her way through them.

'Are you putting up excuses, Caitlin? Don't you want to be with me?' His dark eyes narrowed. 'I can't help thinking I was right all along, that you can't make up your mind to be with me because you're not over Matt yet. You can't move on. There won't be any future for you and me while he's there between us, will there?'

His jaw clenched. 'Maybe I should take up this offer of a job and give you time to decide what you really do want?'

'Are you trying to make me choose?' Her voice broke and she looked at him with tears shimmering in her eyes. 'Matt doesn't come into it. He never did, where you were concerned. I always cared for you, but you weren't around, Brodie. What was I supposed to do? You left. You stayed away for years. And now you want me to choose between going away from here or staying—between being with you or losing you.'

She gulped in a quick breath. 'I don't want to choose, Brodie, and I don't want to persuade you to do something against your best interests. You're the one who has to decide. Stay or go.' She pressed her lips together briefly to stop them from trembling. 'I've made my decision, for good or bad, and I'll live with it.'

CHAPTER EIGHT

'HOW DID YOU get on in London this weekend?' Cathy was keen to know how Brodie and Caitlin had fared when he'd gone to meet his father for the first time.

'It went well, on the whole,' Caitlin answered. 'But I think Brodie found it all a bit strange.' As she finished writing up the prescription for Jason's medication, she glanced across the desk at the nurse. 'He said he didn't expect to feel quite the way he did. It was a bit overwhelming.'

'I can imagine it would be. After all, from what I've heard, his natural father is a complete stranger to him. He didn't know anything about him, his life or his relationship with his mother. Brodie said it was like a bolt from the blue, learning that he was around and that he wanted to meet him.'

Caitlin nodded, handing her the prescription. Young Jason was finally being discharged from hospital today and the medication was to tide him over until his GP saw him next. The little boy was doing really well now, gaining in strength every day. She was glad to see him going home but she would miss him, she acknowledged. Sammy too, was being allowed home on a new regime of medication to help strengthen his bones. He was another one she would miss—he'd started to come out of his shell and was a favourite with all the staff.

'It's true,' she said now, thinking about Brodie and his new family. 'He didn't know they existed. I'm not sure what he expected, really, going to see them… I don't think he knew himself what might come of it but for a first meeting it turned out better than he imagined. We met his father in a pub to start with, so that we could talk in private.'

His natural father had been astonished to find that he had a son he knew nothing about. Brodie's mother had apparently said nothing to him, probably thinking he wouldn't want to know, but he was horrified to learn that she'd kept her pregnancy to herself. He would have stood by her and his son, he'd said.

But Caitlin didn't say any of that to Cathy. It seemed too private, too personal, and it was up to Brodie if he wanted to share that with anyone else. 'Anyway, then he took us to his house and we had a meal together— the whole extended family. It was…surreal.'

They'd all got on well together. His half-brother and half-sister especially had encouraged him to accept the promotion he'd been offered and go to live closer to them so they could keep in touch regularly. Even so, Caitlin still didn't know what he planned to do.

He seemed to be keeping his options open and, much

as she longed for him to stay here in Ashley Vale with her, she couldn't blame him for looking further afield. He'd always worked hard to succeed—everything he did was designed to further his career—and it looked as though his efforts were paying dividends.

'Are we ready for the little girl?' Brodie strode briskly into the children's unit and checked his watch. A twelve-month-old girl was being brought in from the hospital where Caitlin used to work for specialist treatment. 'She'll be here in about ten minutes.'

Caitlin nodded. 'We're all set.' Cathy left them, hurrying over to the pharmacy to get Jason's prescription filled.

'Good. I want this transfer to go smoothly. If it all goes well she'll be able to have the operation tomorrow morning.' He glanced at her, his dark eyes brooding. 'Are you okay with everything? You're prepared?'

'You mean because it's Matt who's bringing her here?'

'Yes, that's what I mean.' His tone was unusually curt.

'Of course. You don't need to worry, Brodie, I'll be fine.' She frowned. 'Look, I know you must have things you need to do, meetings to go to and so on… You can leave everything to me. There won't be a problem. Matt and I are both professionals, after all.'

'Hmm.' His mouth flattened. 'That isn't exactly what's bothering me. I think you know that.'

'I told you, I'm over him.' She didn't try to argue

the point any more. This was a difficult time for Brodie, she recognised that; if he was unusually tense right now it was probably to be expected. His mood wouldn't have darkened simply because of Matt's impending arrival, would it? Matt was his friend and they kept in fairly regular contact with one another. They must have smoothed things over with one another by now.

No, his taut, preoccupied manner surely had more to do with discovering the existence of his real father after all these years of believing it would never happen. It had been a profound experience for him and it was bound to be unsettling.

For now, whatever state their emotions were in, they had to put all that to one side and concentrate on their work. The tot who would be arriving here any minute now had been suffering from symptoms of chest pain, bouts of fainting and shortness of breath. After specialised tests she'd been diagnosed with a narrowing of the pulmonary valve in her heart. This narrowing was causing a problem with the flow of blood to her lungs.

'They're here.' Caitlin heard the faint clatter of a trolley and hurried to meet her new small patient. Greeting Matt with a brief nod, she concentrated her attention on the baby. Connected up to various monitors that recorded her heart rhythm, respiration and blood oxygen, she was wheeled in to the ward and between them Caitlin, Brodie and Matt set about transferring the child to her new temporary home. She was a tiny, vulnerable little thing, and Caitlin wanted to pick her up and cuddle her. 'Hello, Emily,' she said softly. 'We're going to look after you now. We'll make sure you're going to be absolutely fine.'

'Her parents followed us here,' Matt said. 'They should arrive within a few minutes.'

Brodie nodded, acknowledging his friend and listening as he outlined her condition. 'We'll do what we can to get her settled and then I'll go and talk to the parents. It's a straightforward procedure she'll undergo tomorrow, a balloon valvuloplasty; she should be fine afterwards.'

Matt agreed. This hospital was a centre of excellence for catheterisation procedures; if everything went well and her vital signs were satisfactory the little girl would have treatment to widen the valve. Afterwards she should be able to live a normal life. There wouldn't even be much of a scar, because the catheter would be inserted in a vein at the top of the infant's leg and the thin tube would then be passed up to the heart. Once there, a balloon would be inflated to widen the valve. When that was done to the surgeon's satisfaction, the balloon would be deflated and would be removed along with the tube.

Brodie supervised the infant's admission to hospital but, once Caitlin had sorted out the baby's medication, he left the ward and went in search of the parents.

Caitlin saw him glance back once briefly in her direction—that same dark, brooding look in his eyes that she'd seen earlier—but then he continued swiftly on his way. It occurred to her at that moment that she hadn't realised quite how much Brodie kept his feelings locked up inside him. Perhaps the relationship she'd shared with Matt was one more seed of doubt that made him feel unworthy in some way. Maybe she ought to try to do something to get him to open up to her more.

'I heard your mother was back home after the problems with her hip and the emboli in her lungs,' Matt said, walking with her to the cafeteria a short time later. The paramedics who had accompanied the child were in there, taking a break before the journey home. 'How is she?'

'She's feeling much better, thanks.' Caitlin smiled, amazed at how relaxed she was in his company. 'She's using crutches to get about at the moment, and she has physiotherapy every day, but she seems to be doing very well. She's determined to get out and about to see to the animals and so on, so at the moment I'm having to make sure she doesn't overdo things. Of course, the puppies keep us on our toes. They're into everything.'

'I heard about the new additions to the menagerie. She'll be in her element.'

'Oh yes, she is. She's even contemplating keeping a couple of the puppies, though we've managed to find people who want to take care of them when they're old enough to leave their mother.'

'Well, if she's taking a keen interest in things it sounds as though she's going to be all right in the long run. We were worried when she didn't make it to the wedding.'

Caitlin nodded. She expected to feel a pang of dismay at the mention of the big event, but nothing happened, and she felt an immense lightening of her spirits. 'Yes, it was difficult for her.' She glanced at him. 'I thought it all went off very well.'

'Yes, it did.' He bought two coffees and a couple of buns and started to carry the tray over to the table where the paramedics were seated. 'I'm glad you came along on the day,' he told her as they walked across the room. 'I was worried about you. I know I treated you badly…but things just sort of slid out of my control.'

'I know. It doesn't matter. Forget about it.'

'Are you sure?' He studied her, his expression solemn. 'Do you forgive me?'

'I do. It's all water under the bridge. I hope you and Jenny will be very happy together.' She meant it. It was as though a weight had been lifted off her.

He smiled. 'Thanks, Caity. I think I needed to hear you say that.' He pulled out a chair for her and said quietly, 'Brodie's been telling me what a fool I've been and how badly I treated you. I knew it, of course. I hated what I was doing to you and I hated that it was ruining my friendship with Brodie.'

'He's had a lot on his mind this last week or so. I wouldn't worry about it too much.'

'I don't know about that. He seems okay, but he's

had a problem with me for quite some time. It just got worse recently.'

She frowned. 'I think he was jealous at first because you were with me, and then he was worried because he thought I was hurt.'

He nodded. 'I thought it might be something like that.'

She smiled as they approached the table. 'You've always been good friends. I'm sure things will be fine between you from now on.'

They sat opposite one another and chatted for a while, sharing the conversation with the paramedics, who were already well acquainted with Caitlin from her time at St Luke's.

After a while, Caitlin's pager bleeped and she made her apologies. 'I have to go and check up on a patient,' she said. 'I'm sure I'll see you all again before too long. Take care.'

She hurried along to the ward to look in on the youngster who had some time ago suffered an allergic reaction to penicillin. 'How are you doing, Janine?' she asked the five-year-old. 'Nurse tells me you've been feeling a bit breathless?'

Janine nodded. 'My chest feels a bit tight.'

'Okay, sweetheart. I'll have a listen, shall I?' Caitlin ran her stethoscope over the little girl's chest then went over to the computer at the desk and brought up her recent X-rays on the screen. They'd been done that morning to see if the infection was clearing.

'I think we'll give you some extra medicine,' she said, returning to the child's bedside after a while. 'Something you can breathe in to make your chest feel better.'

'All right.' The girl settled back against her pillows while the nurse went to sort out the new medication.

Brodie met Caitlin at the entrance to the patients' bay. 'Is there a problem?' he asked.

'It looks as though she has a bit of scarring on the lungs from the recent infection. I'll ask the physio to come and show her how to clear her chest and do breathing exercises. As long as she has antibiotic treatment for recurrent infections she should be okay.'

He nodded. 'So how did it go with Matt?' he asked. 'I thought you might still be with him, catching up on things.'

'No, I left him in the cafeteria when I was bleeped. Haven't you spoken to him?' She was surprised. 'I'd have thought he would have caught up with you again before he left.'

'I'm sure he will but he's not likely to tell me how he left things with you, is he?'

'Things are the same as they ever were,' she told him. Her gaze was thoughtful. His self-doubt was coming to the fore once again. 'I think you worry too much. He's married now and he only has eyes for Jenny. But you know that, don't you?'

'It's your feelings towards him that concern me,' he answered, but his pager bleeped before he had time to say any more. He checked the text message and immediately became businesslike. 'I have to go and assess a new patient.'

'Okay.' It was nearing the end of her shift and she said quickly, 'Will I see you back at the house tonight? You could come to supper if you like?'

He frowned. 'Thanks but I'm not sure if I can make it—I promised Dad I'd go and see him at Mill House. He seems to be anxious to put things on a better footing between us lately.' He lifted a dark brow. 'I guess you were right about him all along. He's fighting his own demons.'

She was disappointed she wouldn't be seeing him but she tried not to let it show. If he'd wanted to spend time with her, he would have found a way, wouldn't he? 'That's fine,' she said, trying to inject a note of nonchalance into her voice. 'I'm glad you and he are getting on better. When all's said and done, he's the one who brought you up. There must have been good times as well as bad.'

'Yes, there were. I think my memories were coloured by the way I found out he wasn't my real father and by the way he acted towards me when Mum died. He was angry and then he shut me out. I suppose that spurred me on to rebel against him all the more. We were both hurting and we lashed out at one another.'

She reached out and lightly touched his arm. 'I hope you can work things out between you.'

He made a wry face. 'I think we will. We're both up for it, now that we've finally squared up to the truth and realised our shortcomings.'

'Good luck, then.'

'Thanks, Caity.'

Caitlin finished her shift, checking on all her young charges and making sure they were comfortable and happy before she left the hospital.

Then she drove home, taking a route through town and along the country lanes, letting the quiet beauty of the Chilterns soothe her. She wanted to spend time with Brodie but, if he preferred to stay away, what could she do? Maybe she would have to get used to the idea that he wouldn't be around for much longer. David had already gone back to London. Was Brodie planning on joining him there in a few months' time?

'Sorry to love you and leave you, Caitlin,' her mother said shortly after she arrived home. A car horn sounded outside on the drive. 'My friend's arrived to take me to the book club meeting—did you remember it was on for tonight?'

'I remembered, Mum. Enjoy yourself.'

'I will. You'll get yourself something to eat, won't you? Because I'll be eating at Freda's house. There's the makings of a ploughman's lunch in the fridge and I made a batch of scones earlier. You could have them with some of that strawberry preserve.'

'Thanks, Mum. Don't worry about me. I'll have a shower and change and then I'll sort something out.'

'Good.' Her mother looked at her closely. 'You're looking a bit peaky. I hope you're not coming down with something.'

'I'm fine, really.'

'Hmm.' Her mother wasn't convinced. 'Is it Brodie? Is he the problem?' She frowned. 'I wish you and he could sort yourselves out. I thought when he bought the house next door he was all for settling down—but now that's all up in the air again with this job in London on the cards.'

Caitlin flicked her a glance. 'He told you about it?'

'Oh, yes. He said it's a fantastic opportunity. They've told him he can have carte blanche to make changes and there's even an executive house that goes with the job.'

Caitlin's heart sank. It sounded too good to be true and he was obviously impressed with the terms of the contract. Why would he even think of turning it down?

After her mother left with her friend, Caitlin showered and changed into jeans and a fresh, pretty top, then took Daisy for a walk along the quiet lane by the house. The terrier was happy to be out and about, fully restored to health with a shining, shaggy coat. She explored the grass verges, her tail wagging the whole time. Caitlin let her sniff and forage for a while, until finally she said, 'Come on, then, Daisy. It's time we were heading for home. I expect the puppies will be wanting their mum back.'

Daisy eagerly started back along the lane. She was unusually happy to hurry home and Caitlin had no idea what had brought about that enthusiasm until they rounded a bend in the road and saw a lone figure up ahead. He was coming towards them.

'Brodie?' Caitlin's eyes widened. 'I thought you'd be up at Mill House.'

He walked towards her, long and lean; his body was supple, his legs clad in dark chinos, his shirt open at the collar. 'Hi there. Yes, I was. I talked to Dad for a while and then told him I had an invitation for supper at your place. He seemed to think I should take you up on it.'

'And you were okay with that?'

'Oh, yes. I told him I was hoping he'd say that.'

She laughed, letting Daisy off the lead now that they were close to home. 'You got on well with him, then?'

'Yes, it was good. I think we smoothed a lot of things out. We'll be okay.'

The dog ran up to him, fussing around him delightedly, rapturous at finding her favourite person in all the world so near at hand, and Brodie stroked her silky head in return. 'I thought I'd find you both out on a walk along here,' he said.

'Mum's out at her book club meeting and I haven't started supper yet,' Caitlin told him. 'I thought I might make a pizza. What do you think?'

'Sounds good to me. I'll prepare the topping if you want to do the base?'

She nodded. 'Fair enough. There's cheese and ham and sun-dried tomatoes. Does that sound all right to you?'

'Perfect.'

They went into the house together. Daisy went off to find her offspring while Caitlin washed her hands at the sink and started to get organised for supper. She sent Brodie a quick glance. 'Did you catch up with Matt at the hospital before he left? I wondered if you and he had a chance to talk?'

She switched on the oven to warm and then gathered together the ingredients for the pizza, setting them out on the kitchen table. 'He seemed to think you had a problem with him.'

'So he said. Yes, we talked, for a short time. We're all right.' He started to chop ham and then grated the cheese she had put out on a board. 'I guess I just need to get over the fact that he dated you for what seemed like for ever.'

Her brow creased. 'That seems to have bothered you quite a bit.'

'It did. A lot.'

She shook her head. 'I'm sorry but I don't really understand.' She paused in the middle of putting together the mix for the pizza base. 'That all started a long while ago—Matt and me. Why would it worry you? You weren't around.'

He pulled a face. 'Maybe…but I wanted to be.'

She'd started to roll out the pizza base but now she hesitated once more. 'I don't think I follow what you're trying to say.'

He moved his shoulders awkwardly. 'That's probably because I'm finding it hard to say it. I'm not used to baring my soul, Caity, but I suppose it's about time we had this out in the open.' He started to pace around the kitchen.

She frowned. 'Okay.' She spread sun-dried tomato paste over the pizza base and added the grated cheese and ham. 'What is it you need to tell me?' She slid the pizza into the oven and set the timer. 'Perhaps you should stand still and tell me before I get dizzy from watching you walking around.'

He gave a rueful smile at that but stood still. 'I always thought there was something missing in my life, something I was searching for. I thought I felt that way because I didn't know who my father was. I couldn't settle. I thought if I found him, found my natural father and discovered who I really was, that would resolve everything. But then I realised that wasn't the problem at all.'

'It wasn't?'

'No.' He shook his head. 'You see, it was you I wanted, Caity. It was you I wanted all along. You were the one who was missing from my life. I wanted you when we were teenagers but you weren't having any of it… I went away thinking I'd get over you, I'd make a new start…but it didn't happen. I never found anyone who could make me happy.'

He drew in a long breath. 'For a long time, I thought I didn't deserve to be happy. I believed I couldn't make you happy. Back when we were teenagers I wasn't good enough for you… I was so confused and out of sorts. I spent years thinking I wasn't good enough, that I was lacking in some way, not to be trusted. And then I heard you were with Matt and I knew I had to make one last effort to see you again, to see if things might change.'

He started to pace again and Caitlin stared at him, not daring to believe what he was saying.

'Is it true, Brodie? Do you mean it?'

He came over to her and wrapped his arms around her. 'It's definitely true, Caity. I came back here to Ashley Vale for one reason and one reason only. I wanted to be near you. I knew you would come to stay with your mother from time to time, so at least I would see you.'

He frowned. 'Knowing you and Matt were together drove me crazy. I'm ashamed to say I wanted to break things up between you. I couldn't stand the thought of you and him being together. In fact, I didn't want to think of you being with anyone other than me.'

'But you didn't say any of this to me.' She looked up at him, hardly daring to believe him, yet inside her heart was soaring. He'd missed her, he wanted to be with her and he'd come back to Ashley Vale to be near her.

She lifted her hand to his cheek, tracing the line of his strong jaw with the tips of her fingers. 'Why didn't you tell me?'

'How could I, when you seemed to be so much in love with Matt?' He bent his head and rested his cheek against hers. 'I'm sorry, but I was glad when you broke up with him. I thought maybe, in time, you'd come to see me in a different light, that you might come to love me as I love you.'

'Do you…love me?'

'I love you, Caity, more than anything. Being with you since I came back here just confirmed what I believed all along: that you're the only woman for me; my soulmate; my true love.' He held her close and kissed her and she clung to him, hardly able to breathe because she was so full of joy and love for him.

After a while, he reluctantly broke off the kiss to say raggedly, 'When you said you were unhappy because I left Ashley Vale, that you turned to Matt because I wasn't around, I began to hope there was a chance for you and me to be together. I hoped I could prove to you that I'm strong now, that I'm capable of true, heartfelt love, and that I can give you what you need. Tell me I'm right, Caity.'

'Brodie, I love you. I've known it for a long time now.' She kissed him fiercely, passionately, wanting to show him how much she cared for him.

'I think I turned to Matt because he was safe—he was steady and responsible—but as soon as you came back here I knew I'd made a huge mistake. I was in such a state of turmoil. I never felt for him, or for any man, what I feel for you. I always hankered after you but I was afraid to act on my feelings. I was so scared of being hurt, of loving you and losing you. Can you understand that? I think it all goes back to when I lost my father. It was so painful—I didn't want to risk you not loving me in return.'

'Ah, Caity…' He kissed her tenderly, his mouth

achingly sweet as he explored the softness of her lips. 'I love you and I'll never let you down. I want you to know that. I'll always be here for you. All you have to do is say you'll marry me—say the word and everything will work out fine. We'll stay here and look after your mother and they can find someone else to take the job in London. It's not important. You're what matters to me, more than anything. I want you to know that you mean everything to me.' He gazed at her, his eyes dark with passion. 'Say you'll marry me, Caity?'

'Yes, Brodie. Yes. Yes, I will.' She was laughing now with happiness, brimming over with it, still hardly daring to believe this was happening. Was it all a dream? Would she wake up and find it was a fanciful, wonderful fantasy?

But then the buzzer from the oven rang out, signalling that the pizza was cooked, an all too real sign that she was well and truly awake, and that someone would have to do something about it. Then they were both laughing, wrapped up in each other's arms, kissing and hugging, neither one wanting to let go of the other.

Daisy came in from the utility room to see what the noise was all about. She gave a short bark and nudged Brodie's leg.

'I think she wants me to stop the buzzer and get the pizza,' he said with a smile. 'You can tell who's going to be the boss in our house, can't you? A small, raggedy-haired dog with a tail that wags ten to the dozen.'

'"Our house",' Caitlin repeated with a smile. 'I love the sound of that.'

Brodie switched off the alarm and kissed her again, tenderly, thoroughly. 'So do I. Our house—a family home filled with love. Maybe even, some day, if you want it too, our own small brood of children.' He gazed down at her, holding her close.

'Oh, I do,' she murmured. 'It sounds absolutely perfect.'

* * * * *

MILLS & BOON®

It's Got to be Perfect

* cover in development

When Ellie Rigby throws her three-carat engagement ring into the gutter, she is certain of only one thing. She has yet to know true love!

Fed up with disastrous internet dates and conflicting advice from her friends, Ellie decides to take matters into her own hands. Starting a dating agency, Ellie becomes an expert in love. Well, that is until a match with one of her clients, charming, infuriating Nick, has her questioning everything she's ever thought about love…

**Order yours today at
www.millsandboon.co.uk**

MILLS & BOON®

MEDICAL ROMANCE™

THE ULTIMATE IN ROMANTIC MEDICAL DRAMA

A sneak peek at next month's titles...

In stores from 4th September 2015:

- **Falling at the Surgeon's Feet** – Lucy Ryder *and*
  One Night in New York – Amy Ruttan

- **Daredevil, Doctor...Husband?** – Alison Roberts *and*
  The Doctor She'd Never Forget – Annie Claydon

- **Reunited...in Paris!** – Sue MacKay
- **French Fling to Forever** – Karin Baine

Available at WHSmith, Tesco, Asda, Eason, Amazon and Apple

Just can't wait?
Buy our books online a month before they hit the shops!
visit www.millsandboon.co.uk

These books are also available in eBook format!